A Killing Cold

ALSO BY KATE ALICE MARSHALL

No One Can Know

What Lies in the Woods

The Narrow

These Fleeting Shadows

Our Last Echoes

Rules for Vanishing

I Am Still Alive

Thirteens

Brackenbeast

Glassheart

Extra Normal

A Killing Cold

KATE ALICE MARSHALL

FLATIRON
BOOKS
NEW YORK

This is a work of fiction. All of the characters, organizations, and events portrayed in this novel are either products of the author's imagination or are used fictitiously.

ISBN 9781250343055

For Darryl, who read every one

A Killing Cold

In the house in the woods, the girl waits for the monster to come.

She crouches down, hiding as best she can, making herself small and quiet. She's good at that. She has to be. When the monster comes, you don't want to be noticed. You don't want to be found.

We're going to a special place, the girl's mother told her, not long ago. *A forest.*

An enchanted wood, the girl said. *And we're going to live in a castle and all our wishes will come true.*

That's right, her mother said, and pulled her in tight. *Everything is going to be better now.*

The door opens.

The monster is here.

1

I've never liked the way snow makes the world go quiet, stifling sound and creating the illusion of stillness. I can't shake the feeling that the silence is one of waiting. Of watching.

The car crunches implacably along the narrow road. The trees around us are mostly hemlock, wearing capes of snow to conceal their green. Beech and sugar maple appear here and there, branches winter-stripped and grasping. Connor's family owns this land, all the way to the mountain peak.

"Not far now," Connor says for the third time since we left the small town at the base of the mountain. "Once you're out of Datura, it's only about twenty minutes, even with the weather."

"It's a flower, you know," I note idly. "Datura. Also known as devil's weed. The Victorians said it represented deceitful charms."

Connor gives me a look I've come to know so well—half-pleased, half-puzzled.

I've always liked to know the names of things. It's the next best thing to knowing my own.

I'm bunching my scarf in my hands again, twisting it up like a cheap rag. It was a gift from Connor, which means it's anything but. Sometimes I play a game where I guess how much something cost, and then I double it, and then I look up the actual price. I'm usually still a bit low. Red cashmere and wool blend scarf, $490. I wad it up in a ball in my lap.

"They'll love you," Connor says, noticing my expression. Connor is a man used to being loved; I've known it since the moment I saw him. *No scars on that heart,* I thought at the time, though later I discovered I was wrong.

"I'll settle for grudging approval," I tell him, flicking him a smile to show I'm not nervous, though of course I am. There's a diamond on my finger that cost as much as a down payment on a house, and I've never met my fiancé's family—other than his sister, Alexis, who swooped into town two months ago for less than twenty-four hours and greeted me with plastic politeness. We'd been together only three months at the time, which makes this not even half a year and already engaged—I'd be worried if Connor's family *wasn't* skeptical.

Hell, I'm skeptical.

"The person you have to impress is Grandma Louise," Connor says. His voice thrums with nerves despite his words, his fingers drumming on the wheel in an uneven rhythm. "Mrs. Dalton to you, obviously. Granddad's in charge of the business, but Grandma's in charge of the family. If she likes you, you're in."

"And if she doesn't like me?" I ask.

"Oh, we just take you up to the top of the mountain for a ritual sacrifice," he assures me, deadpan, and I roll my eyes at him. "Don't worry, Theo. She'll like you."

My heart thuds hard, just once, and I'm sick with a feeling that might be dread or hope. I need Connor's family to like me because I need Connor. I need the soft touch of his hands and the smell of his skin, and it feels impossible that I didn't know him at all this time last year.

Connor hasn't had to worry about impressing my family—there isn't anyone to impress. I told him that my parents are dead. It's what I tell everyone.

It might even be true.

"The only thing you need to worry about—" Connor begins, and then he swears as a dark shape bursts from the tree line. Connor slams on the brakes, twists the wheel, instinct overtaking sense. The wheels lose their grip and the car swings sideways, sliding alarmingly before coming to a lurching stop two feet shy of the thing we nearly hit. A deer.

The buck's antlers branch to ten long points. Steam rises from its heaving flanks. It stands with its legs splayed, head down, and for a moment I think it's going to charge the Jeep, but then I see the bright crimson rimming its nostrils. Pattering onto the snow beneath it. The black shaft of an arrow protrudes from its ribs, a slash of red and yellow fletching at the end.

Connor's arm is outflung in front of me. I grip the door, white-knuckled. Mist plumes with every forceful exhale from the beast; its dull eyes stare at nothing.

"Theo. Are you okay?" Connor asks.

The deer lets out a low stuttering moan. It collapses—its front legs first, then the back. I unbuckle myself.

"Theo," Connor says again.

"I'm fine," I say. I open the door, stepping out onto the snow. Connor, with the slow reflexes of a man who has never needed to be wary, catches at my sleeve but doesn't get a grip. He fumbles for his own seat belt as I skirt the edge of the Jeep, approaching the deer. Its eyes are closed. Its sides hardly move. Maybe don't move at all. Blood trickles sluggishly from its side.

There is a strange feeling in my body. A tightening in my stomach and up my spine. A need to run. A need to see. The polished prongs of the buck's antlers are the length of my hand.

"Theo, be careful," Connor says, and at the sound, the buck's eyes flash open. It heaves upward, rising to its feet with a horrible bellow, antlers raking upward. I stumble back. My heels catch snow and then I'm on the ground, staring up at the glistening bloodstained muzzle of the deer. Connor shouts.

The buck runs, a broken lope, tracks filling up with blood; it won't run far, but I will it to. *Run. Don't stop,* I think, half-wild. *Don't let them find you.*

Connor hauls me to my feet, knocking snow from my fleece as he checks that I'm whole. I brush his hands away, pulse galloping, and stare after the buck. It vanishes among the trees.

The image remains: branching antlers. A splash of red across achingly white snow. That tightening in my stomach returns, and with it the strange echoing feeling of a memory half-lost.

"Theo, I asked if you're okay," Connor says, and my focus snaps to him.

"I'm not hurt," I assure him, though my bones didn't exactly appreciate being knocked together like that and my elbows are smarting. "That was an arrow in its side."

"It's bowhunting season," he says. "Granddad lets a few locals hunt on the land."

Three sharp barks sound nearby. I start to look toward the noise, but Connor catches my chin with one finger.

"You could have gotten yourself killed," he chides.

Connor thinks I'm reckless. It alarms him, how little care I sometimes take for my safety, but I'm much less valuable by the pound than Connor Dalton. A few dents and dings won't make a difference.

"I didn't," I reply. I squeeze his hand. "But you're right, that was stupid."

A man in a bright orange vest with a matching beanie jammed over his gray curls tramps through the snow toward us. He carries a hunting bow in one hand, a complex contraption outfitted with a scope and pulleys. Beside him trots a large black dog.

"Mr. Vance," Connor says, raising a hand. The dog pricks its ears. The man—Mr. Vance—fixes his eyes on Connor but doesn't say anything as he crunches closer. My pulse quickens. I tell myself there's nothing to be afraid of. Connor knows him, he's not some stranger.

"Everyone all right?" Mr. Vance asks. His voice is gravelly, and nicotine stains his fingertips with yellow. He nods toward our car, still sitting crookedly in the middle of the road.

"We had a close encounter with what I'm assuming is your quarry," Connor tells him. "No damage done." His eyes cut to me, as if to confirm it. I manage a thin smile.

"Sorry about that. Didn't think he'd run toward the road," Vance says. Stray snowflakes cling to his beard.

The dog stands perfectly still at his side, watching us. I force myself to look at Vance, to keep my hands from folding into fists. I've had a fear of dogs for as long as I can remember. There might be a reason for it, some trauma, but like most parts of my early childhood, it's a big question mark. *Good doggy,* I think.

"You're heading up to the camp?" Mr. Vance asks.

"That's right. This is Theo—Theodora Scott. My fiancée." Connor glows; Vance grunts.

"Heard about that," he says. He nods to me in greeting. "Daniel Vance. I work for the family. I'd stay to chat, but . . ." His hand waves to indicate the blood, the battered snow.

"It didn't seem like it would get much farther," Connor tells him cheerfully. "We'll see you up at Idlewood?"

"I imagine so," Mr. Vance says to Connor—but it's me he's looking at, and I don't like the expression on his face. It's like he's sizing me up. Or like he already has, and he isn't impressed. He walks past us. The dog stays put, nose twitching, glistening eyes still fixed on me. My fingers curl. I try not to think about the white of its teeth. Then Vance whistles. "Duchess, heel."

She bounds forward, rejoining him, her every step matched to his. They move at a steady clip, following the trail the buck left, and soon it's just us again.

Connor rubs the back of his neck. "Mr. Vance takes care of the grounds for us. Makes sure everything's all right when we're not here."

This sprawling retreat on the mountain waits empty through the spring and fall. The family converges only twice a year—for a month in the summer and two weeks over Christmas. They never rent it out, even to friends. A firm rule, Connor tells me, as his grandparents didn't want to deal with constant requests. Occasionally, one of the teenagers is allowed to bring a friend along for the summer. Other than that, the only people to step foot on the grounds are the Daltons and those they employ.

And now me.

For the next two weeks, I will be far from civilization, alone in the woods with my fiancé's family. And it will be fine. All I have to do is convince them that I love him, that I'm charming, that I'm not just interested in his money.

All I have to do is ignore the text on my phone, buried in the bottom of my purse. The text that arrived last week from a number I've never seen before.

Stay away from Connor Dalton.

2

Falling in love with Connor was so easy. It didn't hurt that he was good-looking—with his broad jaw and soulful eyes under dark brows, his sandy-brown hair swept to the side just so. He had the good sense to have ears a little too big for his face, or he would have been entirely too pretty.

It started at one of Harper's parties. From the moment she introduced us, I had the unshakable sensation that we'd always known each other. There was a glass of wine followed by another, a conversation on the balcony that neither of us wanted to end. So we didn't end it. We talked until morning, got coffee, walked through the park. He left me at my doorstep after dinner the next night and I went to bed, afraid that surrendering to sleep would break the spell, but he showed up again with breakfast and convinced me to call in sick to work.

It was alarming, how quickly he became as necessary as oxygen. Frightening how rapidly we became entangled. I would burrow against him in the night, the weight of his arm over me, and be seized with the fear that this would end. It was like fingers curling up under my ribs, reaching into the dark cavity of my chest. This couldn't be real. It was too perfect.

Connor just laughed when I told him. Laughed, and gave me the ring.

Sometimes, he said, you just know.

Then the texts started to arrive.

You're making a mistake.

Stay away from Connor Dalton.

They were anonymous, untraceable. And very possibly from someone I'm about to spend two weeks with.

"We're here," Connor says. There's a gate across the road—wooden and appropriately rustic, but with a keypad mounted nearby, which Connor uses to plug in a code. The gate swings open with a faint motorized whir. "Welcome to Idlewood."

Before us, the woods open up, like a curtain drawn back with great ceremony to reveal the marvel beyond. In the middle of it all is a large pond, its edges delicately veiled with ice, the center gray-blue and still. There's a dock; a dinghy; a boathouse painted the same blue as the sky. On the other side of the water, up a short slope set with stone steps, looms a lodge constructed of glass and dark wood, a striking blend of natural texture and ultramodern angles.

"Is that where we're staying?" I ask. It's beautiful, but I can't imagine living in a place like that, even for two weeks—those huge panes of glass, the interior exposed to anyone walking by. Though that's the point of this place, I suppose. There's no one to look in on you. Why bother with walls and curtains when you have a whole mountain to yourself?

"That's the grand lodge," Connor says. "Only Granddad and Grandma stay there. We'll be in the White Pine cabin." He parks the Jeep next to two other cars and climbs out. He grabs our bags from the back. Apart from the cars, there's no sign of anyone else at first—but as Connor comes back around, Alexis emerges from the trees to our left, hand lifted in greeting.

"I thought I heard a car," she says, teeth flashing white. Connor sets our bags down and strides forward to grab his sister up in a bear hug. She's a narrow woman in every dimension, thin to the point of bony, her dark hair falling straight to the middle of her back. A few snowflakes are caught among the strands. She crinkles her nose when she turns to me. "Theo! So glad you could make it."

"Glad to be here," I say, resorting to clichés in my nervousness. The first time I met Alexis was the moment I saw just what I was getting into, dating Connor. I knew he was rich, obviously. But he was nerdy, a little hapless, forgot to iron his shirts. I'd convinced myself that he was just a normal guy, plus money. Then Alexis appeared, oozing effortless polish—expensive haircut, expensive bag, expensive *teeth*, and the way she moved through the world like it never occurred to her that it wouldn't step out of her way. She's thirty-five, eight years older than Connor, a VP in the family company—Dalton Shipping—and by all accounts excellent at what she does.

We hug, that delicate palms-to-shoulders squeeze of reluctant acquaintances. Part of me is disappointed—the part of me that has always wished for a sister, for a family.

"And let me see . . ." Alexis prompts, making a grabbing gesture. It takes me a moment to figure out what she's asking.

I dutifully stick out my hand to show her the ring—a confection of white gold, boasting a frankly enormous diamond in the center flanked by two sapphires, with more minute diamonds glittering along the band. It came with a dizzying education in cut and clarity and what the various grades meant—not that there was any doubt that it was the highest possible quality. When a Dalton says "only the best," it's quite literal. And god, it's gorgeous. I want to say I'd be happy with a Ring Pop, that none of this matters, but the diamonds catch the winter sun and turn it to stars, and I know it's a lie.

Alexis examines the ring with a practiced eye and arches an eyebrow at Connor. "Gorgeous. Excellent selection, Connor."

He shrugs, as if embarrassed. "I just got the one you suggested."

"Exactly," she tells him, and grins. I smile reflexively to hide my surprise—I hadn't known he even told her he was going to propose. Then she's looping her arm over my shoulders, hugging me tight against her side. Together, we walk toward the path she came down. "So are you completely terrified?"

"Lex," Connor chides.

She flips her hair over her shoulder dismissively. "What? We're intimidating, no way around it. But don't worry, with me on your side, you'll emerge triumphant."

"All this telling me not to worry isn't really helping my nerves," I reply, and she laughs. "Is your wife here, too?"

"Paloma and Sebastian are napping," she says. She points at a cabin set back among the trees, far more rustic than the grand lodge.

Sebastian—that's their three-year-old, whom I've seen on the phone screen over Connor's shoulder, gabbing about daycare adventures while Connor listens attentively. Paloma has been more ephemeral: a hand guiding Sebastian away for a bath, a voice calling out that dinner is ready.

"You're in Red Fox this year? I thought they'd stick you in Wildflower," Connor says. The names of cabins, I can only assume.

She makes a face. "Trevor's staying with Mom," she says.

"Ah," Connor says, and they share a look like this means something significant. He cuts his eyes to me. "Wildflower is the only two-bedroom cabin," he explains.

"Oh," I say, and then the conversation hangs and I feel like I should have something more intelligent to contribute. "Is that where you all stayed growing up?"

There's a hitch before Alexis chirps, "Not really."

"Dad never liked it. Too close to the lodge," Connor says.

That's the wound I didn't see at first, the scar tissue both of them carry. Their father died young—in his late thirties, when Connor was a young boy. In photographs, Liam Dalton is his son's doppelgänger—identical grins, the same way of looking at you like they're letting you in on a secret. Sometimes it takes me a moment to work out which of them I'm seeing in the pictures that cluster on Connor's walls.

"Trevor here yet?" Connor asks tersely.

Trevor is the baby of the family, which means he's my age. Twenty-four. I've never heard Connor speak to him, only about him: *What's Trevor done this time?*

Alexis's lips thin. "Not yet. He should be up soon, though. Mom can't make it until tomorrow."

"I thought they were coming together," Connor says.

"Nope. He's driving himself," she replies, voice tight. Her eyes cut to me, and then she gives him a pointed look. "Anyway. You two are in White Pine, of course." To me she adds conspiratorially, "White Pine's always for the newest couple, because it's out of the way. Total privacy." She winks; Connor blushes. "We'll see you both for dinner?"

"We'll be there," Connor assures her.

Alexis releases her hold on me at last. She gives me a look I can't quite read, analytical but with a smile keeping the edges from getting too sharp. She tucks my hair behind my ear, and it seems like she's going to say something.

Someone sent me that text. Could it have been Alexis? She was friendly when we met. I mistook her briskness for distraction at the time, but I suspect she's always paying attention. If she thought I was wrong for her brother, I have no doubt she'd do something about it.

Alexis's lips close. Whatever she was going to say stays sealed behind them. She drops her hand and steps away.

"I should let you two settle in," she says. She puts her hands in her jacket pockets. Her weight rocks back on her heels. "Connor, when you get a minute, there's something I need to talk to you about."

His brow creases in concern. "What is it?"

Her smile is bright and false. "It can wait. None of us are going anywhere." With that, she swings around, putting her back to us. "See you later!" she calls, and she's marching across the snow again, with the same careless grace as when she walks down a city sidewalk.

"She can be a lot," Connor says when she's out of earshot.

"I don't mind," I tell him, which is at least five-eighths the truth.

"She's a bit protective. It comes from being the oldest," he says, still with that apologetic tone.

"That fits," I say distractedly. He gives me a curious look, and I blush a little. "Alexis—it means 'protector.' From the Greek."

"I don't know how you hold all this stuff in your head," he says fondly.

"It comes from being a lonely kid. Fun facts were my go-to social move," I tell him.

"And what does Theodora mean?" he asks.

My throat tightens. "'Gift from God,'" I say, trying to keep my tone weightless, unbothered. I don't tell him that it isn't my name—not really. There are things about me Connor Dalton doesn't know. Can't know.

"Shall we?" Connor asks. He hefts the suitcases again. I know better than to offer to take mine. It's a point of pride for Connor, to carry things. It makes him feel like he's being "down to earth," which I find charming. "I'm sorry my mom isn't here yet. I was hoping I'd get the chance to introduce you before—"

"Before you have to loose the whole pack on me?" I ask. "That would have been nice."

"We aren't ravening wolves," Connor chides. "And you have pretty sharp teeth yourself."

I bare them at him to prove his point.

Connor hauls the bags the rest of the way to the cabin and we step up onto the porch. The brass silhouette of a pine tree is tacked to the door, to match its name.

The interior is warm and well lit with electric lights. I turn in a slow circle. The Scotts took me to a cabin one spring when I was nine. It was cold and wet and the roof leaked; I burned myself on the woodstove, leaving a shiny welt across the side of my hand. This cabin has hardwood floors, a full kitchen. Through the bedroom door I spy a king-size bed.

Connor's watching me with a worried expression—one he wears often. It's hard to say whether it's his natural state or if it's just that I worry him.

"Mm," I say, cracking a smile. "I see we'll be roughing it."

"If you'd rather pitch a tent out back . . ." he begins, and I smack his arm playfully. He catches my hand. He turns it, slides my sleeve up my arm, and kisses the bare skin of my wrist—and the tattoo that decorates it: a blackwork dragonfly, three circles behind it. Then he draws me in toward him, and now it's my lips he kisses, slow and deliberate. I hum against his mouth, content, but break away.

"Give me the tour," I say, faux sternly. He obliges.

The tour doesn't take long; it's a one-bedroom, with a spacious living room and a full kitchen decked out with quartz countertops and top-of-the-line appliances. The bathroom is just as generous, the walk-in shower done in shimmering blue tile.

"Rustic," I say as we walk through the rooms, my eyebrows climbing higher with each new open door. "Charming. Quaint."

"Some of the others are more modest," he tells me almost defensively as I experimentally turn on the rainfall showerhead. I hold out my hand to let it patter against my palm.

"I'm not complaining," I assure him with a laugh, shutting the water off again. "But you can't blame me for being a little awestruck. Your family owns a whole *mountain*, Connor."

"Not the whole mountain," he protests. Then he grins. "Just the nice parts."

"Ha ha."

Connor puts a hand on my shoulder. "If you want to unpack, maybe take a shower, I should really go find out what Alexis wanted to talk about."

"Oh." I nod convulsively. "Of course. No problem."

"Unless it is?" he prompts.

"Don't be silly. I'll be just fine by myself for a bit," I tell him, though I don't want to be alone right now, right here. It's important that I not seem too needy. Too broken.

He kisses me again before he ducks out the door, a blast of cool air swirling past him. I stand alone in the quiet of the house, nothing but the drone of the fridge to drown out the sound of my own breath and pulse.

Connor's left his phone on the kitchen table.

I have a few bad habits. A history of looking where I shouldn't. Of taking what isn't mine. But I've been good, with Connor. I have to be.

It's not the same, I tell myself. All I need is to check one contact.

I pick up the phone, and then cross to where I dropped my purse beside the door. I dig out my own phone and unlock it, pulling up the texts. There are five of them altogether.

I know who you are, the first text says. Followed quickly by the second: *I know what you did.*

And then, a few days after that: *I know what you're doing now.*

You're making a mistake.

Stay away from Connor Dalton.

Each time one of the texts arrived, I hoped it would be the last. But they haven't stopped. It could be someone messing with me. A romantic rival. Someone with a grudge against Connor. There are at least a half dozen explanations that aren't the worst-case scenario.

That someone really does know about my past. The things I have never told Connor—can't ever tell him.

I unlock Connor's phone, using the code I've seen him plug in countless times. I pull up his contacts and scroll through to Alexis's number. It doesn't match. But of course Alexis is too smart to have sent anything through a number that could be tracked to her.

I open their messages. The last one is from Alexis.

When you get here we need to talk. Alone.

There's something I need to show you.

It was sent a few hours ago. And now Connor's out there, finding out what's so urgent.

Is it me she wants to talk about?

I put Connor's phone back where I found it, swallowing against a sick sense of guilt. I go to the bedroom and sink down onto the end of the bed, my phone in my hand.

I should just tell him—tell him all of it. He'll understand.

But what if he doesn't? What if once he knows, he doesn't want anything to do with me?

"I can't," I whisper. My vision swims. I turn on my phone, meaning to message Harper to let her know we made it safely. No signal. I give a hollow laugh and throw the phone on the bed.

Well, at least I know I won't be getting any more texts.

We're completely cut off up here.

3

Connor is gone for an hour. I brush my hair to tame the opportunistic tangles that have cropped up during the long car ride, put on a tasteful amount of makeup, examine myself in the mirror. My hair is a shade between copper and blond, cut just below my chin. I have one of those faces people always call "striking," which is to say slightly off-putting—broad cheekbones and wide-set eyes that look gray or blue depending on the light. Connor calls my face mercurial: I have a small mouth but a smile that rounds my cheeks, and when I'm angry my whole expression tenses into harsh angles.

Tonight I need to try for pretty, which means a smile is a delicate bend of the lips. I put on the outfit I chose for this dinner—a cable-knit sweater and wool trousers, both of them bought with Connor's credit card. I was surprised how easy it was, handing it over. How little shame I felt. Maybe it would have been different if he had ever seemed to care that I wore thrift-store clothes and owned only two pairs of shoes, or if when he suggested I buy clothes for the trip, he hadn't sounded as blithely casual as if he were telling me to get a loaf of bread at the store.

In these clothes, I almost look like I belong.

I almost *feel* like I belong, when I thought that was impossible—that I could belong anywhere or to anyone. There's something different about moving through life with Connor at my side. The world seems to part before us, to watch with admiration and with envy. It's not about the money or the clothes or the fancy dinners, though there are those: meals that melt on the tongue and supple leather boots molded to my ankles, a teardrop of gold set with a sapphire glinting at my throat.

It's about the way the ground suddenly seems solid. How I have room to breathe, to move, to be unafraid. Money isn't just money. It's power, freedom, and protection.

Or so I thought, until the messages arrived and things started to feel far from certain. Far from safe.

I push the thoughts away and loop the scarlet scarf around my neck. I examine my reflection, checking for flaws, for cracks in the illusion. My fingertips trace a fold in the fabric, a strange sense of familiarity shivering through me.

I don't have very many memories of my early childhood. A scattering of images, nothing more. Snow; sitting in the back seat of a car while the radio played; a woman in a red scarf. I can never recall her face.

Did it look like mine?

"Theo?" Connor is back. I hurry out of the bathroom, feeling strangely guilty. It must be snowing again; a dusting of white flakes decorates his hair. He shuffles his feet on the entryway mat. Deep lines crease the corners of his eyes.

"Did you manage to catch up with your sister?" I ask, not prying, not *not* prying.

There is a hesitation before he speaks. "Yeah. It's just a family thing. Sorry about that," he says, eyes dodging mine. The fearful animal inside me flinches. "We can head to dinner soon." He takes in the new outfit and the makeup, looking chagrined. "As soon as I get cleaned up enough that I don't look like a complete slob next to my girlfriend. *Fiancée.*"

"Smooth," I say. He ducks his head. It's not like I have any room to complain. My ring lives in my bedside table most of the time, and at work Connor remains "the boyfriend." Harper has asked me more than once, in her hesitant, just-worried-about-you way, if I don't think I'm moving a little fast. Of course I am, I want to say. Moving fast is the only way to stay alive.

Instead I tell her that I'm fine, that this time is different. That Connor loves me, that I'm safe with him. She pretends to believe me and keeps on worrying.

Twenty minutes later, Connor and I are stepping out the door. It's already dark outside, with only the golden pool of light from the cabin to illuminate our steps until Connor turns on a flashlight. I have always seen well in the dark, been adept at navigating by feel, without making a sound. It was a necessity, growing up. I almost prefer the dark now. The light only blinds you to what might lie beyond it.

Besides, we don't need light to know where we're going. The great lodge is a beacon shining through the trees. At the steps, orchestral Christmas music rises to meet us. The door swings inward to reveal a petite woman with dark hair streaked liberally with gray, sleek as lacquer and drawn back in a severe bun at the nape of her neck. For a moment I think this must be Connor's mother, until I recognize the stance, the warm but restrained smile.

Of course the Daltons didn't come to the mountain without staff.

"Irina," Connor says. "So good to see you." He leans in to kiss the air just shy of her cheek.

"Ah, Mr. Connor. It's been too long," she says in an Eastern European accent, and pats his arm affectionately. "And this must be the mysterious girl we have heard so much about." Does her voice cool as she turns her attention to me? She folds her hands in front of her, head tilted slightly, that smile still fixed in place.

"I'm Theo. It's nice to meet you," I say, not sure if I should extend my hand, but she's already gesturing us inside.

"Irina has been working for my family since before I was born," Connor says as we step in. We shed our coats and boots and slip into the formal shoes we carried with us.

Irina stands to the side, a presence so contained it's like she takes up no physical space at all. "The Daltons have been very good to me," Irina says.

"That's wonderful," I reply, hoping it's the correct response.

The entryway of the lodge has cathedral ceilings, leaving plenty of room for the massive tree that dominates the center. At least fifteen feet high, it's decked with impeccably coordinated ornaments in shades of gold and silver. We skirt it and pass through a short hallway, emerging into what in a normal house I would call a living room, though drawing room or parlor would be a better descriptor. The rustic touches persist: natural wood beams girding the roof, a stone fireplace, a set of antlers mounted to the wall, a fur rug with a black bear's head still attached. The floor-to-ceiling windows and wet bar belie the illusion.

Alexis sits at one end of a long white couch, a martini glass in hand. Her wife, Paloma, sits beside her, sipping what looks like club soda. Her rich black hair tumbles in artful waves over one shoulder, and she wears a form-hugging maroon dress. Their son, Sebastian, plays with a toy car on the rug in front of them, a perfect cowlick in his dark hair and tiny suspenders over his button-up shirt.

"And here they are!" Alexis says, rising to her feet. In another few seconds I've had my cheeks kissed, shaken Paloma's hand, received an adorably formal greeting from Sebastian, and been supplied with a drink.

"I told you she was pretty," Alexis says, draped over her wife's shoulder, not bothering to keep her voice down.

Paloma huffs a little. "Lex, please."

"I know. I'm terrible, you can't stand me," Alexis says; Paloma's nose scrunches. "So. Have you met Grandma Louise yet, Theo?" she asks me.

"Not yet," I say.

"She's the one you have to impress," Alexis informs me.

"So Connor said." I laugh a little.

"He's right," says a new voice, old but strong as steel, and everyone turns toward the woman walking into the room. She stands ramrod straight, her hands clasped before her. She must be in her eighties, but she doesn't look it. Maybe that's what a lifetime of money will buy you—not happiness, but smoother skin, fewer aches and pains along the way.

"Grandma," Connor says, tension in his voice. He wants this to go perfectly. He wants *me* to be perfect, but I don't know how. I feel like I should curtsy or bow or do a little dance; I just stand there frozen.

"Theodora Scott," the old woman says.

"It's just Theo." I try not to sound like I'm correcting her.

"And I am Louise. You can call me Mrs. Dalton." The formality is almost a relief.

"Thank you so much for inviting me here, Mrs. Dalton," I say. "Connor talks so much about all the time he's spent here."

"A venerable Dalton family tradition," Mrs. Dalton acknowledges. "Idlewood was built by my husband's grandfather. Back then, it was only a few log cabins, of course. It's had many lives over the years. This particular structure was our addition, after the old lodge was damaged in a fire."

"It's beautiful," I say.

"It is," she agrees. "Now, why don't you take a seat so I can interrogate you properly?"

I laugh, which seems to be the correct response. Paloma and Alexis make room on the couch, and I sit with hands clasped nervously in my lap.

Her head tilts, examining me. "So, Theo, are you from California originally?" she asks.

"I grew up in Washington state," I say smoothly. "But I left for college and I haven't been back."

An eyebrow arches. "Why LA?" she asks. "No Hollywood aspirations, I should hope."

I make a face. "Definitely not. I guess I always wanted to live somewhere warm, and . . . I don't know. I just always felt drawn to the area."

"And your family?" she asks. "Are they still in Washington?"

My stomach clenches. It's an easy question. A normal question that normal people would have a simple answer to. "I don't have any family."

"An orphan?" she clarifies, brow arched. I nod. It's not a lie. Not really. A simpler version of the truth than I could share, maybe. "My condolences. That must be very difficult."

"It was a long time ago." I smile—just the bend of the lips, pretty, polite. "But I am so grateful to be welcomed into your family."

"Well, we shall see," Mrs. Dalton says. Connor makes a strangled noise. "You mentioned college. You have your degree?"

"A BA in English," I say.

"And employment?"

"I work at a bookstore." This is not an ideal response; her top lip wrinkles. "I'm saving up money to go back to school to get a master's," I add, and Connor gives me an odd look. I avoid his eyes. I have no such intention and I'm not sure why I said it. The last thing I want to do is delve back into academia. But I need to impress these people, and assistant manager at the Magpie's Pen is not impressive.

"In something more practical, I should hope," Mrs. Dalton says.

"I haven't decided," I stammer.

"Theo's brilliant. Top of her class. She could do anything she wants, really," Connor says, acting like this isn't the first he's heard of my academic ambitions. I take a sip of my drink to hide my expression. The only way I could have gotten to the top of my class was if I'd taken out hits on a half dozen other students. I'd had to work full-time, a night-shift warehouse job. I slept through too many morning classes to hope for a perfect GPA.

Alexis waves a hand. "You're, what, twenty-four? Basically a baby. You've got plenty of time to figure out where you want to land."

I flush. Maybe I'm imagining how pointed the remark seems to be, but it's true—I am young. I never imagined myself getting married before thirty, much less twenty-five. I never imagined myself getting married at all.

"Oh, this one isn't so young," Mrs. Dalton says. She meets my eyes. "You can tell when someone has had to be grown-up. It's different when someone is coddled. Allowed to remain in a state of irresponsibility." Her sharp tone suggests she has someone particular in mind.

"I've been on my own for quite a while," I say, choosing my words like I'm picking my way past a snare. Every sentence feels like it's waiting to spring a trap on me. "I don't know if that makes me more grown-up or just more tired." I try for humor, but she doesn't smile.

"Yes, I imagine you've learned to look out for yourself," she says. I open my mouth to reply, but I can't think of anything to say.

Then a gray-haired man steps into the room, and I don't need to think of anything at all. Connor gets to his feet. Magnus Dalton surveys his family. He's a thin man—wiry, really, nothing frail about him. He has Connor's strong jaw and thin lips, the same piercing blue eyes. His skin is sun-weathered, and in defiance of the semiformal dress code, he wears a flannel and jeans.

"Well," he says, "I see you've already terrified the poor girl."

"We're having a conversation," Mrs. Dalton says stiffly.

"We ought to be having dinner," Magnus says, his hands in his pockets. "Irina tells me it's ready."

"Not everyone has arrived," Mrs. Dalton says.

He grunts. "I'm too old to wait on the young for my supper."

Her lips press together briefly. "Let us decamp to the dining room, then." She gets to her feet, her movements just deliberate enough to betray the weakness of age.

Everyone files out. I stand, but don't move yet. I feel sick. I catch Connor's eye, and he hangs back.

"You did great," he says.

"I didn't expect it to be such a literal test," I say. "I can't believe I said I'm going to grad school."

"You could," he says.

"I think I might have to now." I hide my face in my hands. "I can't do this. I'm not—I shouldn't be—"

"Breathe," he tells me. "You belong here because you belong with me. The rest doesn't matter."

"What if it does?" I ask him. "What if I do screw this up, and they tell you I'm not good enough?"

"I don't need their approval," Connor assures me. He takes my hand, running a thumb over my knuckles. His eyes search mine. "You are good enough. I love you. If they can't see that, it's on them."

I take a stuttering breath. He tilts my head up, kisses me softly.

"It's going to be all right," he murmurs. "You'll see."

His life has so rarely had a misstep. He doesn't understand how easily things can fall apart.

"Your mascara is running," he says, touching a knuckle to the corner of my eye. I've teared up again.

"I should go get cleaned up."

"I can wait for you."

"No, you go ahead." I wave him off. He gives me instructions to the bathroom, and after I promise him one more time that I don't need him to wait, we part ways.

In the bathroom, I wash my hands just to feel the cold water over them and dab at the smeared mascara with a piece of toilet paper. My eyes are a little red, but not too bad, I decide.

I'm not ready to go back out there. I'm running over everything I said, second-guessing.

Mrs. Dalton wants to know where I come from. The answer is nowhere. The answer is I have no idea. Theodora Scott is a fiction, but it's the only story I have. The rest is fragments. Less than that. The woman in the red scarf; the echo of a voice that never resolves into words.

A dream of winter and branching antlers and the urge to run.

There's a map on the wall behind me—Idlewood. The year in the corner reads *1983*. Elevation lines chart the shape of the mountain. Trees blanket most of the map. The pond—labeled here *Idlewood Lake*, with more optimism than accuracy—is dead center, with the grand lodge above it and five cabins scattered here and there, each far enough away from the others for privacy. The corner of the map is scorched. I think of what Mrs. Dalton said—about the old lodge being damaged in a fire.

Damaged, not destroyed. This isn't a family that sees something flawed and fixes it up. No. When something breaks, it needs to be gotten rid of, in order for something better to take its place.

So I must not let them see the ways in which I'm broken.

4

I leave the bathroom with my shoulders squared, wishing it felt less like marching to war. In the foyer, a man is in the process of hanging up a heavy winter coat. I slow as I approach. He has short-cropped hair and a craggy face. It might have once had the same boyish appeal as Connor's, but it's settled into something more severe. The click of my heels alerts him to my presence. He turns—and freezes.

"Who the hell are you?" he demands.

I blink, but don't falter. I step forward, sticking out my hand, and smile with all my teeth. "You must be Connor's uncle, Nick. I'm Theo. It's so nice to meet you."

I don't know my real name, first or last, as hard as I have tried to remember. Sometimes I think I detect an echo of it, my head twitching around in recognition, but there's no pattern in the syllables that trigger that little twinge of familiarity. When I was young, I tried on different names for a day or two at a time, hoping one of them would fit. Miranda and Abigail and Evelyn, Ann and Lia and Tara—none of them were me.

The Scotts called me Dora. Theodora Hosanna Scott, their gift from God, the child sent when they could have no children. Maybe to another girl they could have been kind, but I was too wicked from the start. It didn't take them long to conclude that I wasn't a miracle after all but devil-sent.

At least I've torn *Theo* free for myself—the Scotts always hated that nickname, too masculine. It's almost enough to make it feel like I'm telling the truth when I introduce myself.

But with Nick Dalton staring at my hand like it's a piece of uncooked chicken, the lie of it is as keen as ever.

I keep my smile in place, even as it starts to feel absurd, and then at last he stretches out a hand and closes it over mine. His grip is tight enough to hurt, but I don't flinch.

"Theo," he repeats.

"That's right." I'm relieved when he drops my hand. "Sorry if I took you by surprise. I don't know if Connor mentioned I was coming."

"You're the girlfriend," he says. I don't correct him. "Where did you two meet again?"

"LA. We have some mutual friends at UCLA." Meaning just Harper, but this makes me sound less like a complete loner.

"Right." His brows draw together slightly. "Sorry, I forgot you'd be coming. Took me by surprise."

"That's okay," I say. He wags his head, mutters something to himself I can't hear, and then gestures toward the hallway.

"Sounds like everyone's waiting on us," he says, but stays put, forcing me to lead the way. I can feel his eyes on me as I make my way toward the dining room. It makes the hairs on the back of my neck prickle.

When we reach the dining room, the appetizer course has already been served, and Nick isn't the only new arrival—the wayward Trevor is here, his honey-blond hair flopped artfully over one eye and his shoulders stooped in an affected slouch. I find my place at Connor's side as fresh introductions are made. Across the table, Nick's eyes keep finding their way to me. I pick at the food.

"How was the drive up?" Alexis asks Trevor when the introductions are done.

"Lovely," he says with a treacly smile.

"You have your license back, then?" she asks pointedly.

"Yup. All sorted out," he replies, not breaking his tone. "How was *your* trip, dear sister?" He reaches for the bottle of wine that's been left at the table.

"Are you sure that's a good idea?" Nick asks.

Trevor pauses, hand still outstretched. For an instant, anger glints. Then he shrugs. "I was going to offer it to Theo. May I?"

Entirely aware that I'm caught in the middle of things, I tick my chin down enough to approximate a nod, and Trevor fills my glass with exaggerated care. "It's so good to have a sister who looks out for you," he says as he returns to his seat. His siblings are both tense, Connor's jaw clenched so tight I can see a tendon twitching.

Magnus clears his throat. "Alexis, I've been meaning to ask—how is Sebastian liking the new school?" he asks.

Conversation after that is blessedly free of tension, light family catch-up that doesn't involve me. The conversation bounces around the table at a velocity I find borderline dizzying, with threads of old conversations picked up and dropped again before I can begin to discern the context. Even Louise Dalton smiles and laughs as she asks about Sebastian's latest antics, and there's a gnawing feeling in my stomach, emptiness food can't fill.

I think of heads bowed around the dinner table. Utensils clinking in strict silence—*seen, not heard, do not speak unless spoken to*—and a child sitting in front of a plate of stewed greens for an hour, two hours as they turned to cold, congealed slime.

Clear your plate, Dora.

I threw it against the wall. I was always an ungrateful child.

Irina returns with a solemn black-haired young woman I assume by their near-identical features is her daughter. They clear the plates, mine with hardly a bite taken, and replace them with the main course—venison in blackberry wine sauce, roasted vegetables on the side.

"Have you ever had venison before?" Alexis asks as I look down at my plate. The smell is mouthwatering, but I think of the creature on the road, the resignation and the fear in its eyes.

"Yes," I say. "Did it come from the property?"

"Shot it myself," Mr. Dalton says. He slices into the steak. The meat is rare, the interior a deep red. The juices pool. "You're not squeamish about that sort of thing, are you?"

I cut into my own meat, compress my lips into a smile. "Not at all. I've done a bit of hunting myself."

The old man looks surprised. "Really. I thought you were one of Connor's poetry types. Eating granola and quoting Joyce." There's a spark of humor in his eye.

"I do that, too," I reply, and he laughs before taking a bite.

"Not much deer hunting in Los Angeles, is there?" Nick asks.

I lift my fork to my mouth to buy myself time. Something about Nick's gaze unsettles me. His eyes are the same shade of blue as Connor's, but cold.

Connor knows a few broad details of my life. I have not lied to him—much. He's smart enough to guess there is a reason I don't talk about my family, and kind enough not to tug at the stitches holding those wounds shut. "I grew up in Washington," I say, as I did before. Most people will hear that and think of orcas and the Space Needle, not a stretch of sagebrush scrub and scablands spitting distance from the Idaho border.

"Is that where you're from originally?" Nick presses.

"Until I left for college."

"I was just in Seattle for a conference last month," Alexis says. "Lovely city."

"It is," I say. I've been there only once. Connor is perfectly aware which side of the mountains I grew up on, but he sips his wine and says nothing.

"You won't be staying in LA, will you?" Alexis asks. "You're moving back to New York, right?"

"We haven't talked about it yet." Connor sounds uncomfortable.

"I imagine there are a lot of things you haven't gotten around to talking about," Alexis says, and then looks embarrassed. "I'm sorry, I didn't mean—"

"Of course you did," Mrs. Dalton says. "They're rushing into things. The girl is drinking, so I assume *that's* not the reason why."

It takes me a couple of seconds to understand what she's saying, and I just about choke on a blackberry. "No," I say quickly. "I'm not—we're not—"

Connor covers my hand with his on the tabletop. "We just don't see the point in wasting time when we both know what it is we want."

"I think we all know what she wants," Trevor mutters—under his breath but loud enough for everyone to hear it, the implication clear. A rich man rushing into love is a fool. The woman on the other side of the equation is something else entirely. Paloma adjusts the napkin tucked into Sebastian's shirt while Alexis becomes absorbed in the task of refilling her wine.

Nick Dalton stares straight at me.

"I proposed to your grandmother after two weeks," Magnus Dalton declares. "Married four months later. I agree. No sense waiting around if you're sure. Of course, that was because she wouldn't let me sleep with her before she had a ring on her finger. I doubt you have that problem."

"Magnus," Mrs. Dalton says in a voice that could freeze the ocean, but he just laughs, dragging a chunk of venison through the juices on his plate.

"No, that's definitely not a factor," I say cheerfully. Alexis coughs. Trevor guffaws.

Magnus jabs his steak knife toward the blushing Connor. "I like a girl who can stick up for herself. But you be careful. They run your life." At his wife's warning look, he adds, "And I wouldn't have it any other way."

After that, the subject drifts blessedly away from me as Alexis starts talking about her business trip, which leads to talking about the family business—something about tariffs and a big deal they're trying to land. I catch the phrase *Eastern markets* and little else I can decipher.

There's a lump in my throat. I down a too-large swallow of wine to dislodge it. As I set the glass down, Connor's pinkie nudges my arm.

He catches my eye and tilts his head. *Hanging in there?* the look says. I take another sip, locking eyes with him, to answer. He stifles a chuckle. Alexis's voice brings my attention back to the conversation. "We're going to have to build another cabin now, you know," she's saying. "I mean, I assume Trevor doesn't want to bunk with Mom forever."

"It definitely makes it harder to bring home all the girls I meet out here," Trevor replies. Alexis snorts.

I do a mental count in my head. "Aren't there five cabins, though?" I ask. There should be enough for everyone without Trevor and his mother sharing one.

There's a pause. The silence holds weight I can't fathom, a strained quiet no one seems willing to break. Mrs. Dalton's silverware clicks as she sets it down. "Technically, yes," she says. "Five cabins were built originally. But only four have been maintained in recent years. The fifth is in quite poor repair."

At that moment Sebastian begins to cry, great wailing sobs that make everyone at the table flinch.

"Sorry! I just told him what venison is," Alexis says, patting his head frantically. "I thought he already knew."

Sebastian's tears don't stop until dinner is cleared away—and we nearly have a repeat a few minutes later, narrowly avoided when Paloma thinks to reassure him that the chocolate mousse is not an animal.

I'm relieved when the dessert course is done and my interrogation has remained minimal.

"We'd better get Bastian to bed," Paloma says. She has been quiet most of the meal, tending to Sebastian while Alexis chatters.

"You go. I'll stay a while," Alexis says, and Paloma's mouth purses before she nods. Alexis is pouring another glass of wine. I've lost count of how many she's had. Suddenly it occurs to me with apprehension that the end of dinner may not be the end of the visit.

"I think we'd better get back to White Pine," Connor says, putting a hand on my arm. "It was a long drive up. We'll see you all tomorrow."

He's already rising, not giving anyone the chance to extend a forceful invitation.

There is a flurry of farewells, and the next thing I know I'm pulling on my boots and coat at the door, Connor adjusting my scarf at my neck.

"There you go. We survived round one," he says, his voice a low murmur.

"How did I do?" I ask.

"Granddad likes you," he says.

"He wasn't the one I was worried about," I remind him. He wraps the end of the scarf around his hand once, twice, until it's pulling me toward him. My body fits against his, his nose nearly touching mine. I breathe him in. He smells of expensive wool, of cedar and winter air.

"The only one you have to impress is me, and you've already done it," he whispers.

"Connor." We spring apart like guilty teenagers at the sound of his sister's voice. Alexis has appeared, her gait slightly unsteady, the corner of her lip smudged with a stain of wine. "Can I steal your fiancée for just a moment?"

Connor looks at me for approval before he steps away, lingering just out of easy earshot. Alexis regards me. Her thumb massages the pad of her opposite hand, a not-quite-nervous gesture.

"I'm sorry about what I said earlier, at dinner," she begins.

"It's fine," I say. "It has all happened very fast. I'd be worried if you weren't worried, honestly."

She grimaces. "We can be protective. You should have heard the grilling Grandma Louise gave Paloma when we got engaged," she says. "At least you're the right gender this time around." She smooths over the bitterness in her voice by flipping her hair back over her shoulder. "Part of it is just—they tend to judge people by their families? So you're a bit more of an enigma to sort out." Her tone is overtly sympathetic, but probing.

When people hear that my parents are dead, they want to know what happened, but they don't want to ask. That fear of being awkward is one of the main reasons I've gotten away with lying for so long.

For a moment, I consider telling her what not even Connor knows. I'm not an orphan at all. I'm a devil-child; my parents are alive, they just don't want me.

But the moment passes. It always passes—every time the words push themselves up my throat, I swallow them down again.

"You know, I feel like no one's going to say it—I mean, other than Trevor—but I know you're all worried about it, and I promise I'm not with Connor because of his money," I say instead.

Alexis's eyes widen. "Oh, no no no, we wouldn't . . . okay, yeah, we would," she says, covering her mouth as if shocked at her own words.

"Not that I'm complaining about the money, either," I add, a little daringly.

"Ha," she says, more of a declaration than a true laugh. "You know, I think I'm starting to like you. But watch out. Hurt my baby brother and I'll turn on you in an instant. We Daltons don't fuck around."

"I wouldn't want it any other way."

Her expression grows serious. "I just want to see Connor happy again. He hasn't been for a long time."

"Really?" I ask, and at the genuine surprise on my face, she cocks her head curiously. "It's just—he's never struck me as unhappy."

"Maybe that's because the whole time you've known him, he's known you," she says. The next thing I know she's giving me a hug, the glimmer of unspent tears in her eyes. "Oh no, I've had too much wine and now I'm getting all weepy. I'm glad you came, Theo. I can't wait to get to know each other properly."

She relinquishes me back to Connor's care. I find myself stumbling as we leave, a pressure in my chest easing up.

Maybe this can work. If I have Alexis on my side, and Magnus—maybe I can win them over.

Maybe I can have this. Have him.

Connor's fingers lace with mine. I glance back over my shoulder, toward the lodge. There's someone standing in front of one of the massive picture windows, a drink in his hand, watching us go. Trevor Dalton—Connor's brother.

He meets my eyes. He smiles, slow and lazy. And he shakes his head.

I turn quickly away and pick up my pace.

5

That night I have the dream.

I call it the dream, but it isn't as if it's one set sequence—it's different every time. I'll be in my childhood bedroom trying to fit my feet into a series of ever-smaller shoes or running through bookstore corridors that seem to wind forever, and then some piece of the dream will appear, out of place. The red star gleaming between the shelves. Snow falling thickly to blanket that old beige carpet.

The buzz of the dragonfly's wings.

Tonight I'm in Harper's apartment, at a party—not the party where I met Connor, though he's here somewhere, in another room. The dream slews between half-realized conversations, anxiety thrumming through them—I've forgotten something important, and Harper won't tell me what it is. Then the door opens to welcome in new party guests, but instead of a hallway and tipsy grad students, there waits a maw of black, and in it, a single red star. Something buzzes at my wrist. I look down. The dragonfly is perched on my forearm. Its wings gleam, metallic.

Footsteps crunch behind me. I don't want to turn, because I know what I'll see.

He's there. He's always there. The rest is just prelude.

I don't want to turn, but I have to. It's the dream, and in the dream I turn. In the dream I stumble back and fall, and he looms above me: the antlered man. Shadow blackens half his face. Antlers rupture from his temples, branching into razor points.

"Scream," he says, and I do.

And then Connor is shaking me gently awake. "Theo," he says, "you're having a nightmare. Wake up."

The dream bleeds away. I try to speak but can only gasp, and Connor gathers me up against him. I burrow against his warmth, shutting my eyes, waiting for Connor's touch to soothe that fearful animal that lives in my chest.

I don't know what the dream means, only that the pieces are always the same: the star, the cold, the dragonfly, and the antlered man.

I know the antlered man wants to hurt me. That he *will* hurt me.

And I can never escape.

I've wondered if the dream has its origins in a memory. My life before I came to live with the Scotts is a blank—I was young, of course, but my therapist believes the complete lack of memories is a consequence of trauma. *It was clear something had happened to you,* Joseph once told me, on one of the rare occasions he talked about when I first arrived or even acknowledged I'd ever been anywhere else.

I was four years old when the Scotts took me in, and yet I don't even know my real name. I only have the dream, the fragments. *The cold, the star, the red scarf wound around her throat.*

The memory of a fear so intense, it traps the breath in your lungs.

I lie with my head on Connor's chest, listening to his heartbeat. It's slow and steady.

"You know, I used to have nightmares, too," he tells me. He trails his fingers up and down my arm. "After my father died. I used to dream that I was trying to catch up to him, but he kept getting farther and farther away. As metaphors go, it wasn't subtle."

"How did your father die?" I ask. "You've never told me."

"You've never asked," he says. His fingertips still.

"I don't like to talk about my childhood. It doesn't seem fair to ask people about theirs," I reply.

For a moment he's quiet. "It was an accident," he says at last. "A fall. He slipped off a roof, that's all. Random and meaningless. I was seven years old. At least I remember him. Trevor was only three. It was hardest on Alexis, I think—she was fifteen. It really messed her up for a while."

He takes my hand and runs his thumb over the dragonfly tattoo, as he often does. As if he's trying to feel the shape of it beneath my skin.

"Your sister said you haven't been happy for a long time," I say. He looks at me with surprise, his fingers making a bracelet around my wrist. "Is it because of your father?"

"I think that's part of it," Connor acknowledges. "He was my hero. And then he was gone, and my mother—it just about broke her. She's never had another relationship after him. I always felt like I had to fill the void he left. It doesn't help that I look just like him. Anyone who knows my family knows who I am at a glance. It's always 'You must be Liam Dalton's son.'"

"Well, I had no clue who you were when we met," I said. "I assumed you were just one of Harper's insufferable poet friends."

"I am definitely insufferable. But not nearly talented enough to be a poet," Connor replies seriously.

"And what about me? Did you think I was a granola-crunching James Joyce quoter?" I ask.

"The secret is that Granddad *loves* James Joyce," Connor says.

"That bastard."

"You'd better be careful. He's going to invite you out hunting."

"That's a bad thing? I wasn't kidding. I've done it before. Not bowhunting—but with a rifle, a few times," I say. They're some of my few positive memories, some of the only times I felt like I'd figured out who Joseph wanted me to be.

There's a beat of silence. "Why did you let Alexis think you were from Seattle?" he asks.

Because when we met, I told you more of the truth than I should have. I thought you would vanish with the dawn. "I didn't want to correct her in front of everyone. I already felt awkward enough."

"I'd like to see where you grew up sometime," he says.

"There's nothing there worth seeing," I say. I sit up, easing free of him.

"Come back to bed," he urges. I shake my head.

"I'm going to sit up a little while. You sleep." He's too tired to protest much. I wrap a blanket around my shoulders and pad out into the main room, shutting the door behind me. I walk to the window, looking out at the snow-shrouded woods. The moon is nearly full—waxing gibbous, as I would have been sure to call it at thirteen, in love with the sound and specificity of the word. The snow reflects the moonlight, making the night eerily bright. A dark shape slips between the trees: an owl. The scene looks peaceful from here, but somewhere among the roots a mouse is scurrying toward soft wings and sharp talons.

I don't know if I've never liked the winter because of the dream, or if winter infects the dream because I hate it. There isn't always snow, but there's always some element of the season—a cold wind, foggy breath, creeping frost.

But it's only a dream, and there are no men with antlers sprouting from their skulls to chase me through these woods.

I start to turn away from the window, and then I pause. The moonlight shines over the snow, turning it to an unbroken spill of silver—but it isn't *entirely* unbroken. A staggered line of discrete shadows trails from the trees toward the cabin. Footprints. They lead toward the bedroom. Toward the window that looks in on where Connor is still sleeping.

They could have been there all day, I tell myself.

But I think of the crunch of footsteps in the dream, and the winter steals into my bones.

Before I have time to think better of it, I'm grabbing my coat and shoving my feet into my boots. I open the door and then pause, glancing behind myself, waiting to see if Connor will emerge—but there's nothing. I ease the door shut.

Outside, the cold is biting, but I ignore the sting. There hasn't been more than a dusting of snow all day. Our tracks leaving for dinner are as clear as the ones coming back. There's no reason to suppose that this other set wasn't here before.

I follow them.

My own footprints are smaller. At a guess, it was a man who walked this way. As I feared, they continue to the window that looks into the bedroom. The curtain is closed, but there is a gap an inch wide. Easy enough to look in without being seen.

The prints lead toward the window. Then they veer away. I keep following.

This is my problem. I can't turn back once I've started. It's one of the things the Scotts never really understood, what made them afraid of me. How once I had a notion in my head, no amount of correction could stop me from chasing it down. They tried prayer and patience, threats and lectures, but I wouldn't bend.

In the end, what happened was entirely predictable. Everyone knows not to put your hand in a stray dog's mouth. You'll only get bit.

The sugar maple and birch near the cabin have surrendered to hemlock and pine. The evergreen branches shelter the ground, leaving only the thinnest skin of snow and blanketing it in shadows. Not far to my right, the ground drops off in an abrupt slope. If it weren't for the moonlight casting its scant illumination, it would be easy to topple down in the dark. Not far enough to kill you, but enough to break an ankle, maybe, and I think of the way snow swallows sound, how loud you'd have to shout to be heard, out here in the cold.

Without the footsteps to follow, I continue forward cautiously.

There's nothing here, and my hands are aching from the chill. My face, too. Under the canopy of the trees, I can't see a thing.

Except, up ahead, the dark shape of a two-story building. My mind constructs the map from the bathroom, tracing a dotted line from the steps of the White Pine cabin. If I've headed mostly straight, I should be right where the fifth cabin is.

My imagination sparks with images of lurking slashers and skulking fugitives, taking advantage of a disused cabin to set up camp, but I tell myself it's ridiculous. Though the mountain would make a pretty good place to hide—anytime but two weeks over Christmas and a month in the summer.

I creep forward, moving more by feel than sight. The trees give way a few feet from the cabin, and the moonlight makes the wood look pale and gray. Three steps lead up to a small porch. The wood is scuffed, one step bowed. It groans under my boots.

White Pine has a brass tree tacked to its door, and I look for one here, but there's nothing—only, when I brush my fingertips over the wood, a pair of holes where screws might have once been drilled through and a faint silhouette, wood less weathered than what's around it. The shape is indistinct, barely discernible in the pale moonlight flung up from the snow.

Bright light spills across me. I whirl with a cry, flinging up a hand to protect myself from the blinding beam of a flashlight. It lowers quickly, but I can't see the figure who's holding it.

"Miss Scott, isn't it?" says a voice it takes me a moment to place.

"Mr. Vance. You startled me."

"What are you doing out here in the dark?" His tone is thick with suspicion—or maybe just confusion.

He steps closer, the light still down, and as my eyes adjust, I see that Duchess is with him, her attention trained on me, her head held low. A faint rumble of a growl sounds before Vance hushes her.

I consider lying, then decide against it. "I heard something outside the cabin, and when I looked out, there were footprints," I say, watching his face for a reaction. Trying to ignore Duchess's intent stare.

His eyebrows raise. "Footprints?" he echoes. "And you decided to follow them."

"It was probably pretty stupid," I acknowledge. My teeth are chattering.

"That's a word for it," he says. "Don't let the luxury fool you, miss. The cold kills you just as quick here as anywhere else, and it's easy to get turned around in these woods. Even when you've brought a light.

Which it doesn't look like you've done." He sighs. "Come on. I'll walk you back to your cabin. You can show me these footprints."

I don't see that I have another choice, especially as he's already setting off in the direction I came from. It occurs to me belatedly that I didn't see his light until it was shining on me—and that he's backtracking without asking me which way to go. It means he spotted me before he approached. And it means Mr. Vance is as comfortable in the dark as I am.

I glance behind myself again. With my eyes now calibrated to the bright flashlight, I can't make out anything but the rough shape of the door.

There is something about it—some low thrum of a feeling I can't name. It reminds me of the moment a plane begins to ascend, the strange sensation of the ground rising up beneath you.

"Where are these tracks?" Mr. Vance asks, pulling my attention back around. I hurry forward to catch up with him and with the light, putting myself on the opposite side from Duchess, who watches me with wary dark eyes. She's silent as she moves. Something about that strikes me as odd, and then I realize—she's not wearing tags, or they would jangle.

My throat is dry as I point across the stretch of bare earth, toward where the snow layer thickens and the footprints—and mine—are visible. Vance grunts and walks to them.

He has a gun on his hip.

Mr. Vance kicks at one of the prints, caving in the heel. "Could be fresh. Could be from this morning," he says. "You said they went by your cabin?"

"Up to the bedroom window," I say.

"Think someone was sneaking a peek?" he asks.

My cheeks heat, images and sensations ghosting through my mind—Connor's hands stealing under my shirt, Connor's teeth against my neck, Connor pulling me roughly to him.

"Did you see where they came from?" Vance is asking; I've taken too long to answer.

"Just followed where they went. I think they came from the main path, though," I say.

"Probably won't be able to sort them out from everyone else's, then," he says. "They're probably from earlier today. Somebody taking a walk, that's all." He shifts his weight, and I look down at the impression he leaves in the snow. I think his footprints look larger than the others—but I can't be sure.

"There's no chance there's someone else around?"

"Nobody's on the mountain and I don't know about it," Vance says, teetering between offense and pride. "It's just the family here. And you."

"No cannibals hiding in the old cabin?" I ask with a forced note of humor.

"Nobody's stayed there in years," Vance says. "Not since Liam died."

"The accident," I say; he grunts. "Connor said . . . he fell off a roof?"

Vance takes a moment to speak. "A storm blew through. There was some roof damage. I couldn't get out on short notice, so Liam came up. By himself. I should've been with him, but there you go." He sets off again, tramping through the snow. Duchess gives me a *you coming?* look.

Liam came up, he said. Came *here*. Which means that Connor's father died at Idlewood. I look behind me, at the cabin with its shaggy eaves and unkempt shutters. Left abandoned when all the others were gleaming. No wonder, if it was where Liam Dalton died. I burrow into my coat, suppressing a shiver that has little to do with the cold.

The return trip doesn't take nearly as long as it did to get here. Vance follows the tracks the whole way, shines his flashlight on where they stop by the window. He's scowling, but that seems to be his natural expression.

"Well," he says, "it's probably nothing."

"Probably nothing," I agree. My mind is still on the cabin with its blank door, its empty windows. Its history. Why didn't Connor mention that his father died *here*, at Idlewood?

At least now I know why the table fell so silent when I asked about the fifth cabin.

"Still," Vance adds, his light still fixed on the prints, "you ought to be more careful. Wandering around after dark. During the day, too. It's hunting season."

"Do lots of people hunt up here?" I ask.

"This time of year, it's just me and the Daltons allowed. From time to time, we do get folks sneaking up without permission, though." He's quiet, long enough that I wonder if he expects me to leave. Then he speaks again. "Can I ask you, Miss Scott—have you been around here before?"

"Nope. Never been here in my life," I answer. "Why?"

"No reason, I guess," he says, staring intently at me. "Good night, Miss Scott."

He gestures to the front door and stays put until I step inside. I watch through the window as he sets off, the flashlight tracing the course in front of him. He said it was probably nothing—but I notice that he follows the trail of the footprints back the way they came, all the way to where they vanish into the more numerous tracks of the main path.

He stands there for a long time. Then he ruffles Duchess's ears and sets off again.

Why did he ask me if I've been here before? I wonder.

And why does it feel like I answered wrong?

6

I wake with Connor's arm around me, his face burrowed against my shoulder. He sleeps like this often, not holding me so much as half-flung over me, like he's afraid I'll slip away from him in the night. As if, as he once confessed, he'll wake to an empty bed and no evidence that I was ever there.

You came out of nowhere. Like a magic trick, he told me. He meant an illusion. Something that isn't real.

I wriggle out from under the weight of his arm. In the bathroom I press two fingers against my cheekbone as I stare at my reflection. Real enough.

By the time Connor gets up, I'm dressed and the coffee is made. I always wake up before he does—it's an old survival instinct I've never shed. Sloth is one of the deadly sins, and you didn't want Beth finding you still asleep in bed past the appointed hour.

I sit alone, sipping my coffee, letting the sense of Theo Scott seep into my limbs. She's never there when I first open my eyes. I am an empty house without her. Restless, dull. And then she enters in: not something I've constructed, no meticulously planned illusion. More like a visitor—someone who arrives every day and yet remains in some ways a stranger.

Connor stumbles into the shower, then out to press a kiss into my hair, praise me for the coffee. He moves like a bear in the morning. Lumbering, slow, seemingly fifty pounds heavier as he thumps down into a chair and takes his first slurp. He's wrapped himself in a plush robe, one of two left hanging in the bathroom for us. There's something different about him, I think: a lassitude to his limbs I can't put down to sleepiness.

"Something on my face?" he asks.

I hum a nonanswer. "So what do you do in a place like this for two weeks?" I ask.

He scratches his neck, stifles a yawn. "Drink," he says. "Stare at fires. The guys go hunting, the women always bake something. There are walks in the woods and snowshoeing and cross-country skiing, and did I mention the drinking? Or you can read. Mom always brings a stack of books," he says. His eyes glitter. "And we can keep each other busy, of course."

He's looking for a laugh, but I only tilt my chin. I think of telling him—the footprints, the possibility of a presence outside our window. I would sound paranoid. Fearful. Perhaps even delusional. None of these words are acceptable descriptions for an aspiring wife. I'm not an idiot. I know Connor Dalton is out of my league. A step out of line, and he will realize this—or remember it.

So when Connor reaches out, I let him tug me from my seat into his lap. He tips his face up, and I meet his lips with mine. He abandons his mug, freeing both hands to rove up under my sweater, warm palms against the skin of my hips.

"God, you're beautiful," he says. He never tires of this, the marveling at me. But I can't stand it—the way he looks at me so intently. Like he is analyzing every freckle, every pore. Like he will see beneath the skin, assess my sinews, my veins, down to the bone. To the marrow.

So when he nods toward the bedroom, I slide off his lap instead, kneel on the warm hardwood. He's already hard when I undo the belt of his robe, take him in my mouth. His hand grips the back of my head, my nails dig into his thigh, and as he lets out a soft moan, zips of pleasure trace electric paths through every part of me.

After we're done, he sits with his head tipped back, that half-dazed smile curling at the corners of his mouth. I brush my fingertips lightly over his eyelids, drag them down his cheeks, and then I'm slipping away before he can open his eyes again.

I love Connor Dalton. I need Connor Dalton.

And so, I can never let him look too closely.

We spend the morning lazing in the cabin, but around noon, Alexis comes to collect us. "Mom's here," she says without preamble. Her eyes flick to me, half-apologetic. "And it's pie day."

"Pie day?" I echo.

"Remember what I said about the baking?" Connor asks.

Right. An afternoon with "the women," performing the rituals of domesticity—despite the fact that the Daltons clearly outsource these anytime they threaten to acquire the whiff of actual work. The Scotts worshipped work, glorified labor and making oneself useful. *Idleness, ignorance, softness, indulgence,* I think anytime I am sitting on the couch in the evening with a glass of wine and a book.

"We always do pie day first," Alexis says as we set out from the cabin. She has this way of talking like everything she says is about to be followed up with a punch line that never comes, like we're all about to break into laughter. She keeps swinging around backward to look at us as she walks. I have no idea how she hasn't fallen. "Grandma Louise's *famous* recipe. We all have a recipe that's 'ours,' you know? You get to be in charge, order everyone around. I remember being so fucking excited to be the head baker for the first time when I was thirteen. Lemon bars—that's my recipe. You'll have to pick one. But Grandma Louise decides if it'll actually go in the rotation. You might have to try a few times. I made seven variations before she decided it was 'minimally acceptable.'"

"Cool it, Lex. You're going to scare her off," Connor says.

She makes a face—more teenager than thirty-something executive. That's the difference I saw in Connor this morning. He's different *here*. There's a blur at his edges, like twenty-seven years' worth of past selves, twice-a-year snapshots, are layered over him.

Places are like that, I've heard. Childhood homes. Old haunts. The *you* that was left behind settling into your body like a ghost. It's not an experience I've ever had; my life has been a straight line onward, never doubling back.

We skirt the pond—the ice has cinched inward, tightening the circle of open water. A new car sits next to Connor's, and fresh footprints trammel the snow around it. Alexis bounds up the steps of the lodge. Unlike last night, we enter without knocking, stomping snow from our boots before ditching them at the threshold.

The doors at the other end of the foyer open. A woman steps through, instantly recognizable as Alexis's mother in the same way Connor is such a carbon copy of his father—the same straight dark hair, sharp nose, piercing eyes. This has to be Rose Dalton.

"Connor," she says warmly. There are exclamations—embraces—her hand on his head like she's checking if he's grown—a flurry of questions about the drive, the weather, when she got in. I hang back, not part of it.

Until Connor half turns, his hand extended to beckon me in. "And this is—"

"Theo," his mother says. I step forward, into the protective half circle of Connor's arm, which he sets around my shoulders. She takes my hand in both of hers. She smiles, but it isn't the smile she gave to her son. It compresses her lips, draws tight lines at the corners of her eyes.

"It's so good to meet you," I say. "Connor's told me so much about you." *So so so*, I think, cringing, and put the word on time-out.

"I've heard a lot about you as well," she says, a veneer of warmth over a decidedly neutral tone. "I am very much looking forward to getting to know you myself."

"Me too," I say, and with that she drops my hands and her attention is back to Connor.

Five minutes later we're being herded into the kitchen, where Louise Dalton is already standing next to a line of artfully arranged ingredients—tubs of flour and sugar and shortening, green and red apples, cinnamon and whole nutmeg. The last time I did any serious baking, I scooped flour and sugar from yellow and orange plastic tubs older than I was. Every ingredient here is in a glass jar with a neat hand-printed cursive label and a polished wooden lid. The eggs nestle in a wicker basket.

Paloma is absent—watching Sebastian again, Alexis explains breezily, though I have to wonder if that's just an excuse. Louise sets Alexis and me the task of peeling apples. I sit on a barstool two down from Alexis and get to work, quickly skinning long strips of peel.

You get a prize if you get it all off in one piece, I remember Beth telling me once, in a rare moment of good humor that didn't last—my fault. It always was.

Wicked girl.

Of course, then I'd used a paring knife, twisting the apple, the blade skating close to my thumb as I slid it just under the glossy skin. I'd tried and tried, getting more and more frustrated. Every time, the strip broke, until finally I had it, moving with steady intensity, the last half inch coming free in one continuous piece, and I'd looked up at Beth and asked, *What do I get?* And she scowled, called me greedy, and the bowl was in my hands before I knew it, the apples tumbling across the floor, bouncing, rolling in every direction, and a scream tearing out of my throat, an animal sound.

Now I twist the apple and peeler in my hands, skinning the fruit efficiently, and try not to remember the way Beth's face contorted in disgust.

Connor's mother is watching me with one eyebrow slightly raised, a quirk to the corner of her mouth. Alexis gets her smile from there, I think—that corner in particular, only on her it never stays tucked away.

"No need to race. We've got all day," Rose says. My cheeks heat. I'm three apples ahead and the only one in a rush. Alexis, apples already abandoned, hands her mother a glass of white wine. Rose curls her hand around it, holding it to her chest.

A wineglass makes a chiming sound as it's set on the granite countertop in front of me. I jump. Olena, the slim girl with Bambi eyes, stands at my shoulder. She murmurs something unintelligible as she hurries away.

I've misunderstood the point of this exercise, I realize with a touch of irritation at myself as Alexis leans a hip against the counter. It's not the baking after all.

Rose takes a sip of her wine and pins me with her gaze. "So, Theo. You and Connor met at a party, is that right?" she says.

I bob my head. Alexis props her elbows on the countertop, leaning her whole body over. I can see down her blouse—see the sharp ridges of her sternum and ribs where the skin pulls tight. She's so thin her chest almost looks sunken. "She already sat through an interrogation last night, Mom. Cut her some slack," she says, and winks at me. I wonder if you have to practice winking in order for it to look natural.

"I don't mind," I say. "I'm an open book." I don't know why these things come out of my mouth.

"Really? Connor says you're quite mysterious," Rose replies. My teeth feel glued together. She chuckles. "Don't look so stricken. I think he likes being intrigued. And I'll admit, I'm intrigued, too. Connor's never introduced me to any of his girlfriends—even Darcy, and they were together, what, two years?"

"Eighteen months," Alexis demurs.

Rose makes a light noise, a sort of verbal shrug. "In any case, here you are on the mountain. It's remarkable."

"Is it?" I ask.

"We do not generally allow casual romantic partners to join us at Idlewood," Louise says. She, too, has a glass of wine, though she hasn't touched it that I've seen. "Rose, you and Liam were together for three years before he brought you, isn't that right?"

"It's a bit like a proposal in its own right," Rose says. "You get engaged and get your invitation to the mountain."

"Well, we are engaged," I point out. Her lips thin, so briefly that I could almost pretend it didn't happen. My pulse is beating quickly at my throat, like I'm looking into the teeth of a wolf, not just having a friendly conversation surrounded by pie ingredients.

One of these people might have sent me those texts. Louise? Surely not—or could she have had someone send them for her, told some employee to handle things? Rose? She's only just met me, and she's obviously skeptical, but openly hostile? Could it be Alexis after all, covering for it with her friendliness?

I'm being paranoid. But I can't help it. What if one of them knows?

My hands have been still too long. I reach for my wine. It's oversweet; it turns my stomach.

"I brought Paloma up here when we'd only been together a few weeks," Alexis says. I know she's trying to help, but being argumentative is just extending this horrific line of conversation.

Louise scoffs. "Because all you teenagers had license to invite a friend for the summer retreat. We simply didn't expect that any of you would be sleeping with them."

Annoyance—or maybe anger—flashes briefly over Alexis's face, but she doesn't push the point. "We should chill the dough, right?" she asks.

"Toss those peels out first," Louise directs her. Alexis takes the metal bowl we've designated for the purpose over to the pullout cabinet that houses the garbage cans. "The trash is full," she notes as she chucks the peels in with the organic waste.

"I'll have Olena take it out. Where is that girl?" Louise asks.

"I'll take it," I say immediately, eager for the excuse to escape for at least a minute or two.

"That's not necessary," Louise says.

I shrug. "I don't mind."

"The bins are straight out back, behind the cinder block wall," Alexis says, pointing in the right general direction. Before Mrs. Dalton can object again, I scoot in to grab the bag. My sleeves are still pushed up from when I washed my hands, and as I tie the top of the bag, Rose leans forward, a little frown sketched over her lips as she examines my tattoo. My first instinct is to yank down my sleeve, but I turn my wrist instead, giving her a better view. She touches my forearm lightly, as if to fix my arm in place for her examination.

"A dragonfly," she says with the faint note of a question.

"Kind of a personal symbol of mine," I say, though a symbol of what, I could not explain. I'm never sure if the dragonfly in my dreams is a protector or a warning—or an ill omen.

"I see," she says, with an expression bordering on distaste. Her hand drops. Abruptly she turns away. "Louise, let me help you with that," she says, stepping quickly away and leaving me to furrow my brow. Maybe she's not a fan of tattoos. Or dragonflies.

I have to head to the front to collect my boots. When I'm halfway there, a flutter of laughter floats down the hall. I turn my head, and I can just see Olena. Her whole body is canted back, someone's arm around her waist to hold her up. She's bending away from him but laughing, the movement elongating her neck, baring her throat, and Trevor leans in to kiss it. I stand there, frozen. He looks up. Sees me. He grins.

I hurry away.

In my haste, I step out with only my thick sweater to ward off the chill. Instead of cutting back through the house again, I tramp around the side of the lodge. A squat wall of cinder blocks hides the dumpster from view of the house. I deposit the bag and lower the lid slowly, not willing to break the quiet of the forest with a clang.

I have to go back inside. I can't. Mist plumes from my lips. Out here, I can breathe, but the cold air holds a razor's edge that nicks my throat. Inside is warmth and the scent of cinnamon, smiles and laughter, so why do I feel safer with the cold seeping into my bones?

"Something interesting about the dumpster?" says a voice, and I jump. Magnus Dalton stands behind me, maybe twenty feet away. He's wearing a gray jacket, the cuffs stained a dull brown from age and use. I try to picture the man in a business suit—I know he owns several companies, that he spends his days in boardrooms, but the crags of his face belong so clearly to this place.

"Just lost in thought, I guess," I say. I gesture toward the house. "We're baking."

"Ah. Pie day." His eyes glint in understanding, and he jerks a thumb over his shoulder. "I could use a hand. Think the ladies can spare you a minute?"

I nod mutely, relieved and nervous. Magnus takes off without another word. I scramble to follow. Multiple sets of footprints trample down a path that he follows, leading to a small wooden shack. Halfway there, the footprints join up with wide wheel tracks and, following behind them, drag marks. Here and there, blood dots the snow. My stomach knots as the pieces click together.

The door of the shed stands open. Outside, a green ATV—or rather, UTV, with two seats side by side—sits parked, a sledge hooked up behind it. Just inside the door, the deer that must have recently been carried on that sledge is laid out on a tarp, eye glassy, head tilted grotesquely where its antlers prop it up. A bloody hole punctures its side, at the ribs.

"Good shot," I say, trying to keep my expression from twisting with distaste. I know where my food comes from. It doesn't make staring at death any more appetizing. "Rifle?"

He shakes his head. "Wrong season for it. Get a good shot with a broadhead and it'll go straight through just as well as a bullet. Clean kill." He pauses. "Mr. Vance tells me you had quite the encounter." He moves as he speaks, getting a thin rope from a nearby table. He loops it around the antlers and ties a practiced knot.

"I guess Mr. Vance isn't as good a shot as you are." I fix my eyes on Magnus, not the dead stare of the deer.

He grunts a laugh. "No, he is not. You could have been killed, you know. Never go near a deer until you're certain it's dead. No sense getting gored."

I remember, then, Joseph telling me the same thing. How I leaned in close to listen as he crouched down in front of me, showing me the parts of his rifle, his knife. Making me hold every piece until they felt natural. The Scotts were always putting knives in my hand. They shouldn't have been so surprised I'd pick one up myself.

"You said you'd been hunting," he says. "Who took you? Your father?"

That was what I was supposed to call him, at least. I hadn't minded it, not at first. I'd adored him. He didn't have his wife's temper—or his father's. Joseph's father, he'd told me, was a congenial man with a loud laugh and a deep affection for the sound of a snapping belt. Seemed to like that clean, sharp sound even more than he liked the fear it instilled. Joseph tried out his father's favorite method of discipline only once. Often he let me get away with things. Palmed me pieces of candy, just pressed a finger to his lips when he saw me sneaking a piece of bread after Beth ordered me upstairs without my dinner. For a little while I'd thought I could really be someone he loved.

"Yes," I say, realizing I've been silent too long. "My adoptive father."

There's a pulley screwed to the beam that runs down the center of the shed, and threaded through it is a cord terminating in a hook, which Magnus draws down to snag the rope he's used to secure the deer. "Help me haul this up," he instructs, and I step forward. An instinct to please that I haven't felt in years tugs at me like marionette strings. I haul on the cord with him, struggling with the weight of the deer. Watch as its neck distends, as its body heaves from the ground, swaying. Settling.

"Good," Magnus says. He ties off the cord. I step away, palms stinging. "Did you learn how to dress a deer, when you went hunting?"

"It's been years," I tell him.

He takes a folding knife from the table. The handle is carved from antler. The blade looks hand-forged. Joseph had a knife like that—not his best knife, but his favorite, because he knew exactly where it had come from. Magnus holds it out toward me, fingers folded loosely over the handle. "Would you like to learn?" he asks.

I take the knife in answer.

"When you did this before, was it hanging head up or head down?" he asks.

"Down," I say, and he nods like this is expected.

"There are arguments for both, and I could tell you all the reasons why my way's better, but the truth is, it's what my father did, so it's what I do," he tells me. "We are what our parents make us, after all."

He takes hold of my hand, the one holding the knife, and walks me through half-remembered steps. Shows me just how deep to set the knife to slit the skin and the membrane beneath without puncturing the organs. He tells me to step back as he pulls out a slopping mass of intestines and stomach, letting them spill into a metal tub he's placed beneath for that purpose. Gorge rises in my throat, but I don't look away—he doesn't want me to, and I want him to approve of me. Not just because of Connor. There is a yearning inside me, shameful, a thing that twists like a worm in my gut.

I want to be what you want me to be, it says. *I will get it right this time.*

"You don't flinch," he notes. There's no approval there, just fact, but I get the feeling it's as close as he gets.

He removes the liver, heart, and lungs with more care, wielding a second knife. The deer hangs all but hollow. It's shocking, how quickly a living thing becomes a body, how quickly a body is disassembled.

"My grandfather made the family rich. He was afraid it would make us soft, so he made sure we weren't. My father did the same. I did what I could, but I lost track, focused on the wrong things. Liam, Connor's father—he was soft. Not like me. Didn't know what to do about that."

My fingers tighten around the polished antler handle. "Soft isn't a bad thing," I say, thinking of Connor, his arms around me in the night. "Soft doesn't mean weak."

"No, that's true," he acknowledges, to my surprise. "Soft isn't the problem. Soft *and* weak, though. It's only if you're weak that you need to learn to be hard. Need that kind of strength. You're not weak, are you."

"I'd like to think that," I say. My mind skitters over shameful things, secrets and failings and the lights of a police cruiser flashing rhythmically, cast against the shimmering surface of a wet road. No, weakness isn't my sin.

"You're not soft, either," he notes.

No, I'm not, I think. "I work in a bookstore and I quote Joyce," I remind him.

He fixes me with sharp eyes. They're blue, like Connor's, but they have more gray to them. "You might seem it. But there's something entirely different under the skin, isn't there?" he asks. He doesn't wait for an answer. "Your parents," he says. "Were they good people? God-fearing?"

"God-fearing, yes. I don't know about good," I say, a bit surprised to have that question asked here. Connor's not the least bit religious that I can tell, though he has mentioned going to church as a kid. But Magnus is from another generation.

He grunts, like this answer doesn't shock him. "You understand—a family like ours, we have to know who it is we're welcoming in. What kind of stock you come from. You can't escape what's in your blood."

"They aren't my blood," I remind him. "I was adopted."

He pauses. Flicks his knife. Spatters mar wooden boards already years deep with stains. "And your birth parents?"

"No idea. It was a closed adoption," I say.

He looks at me, his gaze intent. I shift uncomfortably under his scrutiny. "You should get back inside," he says at last. He reaches out his hand. I set the knife into it, knowing there's been some kind of test here, not knowing how I fared. I'm at the door of the shed before he speaks again.

"You'll come hunting with me. Thursday. Last day for it until after Christmas," he says.

I nod, feeling for the first time since I stepped into the shed the cold numbing my fingertips, my ears, the end of my nose. My eyes water with it, and the smell of the enclosed place. Magnus is done with me.

I head back out into the snow.

7

Inside, I start to thaw and my skin begins to sting and burn. Somehow it's always worse than the cold, those first few moments out of it. In my thick wool socks, my footsteps are all but silent. I'm nearly to the kitchen doorway when the thread of conversation within snaps into focus.

"What do you think?" Louise is asking. I still instinctively, even my breath going quiet.

"She seems sweet." Alexis.

"That doesn't mean anything," Rose replies, and my heart sinks.

Louise, tone practical: "What do you think he's told her?"

"Nothing," Rose says as my thoughts tilt wildly in confusion. "He wouldn't tell her anything."

A skeptical noise from Louise. "Alexis?"

The moment of silence that follows is suffused with reluctance. "I don't think—" Alexis begins, and then down the hall a door shuts. The conversation in the kitchen cuts off cleanly.

"We can talk about this later," Louise declares. "Alexis, give your mother the nutmeg if you're just going to stand there."

Alexis steps around the counter and into view. She looks toward me, startled—and screams.

Louise and Rose move rapidly to see what Alexis is staring at. "Good Lord," Louise says, and Rose contributes a less restrained "Jesus Christ." I look down at my hands, gore-scabbed, blood in the creases. Despite standing back from the slop of guts I must have gotten splashed, because the soft cream of my cabled sweater is liberally spattered with it. Rose crosses to me and puts a thumb to my cheek; it comes away bloody.

"Shit. Sorry, I was outside and Magnus—" I begin.

"Is he hurt?" Alarm in Alexis's voice.

"She means he's out there butchering a deer," Louise says, a hint of contempt running like a seam of tar through her voice.

"I'll go get cleaned up," I say quickly. I must look like I stepped off the set of a horror movie.

"Not here," Louise says. "You'll need more than a quick washup in the sink. Go back to your cabin. Leave the clothes on the doorstep, I'll have Irina collect them. We *might* be able to salvage them."

I mutter something—I'm not even sure what—and flee. Behind me I hear Alexis again—*Holy shit*—and the scrabble of conversation pitched too low for me to make out.

My skin feels like it's on fire as I make my way back around the pond. The blood on my sweater is like a scarlet flag, and I swear even out here in the woods I can feel eyes on me.

When I reach the cabin, I strip off my sweater and run cold water over the stains in the kitchen sink before they can dry. The water runs red, then pink, slipping down the drain.

I know how to get blood out of clothes.

Blood on my shirt, when I was seven and Beth screamed at Joseph to control me and so he took off his belt the way his father had always done, the first and only time because as he struck out, his grip slipped and the buckle snapped free, caught my back. Skin splitting, me shrieking, Joseph gathering me to him with tears in his eyes, promising never again, and I thought his regret was the same as love.

Blood in my underwear, when I was eleven and terrified and no one had told me enough to know I wasn't dying, but I was too afraid to go to Beth, and I didn't figure it out until one of the neighbors' daughters saw the spreading stain on my skirt and wordlessly handed me a tampon, then laughed when I asked what it was for. Her mother told Beth. Beth told Joseph. *It's early, isn't it?* he asked.

I got mine at fourteen, she said.

She's developed for her age. We should keep an eye on that.

Blood soaking through my skirt, too much of it, not stopping, and my hands covered with it and Beth looking on in horror.

Blood everywhere. On my hands. On my arms. Droplets and scattered lines, an artwork in dull crimson across my chest, and the lights of the police cruiser reflecting off wet asphalt.

I've never minded blood. It's a trail to follow, back through my memories. I always feel as if there's something else there, a final step lost in the gloom—before the Scotts, before any of it. Blood holds a promise that someday I might remember what it is.

I scrub my hands in hot water in the bathroom sink. Scrub my face, too, which is freckled with tiny drops of carmine. I dress again. It's no loss, the sweater. There are so many more.

The Scotts would extract every ounce of value they could get from their possessions. They rarely threw things away—not if it had some kind of use, not if they might find one for it in the future. The Daltons can have whatever they want. A thing needs to be very valuable indeed to bother with it. The smallest flaw, and they'll simply get rid of it.

I dress again, checking every inch of my skin for stray spots of blood. It's only when I've pulled a fresh sweater over my head that I see the small shape on the windowsill, framed by the crack between the curtains.

A box the size of my palm, gift-wrapped in glossy green paper and bound with red ribbon, sits tucked against the other side of the window.

I peer outside. The woods are quiet. No sign of my visitor.

I unlatch the window and open it cautiously so that the box doesn't get knocked into the snow. It falls inward instead, toppling into my waiting hand. It's light, seemingly empty. The tag taped to it bears a single word in a typewriter font. DORA.

My mouth is dry as paper, my blood cold. No one has called me that in years.

I pull the end of the ribbon. It comes undone and drops to the floor. The box is one of those wrapped top and bottom, so all I have to do is lift the lid.

The only thing inside is a slip of paper. Four words, and nothing more.

You shouldn't have come.

8

Connor brings me dinner in the cabin. Chicken thighs in crackling skin rubbed with herbs, roasted new potatoes and carrots, a salad sprinkled with goat cheese and tossed with a bright vinaigrette, a glass of red wine and then another. I smile and say the right words and I don't tell him about the box hidden on the upper shelf in the closet.

The texts aren't from a romantic rival or from someone I used to know back home. They're from someone on this mountain.

Someone who wants me gone.

We eat our fill and then sprawl together, sated, on the couch, Connor's hand on my leg and his cheek against my stomach. I play my fingertips through his hair. No one should have been able to find out about what I did. It was supposed to be buried. Forgotten.

"I can hear you digesting," Connor says.

"Sexy," I reply distractedly.

"Glurb. Glubble. Your stomach is a flirt," he says, and I force a smile. I should be here. With him. Not thinking about my apparent stalker. Blackmailer?

He turns his face to kiss the spot by my hip bone that always makes me gasp. I bite my lip, not willing to give him the satisfaction. He works his way up my side, rucking up my shirt as he goes until he reaches my breasts, and then he lifts himself the rest of the way up—neck, jaw, mouth. I put a single finger over his lips.

"What's wrong?" he asks me, because he can see it on my face.

"I think this was a mistake," I tell him.

He sits up, and I push myself upright as well, settling my shirt back down around my hips. "What part?" he asks, wary.

"Me being here. It's too soon."

"For you? Or for my family?" he asks.

I give him a look. He was at dinner. Does he really need to ask? "Maybe we should come up with some excuse. I can leave, and we can try again in the summer. After they have a chance to get used to the idea."

"You can't leave," Connor says, and for a split second a spasm of panic goes through me. He takes my hand, kisses the point at the base of my thumb where my pulse flutters. "Don't worry, Theo. Everything's going to be just fine."

He draws me to him, arms around me, and for the first time, it doesn't feel like comfort but like a cage.

That night I dream of a knife in my hand and a body before me. I split it open down the center. The guts spill out. I look up into the glassy eyes of the deer, but it isn't a deer at all, it's Connor, antlers sprouting from his temples. He grabs my wrist. I run. I always run.

I'm in a cabin—not like this one, rustic, older. The distance to the door is impossibly far, and I can feel the antlered man's breath on my neck.

I flee outside, slamming the door shut behind me even though I know it won't help, and that's when I see the dragonfly at last, hear its droning as it perches on the wooden door.

I wrench from the dream with my scream still trapped in my throat and I force myself to lie still, trembling beneath the comforter with Connor's arm flung over me, even though every instinct in me is telling me to get away.

I wait until my heartbeat has slowed and the cabin beams above me seem more real than the branching antlers of the man in my dream before I extract myself from Connor and pad out to the living room. I touch things along the way—the doorframe, the back of a table. Real. All of it real, and the dream isn't.

When I woke up screaming as a young child, the Scotts would sit up with me and pray. By the time I was a teenager, I was expected to have sorted the problem out. They brought me to our pastor, who suggested that the dream was because I was allowing something to interfere with my relationship with Jesus, a sign that I hadn't accepted Him fully into my heart.

It's been years since the dream came two nights in a row. But it seems impossibly present here—as if it's just beyond the tips of my fingers, and if I step around a corner, I might find myself toppling into it.

My nightmare usually steals familiar things. The bookstore, my apartment, even the grocery store. The cabin was new. The door—it looked just like the fifth cabin, neglected out there in the woods.

Which means nothing. My mind has just taken fistfuls of whatever's around me and added them to the jumble in my brain.

The dream keeps playing through my mind the next day as I drink my coffee, eat breakfast, tromp out with Connor for a lesson in cross-country skiing.

The lesson takes place a ways from the lodge, out past the cabins. The only tracks here are the spindly ones left by birds hopping along the snow, the pattering footprints of squirrels, the occasional larger track of a deer. There was enough snow last night that the surface is pristine, leaving the paths of these early-morning travelers unmistakable.

"You're doing great," Alexis tells me. It's an obvious lie. "How are you feeling?"

"Fantastic," I lie in return, clutching the poles they've given me for dear life.

Connor laughs. "I didn't know a person could stiffen up that much," he says.

"It's practically rigor mortis," Alexis quips.

For the past hour, I've been doing my best "ungainly baby elephant" impression. Connor is a patient teacher. Alexis, less so. Both of them, though, are antsy to get on the move. As Connor urges me to relax, Paloma glides past, then comes to a stop with a sort of swooshing turn that looks effortlessly natural. She smiles warmly, eyes hidden behind mirrored sunglasses.

"How's it going?" she asks.

"Pretty good," Alexis says, in a tone that clearly means *terrible, but I'm trying to be nice.*

I snort. "I'm utterly incompetent."

"Maybe you're not a completely natural athlete," Alexis allows.

"There's nothing natural about strapping sticks to your feet and hurtling through the snow," I point out.

"Well, you're certainly not going to be *hurtling*. More like . . . inching gradually." Alexis leans over her poles to smirk at me. Paloma smacks her arm, but I laugh.

"You'll get the hang of it," Connor assures me, glaring daggers at his sister. He looks to me. "Ready?"

"I don't think I'm going to get more ready." It's more a statement of defeat than optimism. We set out, joining Rose up the path. The others move slowly to accommodate my turtle pace, and bit by bit I start to understand the rhythm and movement of the thing. At least I'm moving forward consistently.

Still, it isn't long before Paloma, Connor, and Alexis have pulled ahead. Rose hangs back. At first I take her presence for charity. Then I catch Alexis looking back, and she and the others pick up their pace a bit, putting more distance between us—enough for a private conversation.

"I haven't really gotten a chance to talk to you alone," Rose says, confirming my suspicions. "I was going to borrow you yesterday, but . . ."

"Not up for a get-to-know-you conversation with someone drenched in deer blood?" I ask, and Rose's eyes crinkle at the edges in amusement.

"You know, I didn't think that these trips could hold any surprises at this point."

"That's me. Always unexpected," I say, trying to cover my embarrassment with good cheer. At least all the huffing and puffing I'm doing provides an easy explanation for the red in my cheeks.

"I imagine you're pretty tired of talking about yourself," Rose says. I make a noise of not-quite-agreement. "How about the wedding? Tired of talking about that yet?"

"I honestly haven't started thinking about it." Or rather, every time I think about it, I start to panic. Planning a wedding is one thing. Planning a *Dalton* wedding is another. There will be at least one senator on the invitation list.

"You're not one of those girls who's had her wedding planned since you were eight?"

"I never wanted to get married at all," I confess. When I was growing up, marriage wasn't about love. It was about partnership, practicality, shared goals. My husband would be someone vetted and approved by my parents, just shy of an arranged marriage; babies would naturally and swiftly follow.

"What changed your mind?" she asks.

"Connor," I say. She looks at me like she's trying to decide if this is a rehearsed answer. I flush. "Not like—I just mean, I don't think I've ever been in love before. Not like this. Not . . . not real, like this. All of a sudden I understood the point."

"And have you talked about a prenup yet?" she asks.

I choke. "No! Or, I mean, I guess I assume there will be one—"

"There will," she confirms. Up ahead, Connor and the others swing out of view around a curve in the path. "Is that a problem for you?"

A nuthatch on the trail in front of us watches us approach with a cynical eye before taking off in a burst of feathery movement. "Of course not." I'm grateful that I have to keep my eyes on my skis. This isn't the conversation I was expecting. "I'll sign whatever."

"Don't," she says. I look up at her in surprise. "I mean, you'll want to have a lawyer look over everything and negotiate for you. We'll pay for it, of course, but it'll be their job to protect your interests. That's what it should do—protect both of you. It's what I should have done, but I was too head over heels and worried I'd lose it all if I pushed back even a little, and I ended up with a prenup that would have left me with next to nothing when . . ." She stops herself. Speaks carefully. "It would have been better to have some kind of protection."

When, she said, not *if.* "That's . . . very practical," I say.

She makes a sound of amusement. "One thing you will find out quickly is that you have to be the practical one. Connor is like Liam—too optimistic for practicality. He always trusts that things will just work out. Never a mind for the consequences."

"People keep saying how much Connor is like his father." I don't make it a question—not a demand for information. For several seconds, there is nothing but the rhythmic sound of our skis through the snow.

"Liam had his flaws," Rose says at last, and in those words, I sense a depth of complicated grief. Whatever those flaws might be, though, she doesn't elaborate. "When you're a kid, you know the best version of your parents. That's the version of Liam that Connor knew. That's the version of him he's tried all his life to emulate."

I think of Beth Scott on the other side of the closet door, holding it shut with her whole body as I flung myself against it, screeching. There was never a version of Beth I wanted to be like.

Though I can't promise I would have done better, with a daughter like me.

"It must be hard coming back here," I say.

She makes a sound as if to say this is an understatement. "I almost didn't, that first summer. I didn't understand how we could all be here like it didn't happen. But I'm glad that I did. We couldn't let . . . all of that take this place away from us." She squares her shoulders, blinking back tears.

Why do I have the sudden feeling that she had been about to say *let* him *take this away from us?*

I'm imagining it, I tell myself. But that old urge is rising up in me. *Little thief,* Beth used to call me, but I never stole things to take them. I took them to understand. I need to know the names of things. Their reasons.

You would think curiosity was one of the seven deadly sins, the way the Scotts treated it. Questions were defiance. A child should receive the truth and know it is true because it comes from authority, and authority *is* truth.

"I'm so sorry," I say.

"It was a very long time ago," she replies. She inhales. "Cherish your loved ones, Theo. And make sure they stay off the lodge roof." Her lips twist mirthlessly. "But that's enough of grim subjects."

"I'm sorry to have brought it up," I say.

"No, no, it's no problem. We should be able to talk about these things, instead of pretending they didn't happen," she says, and again I feel like I'm stepping into an argument she's had with someone else entirely.

I don't know what to do with this conversation—this talk of prenups and Liam's faults, every topic its own peculiar test. I don't know who it is Rose wants me to be, and whether she would rather I prove worthy or slip up in some way that justifies throwing me out.

The sound of laughter comes from up ahead. My calves and thighs are burning, and we're hopelessly behind. I see a look flit across Rose's face—she wants to be up there, joining in the laughter.

"I think I'm going to head back," I say, seizing on the moment.

"Are you sure?" she asks. It's more polite than a genuine objection.

"If I go much farther, one of you is going to have to carry me back," I reply frankly. I wave a hand. "You go catch up. I'm going to go make myself some cocoa while you all voluntarily get cold and exhausted."

"I'll tell Connor you took off," she tells me by way of acknowledgment, and by the time I get myself turned around—a laborious process—she's winging away at a speed that makes it embarrassingly obvious how much she slowed down to accommodate me.

The trail back is clear, pummeled by our passage already. I make it a short distance on the skis before giving up and unclipping myself, opting to carry them under my arm while I tramp along in boots. The conversation rattles around in my head as I walk.

Connor talks about his father with something like awe. But the way Rose spoke of the prenup made things sound less blissful.

Make sure they stay off the lodge roof, she said. But didn't Mr. Vance tell me it was the abandoned cabin where the accident happened?

I suppose that technically, he didn't. I made an assumption. He didn't correct me.

But if Liam Dalton died falling off the lodge roof, why abandon the cabin at all?

It's none of my business, I remind myself.

I stop. The path snakes out before me. The ruts our skis carved are clear, leading onward. They will take me faultlessly back to White Pine, to the place I am meant to be.

Off among the trees, the fifth cabin stands. I can see its gray-brown flank from here. Icicles line its eaves. I wonder if the snow has covered the footprints leading to its door. Mine, and Mr. Vance's, and someone else's.

There is a reason that cabin was abandoned. But it isn't the one I assumed.

And there's that feeling, tugging me forward. That sense of not familiarity, exactly, but the thing nearest to it. Like looking at a photograph of a family vacation from when you were very young that you don't actually remember but feel like you ought to.

Not that I would know, of course. Other than hunting with Joseph and trips to see family in Idaho, we never went anywhere. I didn't know to be jealous; I thought trips like that were things invented for books, to make them more interesting. It wasn't like I had friends at school to compare notes with. My classroom was the kitchen table and Beth glancing over my work as she moved about cooking.

Beth wasn't a natural teacher, but she did her best. Math came easily to me, and I would devour anything about literature or history. It would be much later, of course, that I found out how questionable the history I was learning was, and discovered that my college classmates did not have a section in their history textbooks about "the men who walked with dinosaurs" or sidebars about why Buddhists were going to hell.

School was the only time I ever pleased her. *You're so sharp,* she'd tell me, wagging her head, but when I started to get older there was worry in that, too. *So full of questions,* she would say, and it meant something much different at fifteen than it did at five.

I learned that if I wanted answers, I had to find them myself.

It's only a few steps out of my way. The snow is ankle-deep here where the trees have sheltered the path. And it can't hurt to look, so I turn. I cross the distance quickly and lean the skis against the steps of the cabin.

In the light of day, I can more clearly see the pale silhouette on the door where the ornament must have once hung. My fingers trace the shape of it. A cross, almost—but not quite. The horizontal bar splits at its ends.

A jolt goes through me. I know what that shape is. Or I did, for a moment so brief all I can feel is the reverberation in the air after it's gone. I recognize it the way I recognized Connor, that night at Harper's party.

I've seen you somewhere before, haven't I? I asked him.

I think I would remember, he said.

My hand falls to the door, certain that it's locked—but as if it has been expecting me, the knob turns. I push the door inward. It catches slightly, the door sitting unevenly in its frame, and then springs open. I let go. The door swings inward, and I try to remember how to breathe.

Dried leaves and pine needles litter the floorboards. The welcome mat inside the door has gone gray with years of dirt. A woodstove stands against one wall, and in the back of the main room is a silent refrigerator. I flip the switch a few times, but the lights don't come on—no power.

I try for a moment to match this cabin to the one in my dream, but of course that's not how dreams work. My dream was more the impression of a place, no precise details or identifiable architecture. Besides,

I've never been here before. I have never been to the East Coast at all, and even if I had, what would I be doing at Idlewood?

It's only some long-faded memory, finding echoes in this place.

You may never remember, my therapist told me. *Or it may come back to you at odd times. The strangest little details make memories return. A smell, a sound.*

I close my eyes, and the image of the woman in the red scarf surfaces. I can never recall what she looked like—even what color her hair was, or if she was old or young. But I remember lying down next to her, our faces nearly touching. Did she smile? Did she say my name, tuck a strand of hair behind my ear?

The answers never come.

I step inside, moving quietly on instinct. I'm not supposed to be here—not that there's anyone to notice that I've intruded.

Pale circles dot the floorboards. Candle wax. I turn slowly, picking out the places where the wax has spattered and dried. A dozen or so candles, arranged in a semicircle. I scratch at the wax with my thumb. It's not as dusty as the rest of the floor. Someone has been in here.

I shiver. Straighten up. The stairs are before me, leading upward.

I inhale the scent of cedar, and memories eddy at the back of my mind.

Where did I come from? I would ask Beth and Joseph.

God brought you to us, Beth would say and Joseph, occasionally more practical, would explain, *You came to us through the church. Some folks who knew we were praying for a child and knew you needed a family.*

Years of infertility. Three pregnancies, three miscarriages. After that, nothing, not even the whisper of a positive on a pregnancy test. But then, out of nowhere, their prayers were answered.

Of course, that was before they started thinking I wasn't so much an answer to their prayers as a trick played by the other side. They might have set out to love me at some point, but it rapidly became clear that I was unlovable by their standards.

Poor lamb, they called me. Abandoned. Voiceless.

Damaged. Demented.

I drift toward the stairs. That other cabin, the one flitting through my memories like a figure at the end of a corridor, always out of reach—I can almost picture it. "Two bedrooms upstairs. One smaller. Flowers on the bed," I murmur to myself without quite realizing it, seizing on a flicker of memory. I try to fix the image in my head before I reach the top of the stairs and the sight of the real cabin chases it from my mind.

The flowers. They were white, I think. I practiced counting them, but there were too many. I always lost track.

There are two doors off the landing above. The one in front of me is shut. I turn my head. This door yawns open. The room is tiny—not much more than a closet. There's space for a single bed, sized for a toddler or small child, with a metal frame and a nightstand. The bedspread is faded and dingy, but I can just make out the pattern.

The white daisies, their stems intertwined, spilling across the fabric.

9

I inhale sharply, and it's like being punched in the gut—the scent of cedar, of pine and dust and something so faint I'm not sure it's there at all, that my mind isn't weaving it in all by itself. Lavender.

Daisies. The flowers on the bed were daisies, I think, but that's impossible. This can't be the same cabin. That can't be the same bed.

I walk to the other door. I put my hand against it, not meaning to go in, not yet, but the latch on the door must not work properly because it simply swings open. I brace myself for a rush of recognition—but there's nothing.

A queen-size bed frame, mattress nowhere in evidence, takes up most of the room. The frame is a heavy wooden thing, handmade, knots giving it character. A wardrobe stands in the corner; to my right, a vanity. The mirror throws back an obscured reflection, speckles of grime blotting out my face.

I let out a long breath as the sense of intense familiarity bleeds away. My shoulders relax, and I realize just how tightly I've been clenching my jaw.

Maybe I have been to a place like this one. A place with flowers on my bedspread and a woodstove and the scent of cedar. Common things—all of them pretty much baked into the cabin experience, in fact, and hardly particular to Idlewood.

My eyes fall from my distorted reflection to the surface of the vanity, and the sensible, rational, comforting thought withers up. Because it's right there.

The dragonfly, cast in dull brass.

It takes three steps and an eternity to cross to the vanity. I touch the thing as if it might burn me. An ornament for a door, two spots for the screws at the nose and the tail. It matches the silhouette on the door: a cross, the bar split at the end where the wings diverge.

Red Fox. White Pine. Wildflower.

Dragonfly.

I pick up the ornament, blowing dust from it with a puff of air. The patterns of its wings emerge. There are brass circles behind the dragonfly, an extra bit of decoration. I hold it next to my arm. Not the same, not exactly. The size and position of the circles behind the body are different.

As if this was the image I was grasping for, when I sketched out what I wanted and handed it to the artist. As if glimpsed in a half-obscured reflection, through memory long submerged.

I sink down onto the stool. My mouth is dry.

Why is this here?

Absurd. It belongs here. I'm the thing out of place.

Trapped between the back of the vanity and the wall is a triangle of white no bigger than a clipped fingernail. It has the gloss of photograph paper, and now I spy the telltale squared-off smudges on the vanity mirror, where other photographs might have been taped. Whoever cleared this place out must have missed one.

My eyes fix on it. My hands are shaking, a tremor that starts in my smallest finger and radiates until I have to clench both hands tight against my body to still them.

I should go. Turn and walk out of this place and put all of it, these strange coincidences, out of my mind. They mean nothing.

And yet instead of turning around, I reach out. I pinch the corner of that little white scrap, draw it out. It's a photograph; apart from a crease where it was trapped against the wall, it's intact.

The photograph shows a man you could almost mistake for Connor. The same mouth, the same slightly gawky ears. He wears a heavy coat, unzipped, a gray sweater underneath. He holds the mittened hand of a very young child. She's cocooned in a bright pink winter coat. Her cheeks are bright red. Despite the cold, she isn't wearing a hat, her brown hair in a loose tumble over her shoulders. In her other arm, she clutches a stuffed bear. It looks brand-new, with a bright red ribbon around its throat. The man is smiling. She isn't.

I know that girl. Of course I do. I don't have much of anything from when I was younger, but I stared at the photos of myself displayed on the mantel often enough. Me at the dinner table; next to a Christmas tree; dressed in my Sunday best with my hair in French braids, eyes still red from crying at how hard Beth pulled to get them flat and even.

I feel as if I am not in my body at all. It has dissolved around me, leaving me untethered. I don't know how long I sit there, staring at the photograph, mind reeling.

The man is obviously Connor's father—Liam Dalton.

And the girl in the photograph is me.

10

I pour myself a glass of wine back at White Pine to steady my nerves. The photo sits out on the counter.

It makes no sense—so little sense that the fact of its existence seems hard to hold on to. Like if I look away, it will vanish.

I can't have been here. I can't have been holding Liam Dalton's hand, because I had never heard of him before I met Connor, had never heard of this place, and it's too strange, too wild a coincidence. If I had been here, I would remember.

Except that something terrible happened to me, and there is a reason no one stays in Dragonfly anymore.

The wine has a meaty, metallic taste. I set it down with a grimace, pick up the photograph again. Try to convince myself that it isn't me. Or to come up with an explanation for how it could be that I happened to find my way back to this place, if it is.

The shadow of the photographer spills across the snow. The wind lifts long hair from their shoulders—a woman? It's impossible to tell anything more.

Is she wearing a red scarf?

I almost don't hear the footsteps on the porch. As the door opens, I grab for the book I abandoned on the table this morning and slide the photograph among the pages as the door swings inward. Connor enters, knocking snow from his boots, his cheeks blushing bright from the cold.

"You're back," I say, sounding guilty. Connor doesn't seem to notice.

"I couldn't leave you all on your own for too long," he says. "Who knows what kind of trouble you could get into." There's something strange in his voice—a flatness, almost like anger, that makes the words sound more accusative than joking.

Tell him.

If that photograph *is* me, then it was taken when Connor was a child. If I was—if the *girl* was about four, he would have been seven. Old enough to remember another child visiting for the winter retreat, surely.

He'll be able to tell me who she was and prove I'm imagining things.

"I'm going to take a quick shower," he says. He tosses his hat and gloves onto the bench just inside the door and doesn't wait for an answer. I sit with my lips parted, words unformed. I could say something. Stop him. But I tell myself I'm only being considerate. I am waiting, that's all, for a few minutes, a more convenient time.

I haven't told him the details of my past. He knows I was adopted. He knows I don't consider the Scotts my family. We've never dug into the reasons for it, but he has to have guessed some of it. The story is common enough. Control. "Discipline." Adherence to a code that prized obedience over love.

He doesn't know that I have four years unaccounted for.

If I was four, it was the year—the same winter—his father died.

I see who you truly are, Beth said to me, the last time we spoke. Pure venom in her voice. When people find out who I am, who I really am, they want to get away from me. They want nothing to do with me. I have spent years telling myself the Scotts were wrong. That I am not the damaged goods they claimed. That I have worth.

But they also taught me I was a liar, not to be believed. And that's a lesson hard to unlearn.

I have to tell him.

The sound of the shower stops. I sit at the table, hands folded. The very edge of the photograph sticks out from between the pages of the book. I'll leave it there for now. Work my way up to it.

Connor emerges, hair wet, wearing jeans and no shirt. "Hey," I say, voice soft.

"Hey," he echoes, slightly curt. "So what did you get up to?"

Tell him. "Just reading," I say, and I've already lied. *I was in Dragonfly.* The words form in my mind but don't reach my lips.

"Really." He sounds like he doesn't believe me—no, that doesn't make sense. He just sounds upset. He walks to the fridge, yanks it open. Grabs a beer. Not his usual drink of choice, though he'll have one occasionally on a hot afternoon—which this certainly isn't—or when he's feeling a certain kind of stress, one he wants to stoke instead of soothe.

"Is everything okay?" I ask. Is he angry? Is he angry at *me*? I can't think why. He can't know about the cabin.

"Fine," he says. Connor has never let his anger hurt me, but that doesn't make me less afraid of it. Of anyone's anger. You have to placate it, quiet it, before it builds up. Beth liked to nurture her anger. It would build and build all day, until it boiled over. As an adult, I can see that half of Joseph's punishments were more like protection—go to your room. You're not allowed to come down for dinner. *Stay out of her way until she calms down.*

I slide out of my chair and around the side of the table, standing next to him. My fingertips touch the inside of his wrist. He runs his other hand down my side to rest on my hip.

"You're upset," I say.

He takes a long sip of his beer, lets it sit in his mouth a moment before swallowing. "It's been a weird day." I almost laugh. Instead I sink into the chair next to him, leaning close with my elbows on my knees. Drawing the world down to the two of us.

"Weird how?" I ask. He rolls the edge of the beer bottle back and forth on the table, doesn't answer. "Did something happen? While you were out?"

"We had a conversation," he says. He doesn't meet my eyes.

"Oh?" I shuttle through possibilities in my mind, but I can't think of an obvious conversation that would upset him, except— Ah. "About me."

His lips part—he's about to say something, but then his teeth click shut. He lets out a breath. "They think I'm rushing into this. That I don't know you."

I rise, only enough to slide into his lap. He tips his face up toward me. I rest my brow against his, my arms around his neck. He presses a hand to the small of my back and shuts his eyes. I don't. I watch him.

I always have to watch him. I have to stay aware at every turn of what it is he's thinking. What he sees. I cannot risk him seeing something I've buried. I have to be perfect.

"You know me," I say, willing it to be true enough to blot out all the things he *doesn't* know. That I don't know. There's a photo of me with his father, and I don't understand why and it terrifies me.

He starts to speak, but I kiss him. Nothing we could say now would help. It's not words that will remind him of who I am—to him, *with* him, which is all that matters. All those other girls—the one hiding from Beth's rage, the one taking photos of her bruises, the one clutching a knife, and the one holding a stranger's hand in the snow—let them stay buried.

"You know me," I say again, and I pull back, look into his eyes. He stares up at me. I stand and put my hand out in invitation. He hesitates for half a second before he takes it. I turn, two fingers hooked around his, guiding him toward the bedroom.

There are two versions of Connor. There's the one who kisses me slowly, reverently. Soft and tender, his touch an act of worship. Like I am something delicate or a wild thing that will fly away if he startles me. But every gentle touch wraps a sense of suffocation around me. His love is claustrophobic, and sometimes I can't endure it any longer.

Sometimes, when he trails delicate kisses down the rise of my hip, I want to scream, to dig my fingernails into his skin, to bite down until he bites me back. But Connor wants to be a good boy, a gentleman. And so I grant him all those whispering touches, until I can't anymore.

Occasionally I meet the other version of Connor. When I bite down on his lip, when I shove him away. When he pulls me roughly onto his lap and traps my hands behind my back. When he tells me I'll have to beg for it—but it only ever takes one whispered *please* before he's pushing me down onto the bed.

He's never been like this before, though—grabbing my hips, pressing me down, his hand on my chest, fingers splayed to frame my throat. I wrap my legs around his waist to draw him deeper, hold him there against me, and I bite my lip to stifle my cries before I remember there's no one nearby to overhear. He slows—that gentleness is back, eyes locked with mine in a silent question. *Please,* I say again, and it's all the permission he needs.

When we're done, he lies sprawled, the back of one hand on his forehead, his body stretched out, strangely vulnerable. He looks up at the ceiling, a faint line already forming a divot between his brows as his worries flood their way back. I start to say his name, stop myself.

He takes his hand from his forehead, resting it on my thigh instead, casual but possessive. His head turns to examine me, his bright eyes intense. "Let's stay here tonight," he says. "I'll cook for you."

Before I understood that Connor was rich, I suggested we cook together to save money on dates. He showed up with quail eggs and fifty-dollar steaks. He loved it, though. Pouring me a glass of wine and telling me to stay put while he flourished his way through fifty-step recipes. He'd produce elegantly plated delicacies on my mismatched thrift-store dishes and wait, eyebrows pinched upward in nervous anticipation, as I took the first bite.

"Your family will be expecting us," I point out.

"We have weeks here. There's plenty of time for togetherness." His thumb makes circles against my bare skin.

"Okay," I say. We'll stay in. We'll talk. I'll find the right moment. I'll tell him about the photograph, about the cabin. I'll tell him everything.

Just not yet.

11

Connor vanishes around five and comes back laden with produce. He has no idea how to cook for only two people; the leftovers from our date nights feed me for a week.

"Step one: pour wine into chef," he says, as he does every time, and pauses for my obligatory chuckle. He fetches us long-stemmed glasses. Wine comes with a history lesson in Connor's kitchen. "Only a small number of bottles were made that year, because of a hailstorm that wiped out the crop mid-harvest," he informs me. "You'll find it's quite peppery, with notes of currant."

"I notice it's a red wine. You can tell, you see. Because of the color," I say, matching his arch tone, and he narrows his eyes at me in mock annoyance. He carts his own glass over to the cutting board, where he swaps the Syrah for a chef's knife and sets to rapidly deconstructing a pair of onions. The rhythmic noise of the knife against the wooden cutting board is the only sound for a minute or two. Our dinners are like this sometimes—neither of us sure what to talk about, worrying suddenly that our ability to hold a conversation has fled entirely, that the novelty has worn off. And then somewhere between the third sip and the tenth something unlocks.

"Are you enjoying the Miller?" he asks. He tilts his head toward the book on the table. I flinch at the sight of the photograph's edge, resist the urge to tuck it in more thoroughly.

"Adore it," I say. "It's gorgeous."

Of course books were the first thing we talked about. After introductions, followed by an awkward pause, Connor asked—lurchingly, with no preamble at all—if I'd read Vonnegut. Only *Slaughterhouse-*

Five, I had to admit, but Connor had read them all, kept a set of signed first editions. He wanted to talk about them. Not what happened in them but *about* them, about Vonnegut, about stories and what he could do with them, and from Vonnegut we ranged from George Saunders to Virginia Woolf and Jennifer Egan, and then I admitted that since I'd graduated, I'd read mostly popular fiction, books either about kissing or death, and he said all books are about kissing and death when you get down to it, and I told him that was the sort of thing that sounded deep but wasn't really once you thought about it for more than two seconds, and he told me that later he was going to ask me if he could kiss me, and then without taking a breath continued our discussion of which of Cormac McCarthy's books we preferred.

We still talk about books. He makes fun of my lowbrow taste; I crack jokes about Jonathan Franzen he pretends to take personally.

He's smiling now. "Ask me to pick out a ring, I'm helpless. Ask me to pick out a book, though . . ." He gives me a satisfied look. "See? I do know you."

The photograph peeks out from between the pages. I say nothing.

Connor twists a fistful of herbs to strip the leaves from the stems. He draws the tip of a blade to part meat from bone, scrapes a grater across the flesh of a lemon for the zest, halves it with neat knife strokes. The wine is a red darker than blood and it stains his lower lip as he drinks it, pours us both another glass. My reflection is obscured in the glass, just the hint of a silhouette. I tilt it, distorting the image further.

"Has it always just been family, at the winter retreat?" I ask him.

The meat is in the oven. Connor props his palms on the counter, leaning toward me slightly. "It can get a bit claustrophobic," he says, not quite an answer. "Usually at least in the summer some friends get invited. It feels more casual. More like a vacation and less like a summit."

"So no guests at all in the winter."

"Only family. And the very-soon-to-be family," he confirms.

I wet my lips. "So there wouldn't have ever been a . . . a family friend? No other kids for you to play with at Christmastime growing up? No epic snowball fights by the pond?" I ask, trying to keep my voice bright, curious. Without an agenda.

He frowns a little. "No. Definitely not. Although . . ." He stops himself.

"Although what?" I ask. I can feel my pulse fluttering at my neck. Quick as the thrum of an insect's wings.

"Nothing," he says. "We never have guests at Christmas." The oven timer beeps. He turns away, more quickly than is quite natural. "Why do you ask?"

Tell him, I think. But he closes the oven, turns to me. His gaze is warm. My breath catches. I want it to be true that he knows me. I want this—here in this cabin with just the two of us, where for a moment his family doesn't matter and neither does my past.

"No reason," I say.

I run my finger along the edge of the photograph, pushing it deeper among the pages and out of sight.

12

I sleep poorly that night, and if dreams trouble me, they've faded by morning. Connor brings me coffee in bed, kisses my forehead, and tells me that he's already told his female relatives that I won't be joining them for the second day of skiing.

"You're my favorite," I inform him.

"I am pretty great," he agrees. "I've got Male Bonding with Trevor, Nick, and Grandpa today. You'll be okay here?"

I nod, shoo him away. By the time I extract myself from the warm cocoon of the blankets, he's on his way out the door. I draw back the curtain to watch him go. The light filters down through the boughs of the trees, making the snow glint. I watch until he vanishes.

I try not to think about the photograph. I tidy up what we left out last night, make myself breakfast, pour another cup of coffee, clean again. I check my phone, wondering if perhaps some ghost of signal has allowed emails and messages to get through, but there's nothing.

"This is ridiculous," I say to myself the fourth time I skirt around the table, avoiding the book with its illicit bookmark.

Yesterday was strange. I was caught up in my emotions, not thinking clearly. I saw a photograph of some random little girl and I got an odd notion in my head. The moment I take that photograph out, I tell myself, this whole thing will seem foolish. She probably looks nothing like me.

I step briskly over to the table. I open the book and pull the photograph out in one fluid movement, flipping it onto the table.

And there she is. The little girl looks up at me. Brown hair. Braids. Sharp little chin. Lots of children look like that.

My fingertips trail along the line of her face, down to her neck. There are two tiny dots along her throat, right above her collarbone. Birthmarks. I missed them before. I touch the matching marks on my own neck.

I shudder, sitting down.

It was supposed to be a dream. Gone with the rising sun.

"Who are you?" I whisper, searching my own memories for the answer, but there's nothing.

A keening wail breaks through the mire of my thoughts. I startle, nearly knocking over the wineglass. A child is crying outside—and there's only one child here. I rush over to the window, the photograph still in my hand. Sebastian is standing outside, wearing nothing but sweatpants and a thin cotton shirt. He's crying, scrubbing at his face with his little fists.

"What the fuck?" I manage, frozen in place—and then common sense catches up and I pull on my boots. I throw my coat on, grabbing a blanket from the back of the armchair as I head out. I have the presence of mind to shove the photograph into my coat pocket as I stride to the trail.

He doesn't even see me. He's staring off into the distance, crying in hiccupping sobs.

"Hey, kiddo," I say, trying for soothing.

He twists around. A river of snot runs from his nose. His eyelashes are all gummed together with tears. My stomach twists with fleeting panic. How long has he been like this?

"It's freezing out here!" I throw the blanket around him. At least he's wearing shoes—not boots, but little tennis shoes with dinosaurs on the toes. "Where did you come from? Why are you all alone?" I ask him, but he's crying too hard to answer.

Olena's supposed to be watching him, isn't she? I look around, rubbing his arms. No sign of her.

"We need to get you back to your cabin," I say. If someone's looking for him, surely that's where they'll go. "It's okay, little dude, we'll get you back to your mommies."

This promise at last seems to calm him down. The wails stop, and he looks up at me with those achingly perfect brown eyes. I smile in a way I hope is reassuring.

I stick out my hand. He lifts both of his in a very clear demand, and I sigh. "Okay. I'll carry you." I grunt as I haul him up. He burrows against me, his face swiping wetly along the curve of my neck as he finds a comfortable spot. I swallow down my distaste and resettle the blanket.

I listen for voices calling out his name. Nothing. No Olena running around frantically. I cut straight through toward Red Fox, relying on memory, and regret it when I have to wade through a drift of snow up to my calves, each step made more laborious by the ungainly weight of a now-quiet three-year-old.

"What were you doing out here?" I ask him.

"I was playing," he says. "I was looking for foxes." It comes out *wooking fuh fot-ses,* which even I have to admit is adorable.

"I think maybe no more looking for foxes without a grown-up, okay?" I say.

"Otay."

Goddamn, he's cute. I was always supposed to love kids. Beth wanted nothing more than one of those huge families, big enough that all the older girls look after the babies. Instead it was just me. I had cousins, of course. Dozens of them. Most of them lived in Idaho, though, and the ones that were closer were all older than me. It never stopped Beth from pointing out babies to me, offering me up for babysitting, telling me what a wonder it was going to be when I had my own children. She would talk in a disturbing amount of detail about what it would be like, having a baby grow inside of me, the way it never had in her. *It's God's miracle,* she would say.

We're at Red Fox. I knock on the door, balancing Sebastian on my hip. There's no answer. I try the knob but it won't turn.

"What are you doing?"

The voice brings me around fast enough that Sebastian squeaks and wraps his arms around my neck. It's Nick, Connor's uncle. He stands with his hands in the pockets of a black wool coat, a scarf around his neck. He's got a lighter complexion than his brother or his nephew, black hair peppered gray, the same square jaw but without the soft cheeks to gentle it. He looks like his father.

"I'm—I—" I stammer. I haven't done anything wrong, but my mind is rifling through the last five minutes looking for things I could get blamed for.

"What are you doing out here with the kid?" he asks, restrained suspicion in his voice. Not an accusation—yet.

"He must have wandered off on his own. I'm not sure who was watching him, so I came to check the cabin, but . . ." I turn slightly in a full-body gesture toward the door.

He looks at me for a beat, like he's trying to decide if I'm lying.

"I'm cold," Sebastian says faintly, and Nick's expression tenses.

"Let's get him inside. Come on, my cabin's closest," he says, and takes his hand out of his pocket to beckon me. I scurry down the steps as best I can, following him. My arms are starting to feel the strain of holding the kid, but Nick doesn't offer to take him from me, and I don't ask. He walks staring straight ahead, his expression dark.

"Any idea where his moms are?" he asks.

"Skiing. I think Olena was supposed to watch him," I say. Then hastily add, "But I'm not sure." I don't want to get her in trouble if I'm wrong.

He grunts a response. "Up here."

This cabin is smaller than ours. The ornament on the door is a bumblebee, and I'm faintly amused at the thought of the glowering man being stuck with a cabin with such a cutesy name. He ushers us inside.

"Put him on the couch. Grab another blanket from the bedroom, I'll get a fire going," he says, and disappears outside again.

I set Sebastian on the couch. I have to prize his hands from around my neck, but then he nestles against the cushions, shivering. I pull his shoes off, and his socks, which have soaked through. His feet are bluish, and I rub them between my hands, giving him an encouraging smile.

"All safe and warm," I tell him.

"I didn't find the foxes," he says mournfully.

"I'll help you look later," I promise, maybe foolishly. I hurry to the bedroom to grab the comforter. There's a suitcase sitting out on it, unzipped and flung open. The clothes inside are folded neatly. Shirts I now know enough to recognize are expensive, a pair of dress shoes, a maroon sweater that probably takes five years of education to clean correctly. There's a pair of simple silver cuff links on top of the sweater, as if discarded there absentmindedly.

Once upon a time, I might have palmed one. Just one. Take two, and it's obvious they've been pilfered. Take one, and the owner will assume it fell somewhere, got lost between cushions or down a vent.

I glance toward the door before shutting the suitcase and moving it to the floor. I pull the comforter off the bed and pretend I wasn't tempted.

A minute or two after I get Sebastian properly burritoed in blankets, Nick reappears with a load of firewood. Without so much as glancing our way, he kneels by the woodstove and begins constructing a careful fire.

I remember Joseph making a fire at our campsite with that same concentration, explaining to me about airflow and trapping the heat and natural sources of tinder. He always explained things to me. Told me the proper names of things. "You can use moss," he'd tell me. "I like Spanish moss the best, but it doesn't grow up here. Though you know, it's not actually a moss? *Tillandsia usneoides*. Related to pineapples, if you can believe it."

Joseph had a degree in biology with a focus on botany. He worked installing air-conditioning units for Beth's uncle, but he delighted in sharing what he remembered with me. I mistakenly believed his delight was about me, not simply about having an audience.

Nick Dalton uses a stick of pressed material meant to catch fire quickly and reliably. He strikes a long match and *whoosh*, crackling flames. He shuts the stove door. "Should warm up pretty quick," he says. "How's he doing?"

I look down at where Sebastian has tipped over to nestle into my side. His eyes are closed, those long lashes sweeping against his cheeks. "I think he's asleep," I say.

"Must've worn himself out with all the excitement," Nick says. He pushes to his feet, hands back in his pockets. "You just found him out there?"

"More like he found me," I say. "I heard him calling."

"He's lucky. Could have frozen to death," he says, matter-of-fact. "Olena was watching him?"

"She must be frantic."

"Well, we can wait for him to warm up and bring him to the lodge. See if we run into her along the way," Nick decides. I nod, glad someone else has a plan.

"Hopefully before Alexis and Paloma get back," I say. "I'd rather they heard he was safe before they find out he was missing."

A grunt, this one in agreement. He's still just standing there, looking at Sebastian in a way like he's really looking at both of us, but trying not to be too obvious about it. "I remember one of the kids going missing once. Connor, or maybe Trevor. Rose was just about out of her mind. At least that was summer, though. Mostly worried about the lake, then." He lets out a breath. "Having kids makes you crazy. First because it's your job to protect them from every little thing and they're completely helpless, and then because it's not your job anymore, and you've gotta let them be out in the world without you."

"You have kids?" I ask, trying to remember the family tree Connor briefed me on.

"Two girls. Madison and Paige," he says. "They're with their mom this Christmas." He's still looking at Sebastian instead of me, but now his eyes flick up to my face. They linger there, the way they did when I introduced myself. "How about you? You and Connor planning on having kids?" he asks. It has the air of a question used to fill the space, to silence another thought he isn't ready to voice.

"We haven't talked about it," I say. Yet another thing we haven't had the time to get to. "I don't know. I've always assumed I wouldn't want any."

"Any particular reason?" he asks. It should feel intrusive, but he just sounds curious.

"I didn't exactly have the best upbringing," I say. "I know plenty of people with great parents, but it doesn't feel real to me. Like that could be a happy thing."

"I always wanted kids," he says. "My dad was always on me about having sons, that old-fashioned 'carry on the family name' thing, but I hoped we'd have girls. Of course I didn't exactly predict what having *teenage* girls would be like." He sounds rueful, and I'm pretty sure I can guess the ages of his daughters.

"Sounds like you're in the thick of it," I say.

"Doesn't help that their mom and I split recently," he says. "They're still pretty pissed about that."

"I'm sorry," I say awkwardly.

He waves a hand. "It is what it is. These things have got to work themselves out."

Beside me, Sebastian stirs. He wipes his nose on his sleeve and blinks up at us. "Can we go home now?" Sebastian asks. "I'm hungry."

"Come on. We'll head up to the lodge. Get you something to eat there," Nick says with a huff. I get up, wiping my palms on my jeans nervously. Nick was around back then, of course he was. He has to know who that girl was.

Who I am.

Sebastian's shoes are still wet. Nick leaves them by the woodstove and we make sure Sebastian's feet are bundled up in the blanket as I carry him—Nick offers this time, but Sebastian clings to me.

As we approach the lodge, several questions are answered all at once. Olena's voice reaches us first, high-pitched and frantic.

"What if he got lost? It's freezing out here! It's literally freezing! I can't believe—"

Another voice answers her, masculine but too quiet to make out; it sounds like someone trying to calm her down. Or at least shut her up. I have a pretty good guess about who it is, and I'm proven right as soon as we step out of the stand of trees to discover Olena, hair mussed and face blotchy with tears, and Trevor, his hands on her arms and wearing an expression of mingled stress and annoyance. Olena spots us—and Sebastian—first, and lets out a cry, rushing toward us.

"Sebastian! You're okay!" she says.

Trevor rocks his weight back on a heel, eyes lazy as he looks us over. The set of his jaw betrays tension, despite his unconcerned expression. "Told you he was fine," he says.

Olena is touching Sebastian all over, like she needs to press her palms to him to prove she was worried, to feel like she's doing something.

"I only turned away for a moment and he must have taken off. I've been looking all over for him—" she begins.

"He's been with us for, what, fifteen minutes?" Nick asks me. I give a mute nod. "Must've been wandering longer than that, given how cold he was."

Olena wrings her hands, grip twisting around her index finger. Strands of her dark hair stick to her tearstained cheeks. "I got distracted."

Trevor's hands are in his pockets. He meets my eye and shrugs slowly. Nick makes a disdainful noise, and Olena bites her lip.

"Please don't—Mrs. Dalton will fire me," she says. "He's okay, right? So you don't have to—we don't have to tell—"

"Why didn't you get help?" I ask, not taking my eyes off Trevor. "Why are only the two of you out here looking for him?"

"I was going to. I . . ." She trails off. Glances back at Trevor.

"Figured we'd probably find him ourselves. Not like he could have gotten far," Trevor says, seemingly unconcerned. "No use causing a huge fuss."

"The kid could have died," Nick says, a growl in his voice.

"But he's fine," Trevor replies. "Right?" A faint quaver in his voice betrays his uncertainty.

"No thanks to you," Nick says.

"Hey, it wasn't my job to watch him." Trevor looks over his shoulder, back toward the lodge. "If we're done here . . ."

"Do you have the key to Red Fox?" Nick asks Olena. She rummages it out of a pocket, hands it over. "Go get yourself cleaned up. We'll take the kid back and make sure he stays where he's supposed to this time."

"Are you going to tell—"

"Go," he says, not inviting disagreement, not offering comfort.

She totters back toward the lodge, still crying quietly. Trevor waits a moment later, then lets out a sound almost like a laugh and heads in the same direction.

Nick shakes his head, a look of pure disgust on his face. "I hope you don't mind babysitting a bit longer."

"I guess not." I try to sound cheerful about it. Sebastian is playing with my hair now, his fingers making jump scares in my peripheral vision as he paws at me.

"That kid," Nick says suddenly, startling me. It takes me a beat to realize he means Trevor. "I know it was rough on them, growing up without a dad, but still. I did my best, you know. Tried to step in, but I got distracted. Had my own life. Then my own kids. I should've done more."

"Connor and Alexis turned out okay," I say, treading carefully. It's one thing to criticize your own family, another when someone else does it. But Nick just sighs.

"It's funny. I keep thinking Trevor turned out like this because Liam wasn't there to set him straight, but in some ways he's just like him. Liam had this way of looking at you that made you feel like you were the most important thing in the universe. Wasn't anyone he couldn't charm. He knew it, too. Always loved to be adored. Worshipped, even. And he got plenty of it."

He's deep in memories, but they're not fond ones. Rose had this same tone, too, only she was more guarded.

Nick shakes himself. Smiles, gentling his expression. "I guess Connor's pretty charming, too, huh? Didn't take him long to talk you into marrying him."

It's the first time it hasn't sounded like a dig at my intentions. "I know everybody thinks we're rushing into it."

"Sometimes you've got to grab what's in front of you," he says. "Nothing in this world is permanent. You never know when it's all going to go wrong. Stand around waiting for the right time and you might lose it altogether."

"Yeah. I think that's pretty much it," I say. We've reached the cabin. He unlocks the door and pushes it open a few inches, but doesn't go in.

"If it's all right, I'll leave you to watch the tyke. I promised Mom I'd drop in at the lodge," he says. I nod. "It was nice talking to you, Theo."

I laugh a little. "You mind telling your mom that?"

He gives a wry smile. "I'll see what I can do." He hands me the key to the cabin and then steps off the porch. Then he pauses, turns back toward us. "*Theo.* You don't ever go by Teddy, do you?" he asks.

My lips part. Breath slides from my lips. *Teddy.* The Scotts chose my name, and they never once called me by that particular nickname. And yet I can almost hear it. *Teddy, let's go.* "No," I croak. "Why?"

He puts both hands in his pockets. "No reason, I guess. Forget I said anything." With that, he's gone. I stare after him until Sebastian starts squirming in my arms, and at last I turn away, stepping inside the cabin.

Teddy, I think again, and it's almost as if another voice is whispering it. A voice that, like everything else in this place, skates on the very edge of memory.

I shiver and shut the door.

13

Fergus," Sebastian insists, for the third time.

"I really don't understand what you're talking about. You're going to have to help me out here, kid," I reply. He screws up his face. Points toward the bedroom.

"Fergus."

I sigh. "Is it a stuffed animal?"

"Fergus!" He stomps his foot. "Read Fergus."

Oh, thank god. A clue. Fergus must be a book. I've been attempting negotiation with a cantankerous preschooler for more than an hour now. First over food—I'm pretty sure I've given him far more than his permitted ration of gummy fruit snacks, but he could sense weakness and I was left without much of a choice. Then we had a brief misunderstanding over whether my imaginary hand-person was allowed to eat his hand (the answer was a firm and horrified no). Entertaining a three-year-old is much harder than I remember. Of course, this three-year-old probably doesn't get spanked for being anything but sweet, silent, and obedient.

At least he hasn't left a single quiet corner of my mind to occupy with my earlier discovery. I have no energy for ghosts from my past when a pint-size tyrant is trying to scale me like a rock-climbing wall.

"Wait here. No adventures." I try to sound stern, but I don't have it in me. I want to tell him to stomp his foot and whoop and yell and tear around the room if he wants to. Of course, I won't be the one wrangling him into bed later.

I hesitate only briefly before opening the door to the bedroom. I'm just here to collect a book for a toddler, not root around in people's private things. Surely I can be forgiven.

Inside, a rollaway bed has been set up against one wall, clearly for Sebastian. There's a small stack of books next to it, but a quick perusal reveals *Where's Spot?* and a grab bag of Sandra Boynton, but nothing that might answer to the name Fergus. I linger briefly over the stack of board books, imagining Alexis and Paloma sitting with Sebastian, reading to him. They'd do silly voices, hiss for the snake hiding in the clock, not let up until Sebastian was shrieking with laughter.

I remember being curled in the crook of an arm, warm and sleepy. My hands fanned over the pages, refusing to let them turn. It's one of the few memories I have that I'm certain is from before I went to live with the Scotts, and sometimes I will myself to turn my head, to see who it is who's holding me.

The woman in the red scarf?

Liam Dalton?

I shake the memory and my questions away. Still no Fergus. I'm out of places to look without digging through their things, and I can't. Sebastian is just going to have to do without.

"Fergus, *pwease*," he hollers right at that moment, and what am I supposed to do, say no? Pretty sure that's illegal.

I'll just take a quick look. There's a set of suitcases in the corner. None of them look particularly kid-like, but I gamble on the smallest one, unzipping it before I can think better of the whole thing. Sure enough, it's full of kid clothes—but no sign of any books.

I close it back up. I take hold of the zipper of the next one along. What the hell. I'm just looking for a picture book, I remind myself, and open it.

I'm relieved to find neatly folded clothes and, tossed on top as if at the last minute before heading out the door, a book about a bear named Fergus.

"Found it!" I report, and I'm rewarded with a singsong "Hurray!" I pick up the book. My fingers snag on what's beneath it. A plain manila envelope. I pause, staring at it.

This is Alexis's suitcase—I can tell from the size zero clothes.

Alexis, who's been so kind.

Alexis, who keeps pulling Connor away to talk to him about something *important*.

The text messages are still waiting on my phone, my little gift hidden away. The envelope probably has nothing to do with any of it—but what if . . . ?

I carefully lift the flap and slide my fingers inside. I touch the glossy surface of photographic paper—several sheets.

I slide the photographs out. The first shows a young woman from behind. She's slim; her hair is honeyed brown. She sits on the edge of a bed, a sheet covering her lower body, her upper body completely bare. She's looking over her shoulder at the camera, but her expression is anything but alluring. The point of the photo is not the woman's body but the marks on it. Bruises at the hip, the shoulder.

I've seen photos like this before. Because I took photos like this once. An inventory of harm. She's not me, but she could be—I recognize that blank expression in her eyes, the way her body is tense and limp at the same time. There's only one reason to take photos like these. As evidence.

As ammunition.

Another photograph. The same woman, this time shown from the front, chin tilted slightly up, an arm covering her petite breasts. A deep bruise at her shoulder. A split lip, not apparent on the first photograph. She's young. Not as young as I was—early twenties, maybe. Like me, she looks lost. As if she's receded inside herself.

A third photo. The woman's side, a bruise mottled deep purple covering most of her hip. More bruises—too many to count. Someone savaged this girl. Someone tried to destroy her.

I slide the photographs back in the envelope, feeling sick. Who the hell is she? And why does Alexis have these?

When I took those photos, it was to protect myself. They were proof. Leverage.

Blackmail, if you want to call it that.

I zip up the suitcase and get to my feet. Whatever the reason for those photographs, they're dangerous to someone. And I could get myself into trouble digging into things that don't concern me.

The safest thing would be to forget the things I've seen.

Someone told me to stay away from here. I thought it was a threat. But now, looking at these photographs—this woman, wounded, damaged—I wonder uneasily if they were meant, instead, as a warning.

14

I read the book to Sebastian until the words don't make sense anymore. I read him all the others, too. By the time Paloma and Alexis arrive, I have come up with a hundred explanations for those photographs and rejected them all. I have tried to stitch them together with the photo from the cabin, construct some kind of narrative that would bind the two together, but I have nothing but questions and a growing sense of unease.

"Theo!" Alexis says with surprise as they enter, stowing their gear by the door. Sebastian throws himself at Paloma and wraps around her leg like a jellyfish. "Where's Olena?"

I stand from the couch, setting *Hippos Go Berserk!* on the cushion beside me. "Apparently Sebastian sneaked outside and took off while her back was turned. He was fine, but she was pretty shaken up. I offered to watch him."

I keep my tone light, trying not to alarm them. Paloma's eyes widen. Alexis looks quickly to Sebastian, who has the deer-in-the-headlights look of a child who suddenly realizes he might be getting in trouble.

"He's all right," Paloma says softly, touching Alexis's elbow. "Everyone's in one piece, so let's be grateful for that."

"I thought he was over the running-away thing," Alexis says, voice a little shaky. She runs a hand through her hair. "He started pelting off the instant he learned to walk."

"Thank you for keeping an eye on him," Paloma says, with a *we'll talk about this later* look at her wife.

"No problem," I say. They're still between me and the door. Alexis gives a little jump and steps aside. Her gaze lights on the couch. On the bright yellow cover of *Find Fergus*. Her brow creases momentarily. "I'll see you at dinner?" I say brightly. Maybe she won't remember where the book was.

"Right. We'll see you. Thanks again," Paloma says, lifting Sebastian in her arms as she moves out of my way. I pull my boots on hastily, and I don't take a full breath until I'm out in the cold, booking my way toward White Pine.

I find Connor's boots by the door, his coat flung over the entryway bench. Melted snow pools under the boots.

I go into the bedroom. Connor's phone is in its customary place on the nightstand. A man of habit. As I listen to the sound of the shower, I unlock it and open up his files. He keeps his photos meticulously organized, and it doesn't take me long to find a folder of old family pictures. Many are from more recent years, but there are older photos saved as well—photos of Connor as a child. Of Liam Dalton.

I pull them up one after another, zooming in on his face. Does he look familiar because he looks so much like Connor? Or because I've seen him before?

I can't tell. The gaps in my memory are too thorough, too impenetrable.

The water has shut off. I close the app just as Connor steps in, the towel loose around his waist, hair slicked back and dripping.

"Snooping?" he asks, and my stomach braces before I realize he's joking.

"Just checking if you have any signal," I lie.

"Nope. There's a landline in the lodge for emergencies, but that's it," Connor says. "Granddad absolutely refuses to do anything to improve signal up here. The isolation is the point, after all."

"Right," I say.

He puts a hand to his mouth like he's whispering a secret. "But there's a spot down by the gate that can usually nab you a couple of bars," he confesses. Then he frowns. "Are you all right? You look . . . rattled. Where were you, anyway?"

My mind flashes immediately to the brass wings of a dragonfly. "I, um . . . I was just with Sebastian. He wandered off, I guess, got a bit lost. I was looking after him until Alexis and Paloma got back."

"Is he hurt?" He sounds alarmed.

"Not a scratch," I assure him. "Honestly, the hardest part was keeping him entertained. He's a bit, um, insistent."

"You got bossed around by a three-year-old, you mean," he says.

"Have you met three-year-olds? They are very intimidating," I say defensively, and he laughs. He heads over to the dresser, dropping the towel. He catches my eye in the mirror over the dresser, watching me watch him. His wet hair curls around his ears.

I've seen you somewhere before, haven't I?

Some part of me recognized him from that first moment. But not because I'd met Connor before. Because I'd met his father.

Liam Dalton and I were together here, right before he died.

Right before I showed up on the Scotts' doorstep, a girl with no name and nightmares that woke her screaming in the night.

"Are you sure you're all right?" Connor asks, buttoning up his shirt.

I don't answer.

As before, we gather for drinks well before dinner. When we arrive, Alexis and her little family are there; so is Nick. Olena brings in a tray of Manhattans. Her tears are long gone, but she keeps her head down and her shoulders are tense, her whole body wound inward. When she passes me, she gives me a frightened look before scurrying away. I catch Nick's eye. He's the only one not drinking. He has a glass of water instead, topped with a wedge of lemon. He lifts it to me in a casual gesture, and I return it uncertainly. Given the unworried way Alexis accepts her drink, I doubt he's told her exactly what happened. Maybe that's for the best.

It's a different story when Trevor enters. His hair is mussed, and he slouches about with a can't-be-bothered attitude that pairs perfectly with the faint sneer on his face. He plops down next to Alexis. She pulls away from him. Either not noticing or not caring, he wings his arms out along the back of the couch, legs crossed, and surveys the room.

"What a festive bunch," he declares. Paloma rolls her eyes. Sebastian wanders over and thrusts a T. rex toy at Trevor, who takes it. "Rawr," he says, menacing the brontosaurus in Sebastian's hands. "I'm going to eat you."

"They friends," Sebastian informs him gravely.

"Sure they are, kid," Trevor says. He ruffles Sebastian's hair. "You're all recovered from your little adventure, then?"

Almost to the door, Olena misses a step. Empty glasses clack on her tray, and she steadies them as Alexis's head rotates to fix her brother with a cold look.

"Oh, you heard about that?" she asks.

"Bastian the Abominable Snowman," Trevor says. "It has a ring to it. No harm done, though. And I bet you had a good time with your new auntie." His voice is almost singsong, and despite the unobjectionable wording, it feels like mockery. Connor's hand settles on my knee.

"What's this?" Rose asks, entering the room. She looks stunning—dressed in a gray wool top threaded with something that shimmers in the light, complemented by a pair of pearl earrings set in white gold. The few streaks of gray in her hair only add to her loveliness, which otherwise might seem too unreal, manufactured.

"Oh, Sebastian decided to take a little hike on his own," Nick says, cutting in. "Gave Olena a hell of a scare, but Theo intercepted him before he got too chilly."

"Oh dear," Rose murmurs. Her eyes track to me. "Thank you."

"I didn't really do anything," I say quickly, not wanting to claim credit when I haven't mentioned exactly *why* Sebastian was able to wander away unnoticed.

"He's so sweet ninety percent of the time, and then the other ten percent he turns into the Tasmanian Devil," Alexis says. She commandeers the T. rex and makes it stomp on Sebastian's head. He shrieks and twists away, delighted, and Alexis scrunches up her face at him playfully.

"Wonder where I've heard that before," Nick says. He and Rose share a look, and Rose laughs a little.

"All three of you were little terrors," she says.

"No! I was perfectly behaved," Alexis says. A laugh slips from my lips. She cuts me a look. "You don't believe me?"

I cover my mouth. "I'm sorry, I didn't mean—"

"Oh, she was the very worst," Nick tells me, a twinkle in his eye. "We should have just installed a ladder under that window when you were a teenager. It's not like we didn't know you were sneaking out every night."

"I was sneaking out to do extra math homework," Alexis says, deadpan. "And practice clarinet."

"Is that what that was?" Paloma asks, feigning confusion. "Because I definitely thought we were making out."

"Embouchure exercises," Alexis parries, eyebrow arched. Paloma laughs. Trevor rolls his eyes.

"I have trouble thinking of you as a rule breaker," I say to Connor. It's little more than a murmur, but Nick catches it. He tips his drink toward Connor.

"Oh, he was a mellow teenager. But as a kid? I think he must have run away, what, five, six times? Never got much farther than the park, but we did once find him building a tree house to live in. He'd picked out a plot of land to grow his own crops. It was ten feet away from the swings, but still." He chuckles. Connor doesn't; his leg stiffens beside mine.

"Did you live together?" I ask, head tilting a little. Connor hasn't mentioned much about Nick. I'd gotten the impression they didn't see much of each other.

"Not exactly," Rose says. She smooths her skirt in her lap. "After Connor's father passed, Nick came to stay with us now and then, to help out. He was a godsend." Nick looks faintly embarrassed.

"You needed the help. I did what I could, that's all," Nick says. "Anyone would have done the same."

"You know that's not true," Rose says warmly. "You were like a father to these kids."

"Dad was our father," Connor says curtly.

Rose's mouth purses, ever so slightly. "Of course he was. I'm just saying that your uncle helped us out when we needed it the most."

"I was just glad to be part of your lives," Nick says. I watch Connor in my peripheral vision. The hand on my knee has tightened, just enough to dent the skin. I put my own hand over his, and his fingers relax.

He smiles a little. It looks false. "Right. You were very helpful," he says, politely enough. "Sorry. It's just still hard to talk about sometimes."

"Of course," Nick says, his voice rough.

Conversation moves on to less fraught topics. By the time Louise and Magnus join us, the tension has bled out of the moment. Connor hadn't mentioned anything about having a problem with Nick. In fact he hadn't said anything about him at all, really, except that he exists. What's his problem with his uncle? Is it only what Connor said—that Nick acted like a replacement for his father but couldn't be?

At last it's time to move to dinner. We traipse out, Connor with his hand on the small of my back. In the foyer, a small mountain of gifts has gathered beneath the tree. I find myself searching for green paper and red ribbon.

I only ever got one gift at Christmas each year. The holiday was an occasion for worship, not consumerism. I might not have held on to those religious teachings, but Christmas is one of the few periods I've looked back on with a pang of nostalgia—the sense of peace around that time, the single present carefully selected. It was Joseph who picked them out for me each year. They never told me as much, but it was obvious. Only Joseph would have bought me a flower-pressing kit that included handmade cards with sketches and the botanical names of every flower in our yard, or picked out a collection of polished rocks and a book for identifying them—citrine, jasper, carnelian, quartz. I lined them up on my windowsill and memorized their names.

A teddy bear under the tree. A ribbon around his neck. Soft fur tickling my nose.

"Theo?" Connor says. He's pulled away from me, continuing on as I'm rooted to the spot. I don't answer, don't move.

I remember—

The girl reaches greedily for the gift when it's offered, tears off the paper.

"Here. Just for you. Merry Christmas. A bit late, admittedly," the man says with a grin as she uncovers her prize. She squeals. Launches herself at him in what's meant to be a hug but is more like a headbutt, her arms wrapped around her new treasure. He laughs, ruffles her hair.

"Mama, did you see?" the girl demands. She holds the bear out. "It's a teddy, just for me."

"A teddy for Teddy," the man tells her.

"This is too much," the girl's mother says. A red gift bag sits on the floor beside her; a blue scarf pools in her lap. Her fingers ball it up, smooth it out.

"It's nothing," he says. He sounds strange. Neither of them sounds exactly happy, but they don't sound mad or sad, either.

"It might be nothing to you. But it isn't to us," she says.

It's wrong, I think. *The scarf was red.* It's a nonsense thought—as if a person could only own one color of scarf—but something in it makes me shudder. I reach for the memory again—reach for Liam and my mother and the scent of pine and cedar—and then a tiny body crashes into my legs. Sebastian, running at full tilt. He keeps his footing but loses his dinosaurs, and they tumble to the ground.

"Whoa there," Connor says with a laugh. Half-gripped in memory, I stretch a smile into place for the nervous-looking Sebastian and crouch down to help him retrieve his prizes.

"There you go," I tell him, pressing his tyrannosaurus into his hands.

"What do you say?" Paloma prompts him, coming up from behind to collect her son.

"Thank you. And sorry," he says, and then he's scampering off again, Paloma in his wake. I stay crouched a moment, elbow braced on one knee, watching them go, my mind still chewing on it all—

Red scarf. Blue. The image flickers in my mind.

"Coming?" Connor asks. I turn to look at him—and freeze. Where he's standing, my angle near the floor puts him perfectly aligned with one of the trophies mounted to the wall. With the light half behind him, it only magnifies the illusion.

The illusion of antlers springing from his temples. Curving upward, sharp prongs the length of my palm reaching toward the ceiling. A being out of myth, out of the heart of the woods, out of a dream of cold winter.

Like a frame coming into focus, I see it clearly—the man in my dream. His face has always been occluded in shadow, but I know it. I've always known it.

Connor looks so much like his father. A man I knew, once upon a time.

A man who I've seen in my dreams ever since.

15

My dream has always felt like something out of a fairy tale—the sort of fairy tale where girls get their hands cut off and witches are forced to dance on hot coals. The man with antlers chasing me through the dark wood, the dragonfly, the single red star that glows like an ill omen. They were pieces of a story, not real.

But in that moment, looking up at Connor, I knew I've been wrong all this time. It was real. Parts of it, at least. Liam Dalton is the antlered man in my dream, and I was terrified of him.

There is no question of staying in White Pine tonight.

I make it through dinner and everything after, feeling absent from my own body. I answer questions without knowing what I'm saying, eat without tasting the food.

That night in bed, I wait until Connor's breathing is slow and steady. I envy that sense of safety that lets him sleep so deeply. He lies with his head flung back, his throat exposed. The pose of a creature who has never been prey. I drag my fingertips along the line of his jugular, and then I slip away.

This time I remember the flashlight. Because the clouds are covering the stars, I don't get far before I have to turn it on. I hate the necessity of it—how it constricts my world to the circle of light, marks me out as separate from the dark of the world around me.

The door is unlocked again. I step past the wax stains on the floor; tonight, I head straight upstairs. Again I pause at the bedroom doorway, waiting for memories that don't come. Trying not to permit myself disappointment, I go over to the vanity. It's still there: the dragonfly.

I run my fingers over its bumps. It's too big to slip into a pocket.

Not like the little treasures I used to collect. They were all meaningless: a stray button waiting to be sewn back onto Joseph's shirt, a lighter, a tiny pink shell.

I've been so good. So *mostly* good. There were the photographs in Alexis's bag, but I hadn't meant to find those, had I? I was only looking for a book. There's this place. But does this even count? It called me here. I only answered.

I walk over to the bed frame, trying to imagine it with a mattress, a bedspread, a blanket rumpled after a night of sleep. I shut my eyes and think of fingers running through my hair, picking out tangles.

Hush, my baby. Only good dreams allowed.

My eyes snap open. The voice was as clear as if it whispered in my ear.

Red scarf, I think, and I try to picture it, but all I can see is blue fabric. And then the other image arises, the one I can't escape—a face that is now familiar, half-steeped in shadow, antlers jutting from his brow. With it comes the sensation of a scream at the back of my throat, and my heart races—

No. I can't go there. Not yet.

Red scarf, I think. And a ghost whispers in my ear.

"There you are," her mother says. The girl doesn't know why her mother sounds so upset. She isn't hiding. She's lying on her floor with her crayons spilled out around her. On her paper, spindly trees stand crookedly around stretched figures in triangular dresses, blobs of yellow on their heads. The princesses. She's working on their castle now, carefully angling the V of the roof.

"Look what I made," she says, but Mama doesn't even look at it. She grabs the girl's backpack, starts shoving clothes in. "Mama?"

"We have to go," Mama says. Her voice is tight and angry. No—scared. "We have to go before he gets here."

"But—"

"Now," Mama says. She zips the backpack shut. The zipper catches.

She swears and yanks on it, then puts the straps over the girl's arms. Grabs her hand. Then they're heading down the stairs. A suitcase waits by the door already, and Mama lifts it in her other hand, grunting from the effort.

The girl isn't wearing her coat. The snow immediately begins to soak into her sneakers—her boots are still inside, by the door, but she doesn't say anything, too scared to object. Her mother drags her along, and the girl has to scramble to keep up. The car is up ahead, the door already open, suitcases in the back. Mama picks up her pace.

"Wait!" the girl cries. "We forgot Teddy Too."

"There's no time," Mama says. Her eyes flash with regret. "I'm sorry, honey. I'll buy you a new one later. Here, give me your backpack." She takes it from the girl's shoulders. Half-inside the car, she rearranges bags, shoving them into place.

She isn't looking. And it isn't so very far back to the cabin. The girl backs away, step by careful step. And then she turns and runs. She'll be so quick her mother won't even notice. And she doesn't. There's no cry, no hand grabbing the girl's arm, just the trees around her rattling with a harsh wind. There's a crack—she's heard that sound before. Trees crack when it gets cold sometimes. The sap *expands*. Mr. Liam taught her that fact. She'll tell her mother when she gets back to the car.

She will be so fast, the fastest ever. And she will get Teddy Too and she will be back before her mother even notices she is gone. There he is now, right on the bed with the daisies crawling across it. She has him in her arms and she is pelting back down the stairs again in a blink.

Hanging on the hook by the wall is her mother's blue scarf, the beautiful one that Mr. Liam gave her the day he gave the girl Teddy Too. Her mother says it is Too Expensive, but she wears it every day and the girl knows she'll be very sad if it's gone, and maybe if the girl remembers it, Mama won't be quite so angry that the girl went back (even if she did go so so so fast).

With the scarf in one hand and the bear under her arm she runs back, grinning. She holds the scarf aloft. Her mother will see it and she will see that it was a good idea, the best idea, to go back and there will be no yelling.

But her mother isn't there. The car is where it was and the back door is still open but she doesn't see her mother. And then she sees—

Her mother's feet. She's sitting on the ground, her legs stretched out in front of her. Teddy can't see the rest. She's hidden behind the door.

"Mama?" Teddy says. She steps around to see.

Her grip goes slack. The wind gusts; it rattles the trees. The blue scarf lifts from her hand, and for a moment, it flies.

The memory is not a cohesive thing. It is moments, images, convictions, a feeling in my gut. Blue spills across the snow; it becomes red. Sun shines between the trees, but the next moment I remember night, and in it, the single crimson star. My mother's voice is clear and vivid and then it's gone, wind between my outstretched fingers.

We were here, and then we had to leave. But something happened. Something terrible.

The scarf was blue, I think, and that's correct—but it's wrong, too, somehow. I'm missing something. But I can't reach for it. I don't want to.

There's a thump downstairs. Another. And then a creak. The front door opens.

Someone is here.

16

A sound bubbles up from below. A laugh—a giggle. I stiffen, sitting up.

Footsteps clomp on the porch. I rise, the urge to run suffusing my body, but I freeze. There's only one way out of here, and that's down those stairs, in plain view of the front door.

The door wheezes, opening wider. The giggle turns into a voice—

"Give me five minutes." It's Trevor.

Olena answers. "I hope it'll take longer than that," she says. There's no sign of the guilt that so tortured her the last time I heard her; she sounds giddy. I stay frozen in place, not daring to move, but the fear in my chest eases. No one knows I'm here—they're not here for me.

There's a thump, then noises of movement, of objects being set down. Then the rasp and hiss of a match being lit. I think of the circles of wax on the ground. Not some arcane ritual, of course—a romantic candlelit evening.

"Much better," Trevor says. "Come here."

Of course—Trevor is bunking with his mother. There's no way he could sneak Olena in there, and there's only so much ducking into rooms in the lodge they could get away with. They need a place to meet up, and what better location than the cabin that no one uses, that none of the family will even talk about?

Their voices drop to murmurs. My legs are starting to cramp up. I ease myself back toward the bed. I sit slowly, stilling when the bed frame creaks. Then Olena lets out a little sound of mute pleasure, and I relax.

It's almost funny, really. Almost. My heart is still pounding and my hands are shaking, but it's impossible for the pull of memory to drag me under while I'm trying desperately to block out the sounds below. People carrying on with their lives, completely unconcerned with mine.

"That's right. Get on your knees for me," Trevor says huskily. I try not to listen to the metallic sound of a belt buckle, Olena's soft-voiced assent.

I was so confused the first time a boy asked me to put his dick in my mouth. And then entranced with how quickly it undid him, the way he sat there with his head tipped back and no words, just incoherent sounds of pleasure. I watched him the whole time, and when it was over, he looked at me with something like wonder and said my name, and I would have done anything for him.

Trevor tells Olena what to do. Where to be. Where to touch him, where he's going to touch her, and she whimpers her obedient pleasure. I bite my lip and try not to pay attention as her moans grow louder. My cheeks are hot. I put my hands over my ears, trying to pretend I don't hear, feeling like the worst kind of intruder.

Take your shirt off, that boy had whispered to me, his eyes gleaming. His name was Peter Frey. By then I was already sure I was in love with him. I carried a silver dollar his father had given to him with me everywhere, hidden in the heel of my shoe. When Beth visited with his mother and took me along, I crept into his room and ran my hands over the brim of his baseball cap, pulled on his catcher's mitt, and imagined I could feel his warmth held inside it.

So I did what he asked. I did the next thing, too, and the next, so long as he looked at me like that, and I memorized the books on his shelf and the smell of his clothes. I never loved him, but I thought I did, and so I made all the same mistakes you make when you're too deeply in love with someone who isn't.

The muffled quiet I've created with my pressed palms turns to true silence, and the only sound is the whoosh of my blood in my ears, so I lower them. The breath and murmuring have a different quality now. There's the bright tinkle of laughter from Olena.

"We could stay," she says. *Go*, I will them, but it doesn't take wishing. Trevor's gotten what he wanted out of the encounter, after all.

"I'm afraid my absence will be noted if I stay out too long," he says with a long-suffering sigh, unconvincing. I can't see Olena's pout, but I hear it in Trevor's next words. "Oh, don't do that. You know I'd stay all night if I could."

Leave now, and don't come back again. This place doesn't belong to you, I think.

More sounds: rustling, steps. They're both getting dressed again. I rise, cautious, and make my way to the door, three steps from the top of the stairs. It's a risk, but it's dark up here, and what reason do they have to look in the first place? I watch as they exit. Olena first, Trevor holding the door for her. She's wearing a white wool cap, a bright red coat—the same color as mine, and for a foolish instant I have the conviction that she's taken that from me, too, like she's taken my solitude, intruding on this place. Then she disappears outside, Trevor a step behind her. He shuts the door and I listen to footsteps crunch in the snow.

The faint smell of smoke reaches my nose: the extinguished candles. I wait a full five minutes, counting seconds, before I make my way downstairs, wincing at the noise the steps make. Still in pure darkness, I cross quickly to the front door and let myself out onto the porch. I don't see the bright spot in the darkness to my left until Trevor moves, straightening up from where he has been leaning against the wall.

I go still, like a deer not yet sure if it's been spotted. The cigarette in his hand is the only light, a dull orange glow.

"Enjoy the show?" he asks, his voice a rasp. I hear his exhale, taste the smoke as it furls around me. I say nothing. "You following me, Theo?"

For a moment I don't even process the name. It doesn't feel like mine at all. "I was already here," I say. "So, no. I wasn't following you."

He makes a sound like *hm*, skeptical, back of the throat. "What *are* you doing here?" he asks. "Snooping? I doubt there's much to find. Place has been empty for years."

"Why?" I ask. My voice is strained, my desperation too plain. It startles him; he shifts back, as if to get a better look at me. "Why leave it empty like this? I thought your dad died here, but your mother told me he was at the lodge when he fell."

"Right," he says softly. He takes a drag, and then he holds the cigarette out to me. I'm not quite sure why I take it. It's only that I've always liked to touch things someone else has touched, taste what they've tasted. It's a need to know.

I haven't smoked in years, not since my boyfriend in freshman year, a boy with a patchy beard and soulful eyes. Yet at the first taste of the cigarette, memory rushes back—I'm nineteen again and staring up at Brandon while he talks to his bandmates, his arm around my shoulders and his attention anywhere but on me. Cigarettes and bad folk rock: the things I loved because I thought it was the same as loving him.

"My dad did *something* here. But dying wasn't it," Trevor tells me. I pass the cigarette back. He inhales, and the light of it spills across his face, illuminating the harsh planes of his features for hardly more than a second. "Connor hasn't told you."

"Told me what?"

"He has a rosy view of our father. Really got in that sweet spot where he was old enough to worship the guy but not old enough to see what he was really like. Me, I don't even remember the fucker, so I don't have any attachment to some perfect version of him," Trevor says. "He was keeping a woman here. A fuck-buddy stashed away where he could visit her without anybody knowing about it." Rage stabs through me—how dare he talk about her that way?—but I swallow it down.

"He had—there was a woman living here," I say.

A woman in a red scarf—*blue scarf*—her face inches from mine. *Hush.*

"Kid, too. They were up here for months." He's trying to sound like he doesn't care.

"A kid."

"I mean, she wasn't *his* kid," Trevor clarifies, and I am glad the darkness hides my relief. "She was up here when he died, you know. So Mom has to deal with her husband being a cheating piece of shit *and* being dead, all at the same time. Bastard."

This is confirmation. Proof that I'm not just imagining things, stringing together broken memories and fantasy. I was here. *We* were here.

"What was her name?" I ask. My voice cracks.

Trevor's head tilts, shadow against shadow, his pause pregnant with curiosity. "I don't know," he says. "Does it matter?"

"Do you know what happened to her?" I ask.

"Why would I know that? She probably moved on and found some other rich guy to leech off," Trevor says. "Don't get me wrong. I don't blame her. You've got to get what you can out of life, it's not going to be handed to you."

Says the boy with a trust fund. He offers me the cigarette again, but I don't reach for it, and he shrugs. "Suit yourself."

"Your mother will be missing you," I remind him.

"Nah. She takes a pill. She'd sleep through an avalanche," he says. "Connor's a sound sleeper, too, right? We don't need to be in any hurry. We could duck back in and . . ." His tone makes it clear what he's suggesting.

"For fuck's sake," I say.

He laughs. "Just kidding. Or checking. Gotta make sure you're not *that* kind of girl, you know?"

"Sure." The kind of joke that's only a joke until it isn't. "That's why you were spying on us? I saw your footprints under the window."

"Don't worry, I didn't see anything R-rated," he quips. He tilts his head back, releasing a thin stream of smoke. "He's really crazy for you, you know," he says, like this is pitiable. "Tracking you down like that. He's never done anything like that before. You must be something special."

"We met at a party," I say.

"Yeah, but before that," he says. I stare at him. He gestures, frustrated. "The photo? The art show? Alexis told me. About how he saw your portrait and he had to meet you and blah, blah, blah."

I'd almost forgotten. Harper had a photography show, and she'd used a photo she took of me to round it out. She'd mentioned it to me in an offhand way, making sure I didn't mind, and I didn't. It would have scandalized anyone I grew up with, of course. I was topless, knees to my chest on a wooden chair, my spine a perfect curve, staring straight at the camera. One arm was bent, hand in my hair, showing off the bold lines of the dragonfly on my wrist.

It wasn't a particularly remarkable photograph, but it was lovely and Harper insisted she had to have at least one "seminude hottie" to spice up the collection. I hadn't been able to get out to the show, so I'd never seen it, hadn't really thought about it after she got permission.

"Right," I say. "Harper's show."

He reaches out. His palm catches my hip and he tugs me toward him. Startled, I come forward a step. "You're not very pretty, are you?" he asks.

"Is this your attempt at flirting?" I ask. His eyes search mine, the pinprick of light reflected in them.

"There are millions of pretty girls. You're something else," he says. "People say pretty because they don't have a word for it. It's a lack of imagination. I thought it was ridiculous. Falling for you because of a photo. But I can see it now."

There was a time when I would have easily toppled into the empty hole that is Trevor Dalton. All it took was that look—that look like someone saw me. What had Nick said? That Liam wanted people to worship him. If he was anything like me, that isn't quite right. It's the inescapable power of being seen.

Once upon a time, I would have made a study of Trevor Dalton, learned every inch of his interior, reflected it back at him. Because boys like him, they love nothing so much as staring into a mirror.

"Trevor," I say softly. He shifts his weight, leaning in without leaning in, and I rise on my toes enough to put my face close to his. "Fuck off," I say.

He laughs. And then, before I can react, he reaches out, grabs my hand, and jams the lit end of the cigarette into my palm. I let out a muffled cry of pain, but he's already let go, stepped back. He flicks the cigarette into the snow and vanishes in the pure darkness of the porch.

"Have a nice night, Theo," he bites out.

My hand throbs with pain. I grit my teeth, not wanting to give him the satisfaction of a whimper, an exclamation. I stumble off the porch, wrestling my flashlight from my pocket. Behind me I hear the rasp of a lighter as he starts in on a new cigarette, but I refuse to turn around, even as tears well in my eyes.

I don't slow down until I reach White Pine.

17

I sneak back into the cabin like a criminal, clinging to silence and shadows. I shed my clothes layer by layer in the dark. The burn on my palm provides a slithering sense of pain, building and receding but never entirely vanishing. I ignore it for now and pad into the bedroom. Connor sleeps on his back, one arm above his head, the other across his body. Even in his sleep his brow is furrowed, his face a picture of unhappiness.

I go over to his suitcase. I don't know what I'm looking for, exactly. Probably nothing. But I have to begin somewhere. He's finally unpacked his clothes into the dresser, but I run my fingers inside every little zippered pocket, moving slowly, checking every few seconds to be sure he hasn't stirred. I come up empty except for a creased boarding pass from six months ago—just before we met. LAX to SEA. First class, obviously.

I tuck it carefully back in where I found it. Make sure all the zippers are closed or open according to how I found them. There are little details you have to keep track of. What direction someone closes their suitcase in, whether they left the drawer fully closed or a quarter-inch open, whether a book was straight or crooked on the bedside table. It's important to follow wilderness rules when you are mapping your way through a person's life. Leave no trace.

I try his drawers next, sliding my hands between each of his shirts, feeling along the folds in case something is tucked inside. Nothing.

His phone. It's in the drawer, fully charged despite the lack of signal—he's conscientious about that, at least. I put in the code, flip through his messages. The same messages from Alexis I've already seen. Texts to and from his mother, simple pleasantries, checking in.

Are you sure about bringing her? she asked, weeks ago. He told her he was.

I scroll back. Names I know and names I don't. He's not huge on texting, really. He prefers phone calls, hearing another person's voice. I pause when I recognize another name. Harper. The last text message was eight months ago. I click through.

Hey, Connor again. It was great chatting with you at the show.

Of course!
I am so glad you connected with my work.
I hope you enjoy the pieces.

I know I will.
Actually, I wanted to ask you about that portrait, the black and white one.

Right. Like I said, that one's not available.

You said she was a friend of yours, right?

Yeah, she was my roommate sophomore year. She's an interesting gal.

I was wondering if you could introduce us.

It's several hours later that Harper responds.

I guess I could do that. But you should know, Theo can be a little intense.

I don't mind intense.

Should I give her your number?

No. I'd rather you introduce us in person.

Um, okay. I'm having a party next week she said she'd be at, if you want to drop by. I mean, you did buy enough prints to cover my rent for, like, three months. Least I could do is invite you over for cheap booze and pretentious conversation with failed poets.

Perfect.

Don't do anything sketchy or I'll cut you up into tiny pieces and bury you in the park.

Cross my heart.

I stare until the screen goes dark.

Trevor was telling the truth. Connor and I didn't meet by happenstance. He saw my photo and tracked me down.

Why?

Had I looked familiar to him, too? My hand goes to my wrist. To the dragonfly that almost perfectly matches the ornament on the cabin door—a tattoo that was on full display in that portrait.

He hunted me down.

He brought me here.

I thought all this was a coincidence, too wild to be true. But what if it wasn't? What if I didn't stumble my way here?

What if I was led?

18

I put the phone back in the drawer, adjusting it just so.

I fall in love so easily. It's always been one of my worst qualities. Because I don't know how to love. I don't know how to *be* loved. I always thought it went back to the root. My first parents didn't want me, and neither did the second set.

But that can't be true. It can't be. My mother loved me, I remember it now, but something terrible happened. And so maybe that's what it is, this desperate hunger to get that love back.

It was stolen from me, and so I try to steal it, too.

When I was a child, I stole things from the man who called himself my father, in love with him the way a child loves someone they think will save them. I took from him a book of native plants, well thumbed; a spider trapped in amber. (*He didn't save me. He didn't do anything at all.*)

When I was thirteen, I fell in love with a girl named Sarah Baker, the way a child loves someone they wish they could be. I stole a pretty pink shell from her jewelry box and a bracelet made of twine and beads. (*She kissed me in the old barn; she told me my real parents got rid of me because I was ugly; she never spoke to me again.*)

When I was sixteen, I fell in love with a boy named Peter Frey the way you love someone because they look at you with desire, and I took his silver dollar and a third-place track medal and four hundred dollars to take care of things. (*He told them it was me he told them it was my fault he told them he told them he told them.*)

When I was nineteen, I fell in love with Brandon, who tasted of stale ash and told me I was strange, warped, broken, that he liked me anyway, that no one else would. I took his guitar pick and a letter from the girl who broke his heart. (*He told me I was crazy. He grabbed my arm so hard it bruised. I stayed another month.*)

Connor was supposed to be different. I didn't have to sneak my way in. I didn't have to figure him out, become just right so he'd love me, tolerate me, find some use for me. He loved me. From the start, he loved me, and it was fortune, it was fate.

It was a lie.

I look down at my hand. The pain in my palm keeps tempo with my heart, waxing and waning with each beat. He'll ask me where it came from. It's obvious what it is—round, ragged at the edges, oozing clear liquid.

I walk back out to the living room. The flames have long since died down in the woodstove, but I know from experience how hot it still is, with the embers smoldering within. When I was a child, I barely touched the stove and it left a welt on my palm for days. I curl my fingers. I think of Trevor's face, the moment before he jammed the cigarette against my palm.

I think of the end of it, an orange glow in the night.

A single point of light. Like a star. Not a red star, but an amber one. I close my eyes. I can see it. The star in the dark, among the trees. Cold seeping into my bones, and I need to find the woman with the red scarf, because something terrible has happened here.

Something terrible is still happening.

I open my eyes and press my palm against the edge of the stove.

19

Connor is horrified by the burn. I bandaged it myself the night before, but he insists on unwrapping it to examine the damage, fretting over it. The heat of the stove has obliterated the small circle at the center of my palm; it's a solid welt now, stretching from one edge of my hand to the other. I watch Connor with a sense of detachment.

He's been lying to me ever since we met. He's never pried about my past, but was that only because he knew it would make me run away?

When I first told him about the dream, he asked if I thought it might be a memory. *Pieces of one, maybe,* is what I told him.

He leaves me in the cabin. Insists on going to the lodge to get us both breakfast. I pace uneasily. I need to talk to Harper.

I need to get out of here.

I need to know what happened in this place, all those years ago.

What I can't do is just sit around here. I start for the door, grabbing my coat and yanking it on as I step outside. I'm in such a hurry that I don't notice Nick on the stoop. I yelp, stumble. He reaches out, catching me with one hand as I come down the stairs. He hauls me upright, carefully balancing a wooden tray on one hand. It's loaded high with what looks like a waffle buffet for five.

"Whoa there," he says. He looks amused.

"Sorry," I stammer.

"No worries," he assures me. He tips his head toward the waffles. "Connor got held up at the lodge. I've been dispatched to bring you breakfast and check your hand," he says after a beat of silence. We can't seem to get our rhythm right, keep spending moments staring at each other like this.

"My hand?" I echo. I sound calm, at least.

"I'm a doctor," he says. I flush. I should have remembered.

"It's really fine," I tell him. As if to contradict me, my hand gives a stubborn throb of pain. My fingers twitch.

"Connor seemed pretty worried. Let me just take a look. So I can reassure him," he says.

"What if I refuse?" I ask.

"Then I guess you don't get any waffles," he tells me gravely, and I laugh a little, because that's what I'm supposed to do.

"Right," I say. I turn back to the cabin, heading up the two steps.

"Hold on, you dropped something," Nick says. I turn in time to see him crouching down, makeshift tray carefully balanced, to pick up the white rectangle that's fallen to the snow.

The photograph. It was still in my pocket. It must have come loose when he collided and now he's picking it up, turning it over. His face goes blank. He stares at it for a long moment. And then he stretches out his hand.

I take it from him, fingers trembling. "Thanks," I say.

He says nothing. Nods. I turn and walk quickly inside, listening for his footsteps and the thunk of the door closing behind me. I set the picture on the counter, face down. He carries the waffles over to the counter and then pulls a kitchen chair out.

"Take a seat," he says.

I do as directed. He sits in the chair opposite me. I hold my hand out. He doesn't meet my eyes as he examines it.

"Pretty decent job on the bandages, given that you're operating one-handed," he notes. He peels off the adhesive, pulls it aside. He grimaces. "Jesus. You did this on the stove?"

"Just clumsy, I guess." The skin has blistered badly at the edges of the burn.

"Well, you did everything right," he says. "Top marks for the first-aid knowledge."

"My family wasn't big on doctors," I say. He looks up at last, curious. I arch an eyebrow. "They're all crooks and quacks trying to take your money and pump you full of pills."

"Obviously," he agrees, nodding.

"Though really, I think we were broke and the philosophical objections were cover," I say. "Anyway, short of actually getting impaled on a piece of rebar or something, I was taught to take care of things myself." I'm talking too fast. My nerves make me chatty.

"That's why I bribed you with waffles," Nick says. "My dad's the same way. Especially now that he's getting older."

"It's a hard instinct to unlearn," I admit. You don't ask for help. You just get it done, and you don't complain, and you don't let anyone see that you're weak.

"Well, you're doing the right thing. Keep up the ointment or petroleum jelly, and wash and rebandage it a couple of times a day," he says. "Nasty spot, but it should heal all right. Try not to use that hand too much."

"I don't think I have an option," I say ruefully.

"On that note, let me help you with your breakfast," he says. I start to get up. He waves me back into the chair. "Nope. I've got this. As your doctor, I absolutely forbid you to do it yourself. Strawberries? Blueberries? Whipped cream?" he asks.

My answers produce a pair of waffles piled high with all three. I try in vain to cut the waffle with the edge of my fork. He leans in, takes it from me, picks up the knife. I sit back, feeling like a child. Joseph cutting up my meat for me, because I wasn't allowed sharp things.

"That photograph," he says.

"I found it." I try not to sound defensive.

"In here?" he asks. I don't answer. "Dragonfly." He sits back, setting fork and knife on the plate. He regards me from beneath dark brows. I feel cut apart under that gaze. Carefully sectioned and considered. The kindness is gone from him, replaced with wariness. "Mr. Vance said you'd been going out there at night."

"Not every night," I say. So Vance has been watching me, tracking the movement of my flashlight in the dark. I imagine Duchess with him. His hand on her ruff, restraining her.

"Why would you do that?" he asks. His tone is impossible to read.

"Curiosity, I suppose," I say.

"You were prying."

"It's just an empty cabin." I don't tell him how much I hate closed doors, locked cabinets, things kept up high out of reach. How I've always had the need to know, to have, to inhabit. "Anyway, I found the photo and thought I should give it to Connor or something, but I completely forgot I had it." Voice bright and innocent, like I've got no idea what it might mean.

"Do you know who it is?" Nick asks.

"I know the man is Connor's father," I say. I take a bite of my food. Swallow it down without tasting it. "Who's the little girl?" Does he see how much she looks like me? My face has changed. The girl's cheeks are rounder, her features softer.

Nick's fingertips tap a slow rhythm against the tabletop, like he's thinking. It reminds me of a heartbeat, but mine's so much quicker, pattering away in my chest. "She was called Teddy," he says. "It wasn't her real name. A nickname—pet name, really. Her mother was . . . a friend. Of Liam's." He's careful when he says it. Not sure how much to say. His eyes give him away—the anger in them.

I think of the way he and Rose looked at each other, how he stepped in. He'd taken it personally, what his brother did.

"You asked me if I ever went by Teddy," I say.

He dips his chin. "I was being ridiculous. It wasn't even her real name," he says. "It was because she was obsessed with teddy bears."

Like the one in the photo. In my memory. *Teddy Too,* I called it, because we had the same name.

"You do look a little like her. Mallory, I mean—and I guess her daughter, though it's hard to say with little kids, you know."

I'm glad that I'm wearing the high-collared sweater. That he can't see the two little birthmarks on my throat, their perfect match in the photo.

"Mallory. That was her mother's name?" It stirs no recognition in me. But of course it wouldn't—for a little girl, *Mama* is the only name you need.

"That's right. Beautiful woman," he says.

"You knew her."

"Not well." He shakes his head. "I wouldn't go mentioning any of this to Connor or Rose. It brings up painful memories."

"Because Liam was sleeping with her," I say bluntly.

"Who told you that?" he demands.

I skewer a strawberry. "It seemed pretty obvious." He doesn't need to know about Trevor. "I wouldn't have guessed it. From the way Connor talks about his father, I mean."

"We didn't want any of the kids finding out about Mallory. Hell, I didn't even want Rose knowing, she was dealing with enough already, but there wasn't much way around it. Mallory and the kid were here when the accident happened."

I school my face in a picture of appropriate surprise, sorrow, and awkwardness.

"Alexis found out, and she told her brother. Alexis . . . she took it hard. Barely came out of her room for months. Wouldn't eat. Hurt herself." He doesn't specify. I picture a razor against pale skin, Alexis's face set with concentration and intent. "Connor just pretended he hadn't heard. Kept on building up his father as the superhero he wanted to remember. I don't blame the kid. Anyway, you can see why no one would talk about a thing like that."

Some secrets stay that way because of the trouble they could cause. Others because the pain of silence is slightly more bearable.

"What happened to them after the accident? Mallory and Teddy, I mean?" I ask. It feels strange to speak the name without claiming it. Teddy. A bear with a red ribbon and soft fur and arms wrapped around me. *Everything's going to work out, Teddy. You'll see.*

My breath catches in my throat. Nick doesn't seem to notice. "She took off. I have no idea where to. I didn't exactly care, at the time," he says. "We weren't terribly kind to her. Maybe she deserved it, I don't know. We were all just so shocked and grieving, and then finding out what Liam was doing up here . . ." He scrubs a hand over his face.

What Liam was doing up here. The phrase sticks in my mind, and I give an involuntary shiver.

"You look so much like her," he says again. His eyes trace the contours of my face. I want to hide, to turn my face away. I make myself hold still under his scrutiny. "I wondered if there was some way you could be her. The name, you know."

"But her name wasn't Theodora," I say.

"No. No, it wasn't," he says. I wait. I want him to say it. I need him to say it. But he sighs, straightens up. "I should let you eat that before it goes completely soggy."

I look down at my food. A moment ago I was ravenous, but now the sight of it turns my stomach.

"Thank you for coming by," I say.

He dips his head. "Not a problem. No, don't get up, I'll see myself out." I cancel the obligatory move to rise. He lumbers his way to the door, pulls on his boots.

"Nick," I say suddenly. He pauses, hand on the door. "Did Liam smoke?"

A line appears between his brows. "Now and then," he said. A laugh rumbles in his chest. "We picked up the habit here. Sneaking Dad's cigs out in the woods. I still get that urge when I roll up to the gate. Kicked it a long time ago, though. Patients don't like a doctor who smokes. Why?"

"No reason," I say. He looks puzzled but doesn't press. He lifts a hand in a final farewell, but after the door is open, before he steps out, he pauses.

"Curiosity's one thing, Theo. But digging up the past like this . . . it's not good for anyone," he says. "Just opens up old wounds. You should throw that photo away. Don't let Connor see it. And I'd stay away from Dragonfly, if I were you. There's nothing there but bad memories."

"I understand," I say. He takes that as agreement, and leaves at last. I don't tell him that I knew that already.

That the bad memories are exactly what I'm trying to find.

20

It's cold in the cabin. The fire went out in the stove, and no one has relit it. I wear layers of sweaters and sit in silence at the kitchen table, waiting.

Connor returns at last with cheeks red from the cold and an apology muffin for being late. He's been gone more than an hour. I'm still stuffed from the waffles but accept the muffin as the tribute it's intended to be, and he kisses me tenderly as if he can't be sure what kind of touch is safe, won't hurt me.

"What did Nick say?" he asks. At my startled silence he adds, "About your hand."

Right. "That I'm an unbelievable klutz. Not in so many words." I waggle my eyebrows, going for playful. *Why did you lie to me, Connor?*

He sought me out. And he hid it. He never told me about the art show, and neither did Harper. There must be some innocent explanation, because this is Connor, the boy without scars on his skin, whose only wound is sorrow. He wouldn't hurt me. He wouldn't spend all these months hiding things from me to lure me here for some unknown purpose.

He goes to start a new pot of coffee. "Does he think you need to get it looked at?"

"No, it should heal just fine. I took a couple of ibuprofen to help with the pain. Should be much better in a few days, and look completely disgusting until then."

Connor starts up the coffee and takes the same seat where Nick installed himself. "I've been thinking," he says.

"That's unusual for you," I tease; he huffs.

"My family—okay, mostly my grandparents—are worried about me marrying you. They think we don't know enough about you," he says. He scratches the side of his face. "I know that you don't like talking about your childhood. But maybe if you laid it all out on the table, they would see that there isn't anything nefarious there."

"Nefarious?" I repeat. He lifts his shoulders, lets them drop. My spine stiffens. "My past is none of their business."

"But isn't it mine?" he asks. "I don't even know your parents' names. I don't know how they died, if you have other family, if you liked school or if you got good grades or . . ." He spreads his hands.

I look away, staring at the wall, at the window, at nothing. "Elizabeth and Joseph Scott," I say. "And I was homeschooled. They weren't good parents, Connor, and I don't like talking about it."

"You know, maybe we could find your birth parents," Connor says. "I know you hit a dead end before, but you didn't have the same resources that we do. I bet you anything Granddad has somebody who could—"

"Why are you pushing so hard on this?" I ask him. "For me? Or to make your grandparents happy?"

He taps a fingertip on the table, thinking over his next words. "My family is very rich, Theo. If we don't look into you, someone else might. And my grandparents need to know that there isn't anything to find that might damage the family. I know that it's intrusive. But think of it from their perspective."

He puts his hand on my thigh. He sits on the edge of his chair so he can lean in toward me.

"You have to help me out here," he says. "You have to start telling me things."

"I tell you the important things," I say.

He shakes his head. "You're so hard to read. Hell, you're a blank book."

I flinch back. He's dug his fingers into a wound, a fear I always hold myself curled protectively around. Who am I? Maybe I'm no one and there's nothing inside me except all the little pieces I've collected from the people I've wanted to love. Maybe I'm just a silver dollar hidden in a shoe, a pink shell, a polished piece of tiger's eye, a knife.

"What's so terrible that you can't tell me?" he asks. "What's so important to keep secret?"

Blood in my teeth. On my shirt. Blood that won't stop. The cruiser's lights flashing.

Yes, I'm keeping secrets, Connor. But I'm not the only one.

"The night we met, why did you come over and talk to me?" I ask. His head jerks up. Just a twitch, really. It could mean anything. It could mean nothing.

And then he smiles. "I need a reason to go talk to a pretty girl?" he asks. He rises, coming around the side of the table. He leans against it facing me so I have to crane my neck to look up at him.

"I'm not pretty," I say, Trevor's words an echo in my chest.

"Of course you are. You're beautiful," he says. They're different things, I don't tell him. "You looked intriguing. I wanted to know who you were. It turns out that was a harder proposition than I was expecting." He says it like he's teasing me, but also like it's true.

"You looked familiar. But we'd never seen each other before," I say. I'm leaving him the opening, the option. If he tells me, I'll tell him everything, I think. But if he keeps his secrets, I have to keep mine.

"Maybe it was just a sign that we were fated for each other," he says.

"You didn't recognize me?" Trying not to sound like I'm pressing. That I know there's anything to press about.

"I don't think we'd ever run into each other before," he says. "I wouldn't have waited to talk to you." He cups my chin in his hand, his thumb against my lower lip. He sighs. "I love you, Theo."

Any other day, any other point in my life, it would be enough to undo me.

Today I only turn my head toward his palm to kiss the inside of his wrist, and I say nothing at all.

21

Connor lied to me about the night we met, but he isn't the only one. Harper arranged that meeting, and she never told me. I want to know why.

My injured hand gets me out of family time at the lodge. I charge my phone for a few minutes, long enough for a few calls, and dress for the cold. Connor told me there's signal down by the gate, so that's where I'm heading.

The whole walk, I'm waiting for someone to stop me. But in the brightly lit lodge I can see people moving about, wandering past the giant windows; they're all occupied with more important things than me.

I take my phone out as I approach the gate. Nothing. I have to haul myself over it and go another fifty feet down the road before my phone finally connects to the network. It offers up a scattering of alerts—emails, texts, nothing urgent. I dial Harper's number. She answers immediately.

"Theo!" she says. "Thank god. I was starting to worry you'd been eaten by wolves. So how is it going? Do you have them all wrapped around your finger yet?"

Harper speaks with rapid cheer. She's always like this. So much energy it's constantly overflowing. She's my oldest friend—the first person I met at UCLA when I showed up clutching a single ancient suitcase, with forty dollars to my name. It took her three seconds to decide to make a project out of me. She was fascinated by my upbringing. Protective. Warned me Brandon was bad news, for one thing, and nursed me through the aftermath of him without ever saying *I told you so.*

It doesn't make sense, Harper lying to me.

"Harper. Sorry to bother you," I say, my voice strained. I've never had trouble talking to Harper before, but now I have to force the words out.

"You're never a bother," she tells me. "What's up, babe? You sound dreadful. Don't tell me you're ready to flee in terror from the one percent already."

A sound escapes me—a horrid, animal whimper like a wounded dog.

"Theo?" she says, startled. "What's wrong? Did Connor do something? Do I have to murder him for you? Because you know I will."

My back teeth clench. Yes, Connor did something. But so did she. "Harper, Connor asked you about me, didn't he? Before the party. He asked you to invite me. To introduce us."

"What's this about?" Harper asks carefully.

"It's about you lying to me," I snap. "I'm right, aren't I? He asked you to introduce us. And for some reason you never told me."

"He asked me not to," Harper says with a nervous little laugh. "He said it was, you know, the Dalton thing? He didn't want you looking him up before he actually got to make a first impression. Apparently there have been a lot of girls over the years—guys, too, even the ones who didn't want to sleep with him—who got all weird when they found out how much money he had. He's sensitive about it. Then, I don't know. It got awkward to bring up. I wasn't—it wasn't really a *lie*. I wasn't hiding something. You liked him. I thought . . ."

I suck in a breath, anger washing through me, followed by the faintest edge of relief, because this sounds exactly like Harper. She's never been known for thinking things all the way through, and she wants more than anything for people to be happy. This is exactly the sort of thing that she would convince herself was an innocent omission.

But that doesn't let Connor off the hook.

"Harper, the thing is, I think he knew who I was," I say.

"Right. Because I told him. He saw that photo of you. The one where you're a total smokeshow? He is not the only one who asked for your number, let me tell you. Just the only one I thought was worth my baby girl's time."

I shake my head, even though I know she can't see it. "No. I mean before that. Way before. I know this sounds crazy, but when I got here, it all felt familiar. And there's this cabin that no one uses anymore, and I was just looking around and I found—"

I stop. I'm talking so fast I'm not making much sense, words running into each other.

"There was a photo of me," I say, slow and deliberate. "As a child. Before the Scotts. It's a photo of me with Connor's father."

"That doesn't make any sense," Harper says, baffled.

"Except it does. Because I was here," I say. "I've started to remember things. Find out things. My mother—her name was Mallory. She was having an affair with Connor's father."

"What? Ew, wait, does that mean—"

"No," I say quickly. "No, I was already around. But he stashed her up here, apparently. And then he died, and she just dropped off the map completely and no one can explain where she or her daughter went. Me. Where I went."

"Theo," she says. She's worried. "That's a pretty wild story."

"I know, but I promise you it's true," I say.

"Okay." She's skeptical but trying not to show it. She's doing a shitty job.

"Something happened up here—something they're not telling people. My mother wouldn't have just abandoned me. I think—I think something happened to her."

I see the image again—her feet, sticking out from behind the car door. The scarf fluttering free of my hands.

I was so afraid.

Liam Dalton died here. His death was an accident, Connor says, but I'm beginning to doubt that. Liam Dalton is the monster from my dream. He did something to her. To us.

Or did she do something to him?

"You know that based on what? A photo?" Harper is asking.

"It's more than a photo. I'm starting to remember things. From before."

"And you're sure."

Doubt creeps through me, a scuttle of tiny insect feet.

"I . . . I don't know," I say, and it feels like a betrayal. Of myself, of my mother. Like I'm denying her existence. "Harper, I don't know what to do."

"Theo, we're talking about very rich, very powerful people," Harper says. "If you break up, whatever—they won't care. But if you start making accusations, make them look bad . . ." She trails off.

"What do you think they'd do to me? They're good people, aren't they?" I ask with an edge of irony. "They're respectable people."

"I've heard things," Harper says. "The Daltons don't like to be challenged. And rich people are ruthless."

"So what are you saying? What am I supposed to do?"

Harper takes a breath, lets it out in a rush. "I don't know what's going on, but whatever it is, you're obviously in trouble, and you're not safe there. You need to come home."

"I can't."

"Theo . . ."

"How well do you know Connor, Harper?" I ask her. "Tell me he isn't like this. Tell me I can trust him one hundred percent, and I'll let it all go."

She's quiet for too long. "Theo," she says softly, singsong. "Baby . . . I met Connor at my show. When he bought those prints."

"You said you were friends."

"You know me. I call the lady next to me on the bus my friend because she gave me a stick of gum," Harper says with a little laugh. "I'd only met Connor that one time when he came to the party." There's another pause, because I have no idea what to say. "You should come home."

"Thank you, Harper. I'll talk to you later," I say mechanically, and end the call, cutting off whatever she tries to say next.

I stare down the road. Wheel ruts rake through the snow. Crows quarrel in the distance. I can almost imagine I am completely alone up here.

My phone buzzes. I look down, expecting Harper. Instead, it's an unknown number.

Dora, it's Joseph. We need to talk.

I blink at it, expecting the words to rearrange themselves into something that makes more sense. Joseph is not supposed to contact me; I'm not supposed to contact him. That's the deal. It's the agreement we came to, after everything with Peter, after the way I left.

There's only one reason I can think of for him to break that agreement.

Those anonymous text messages weren't a bluff or a guess.

Someone else knows.

22

When I met Peter Frey, I was sixteen years old. He wasn't much older—seventeen and change. His father was our new pastor and Beth was always good at courting power. In our little corner of the world, Peter's dad was as good as a king. So we were over there often enough, and Beth did her best to cultivate a friendship with Peter's mom, though she never got beyond arm's length. Her big mistake was asking for a family biscuit recipe too early. That kind of intimacy needs to be earned. I will never forget the subtle and stinging rebuke of the recipe card slotted back in its little wooden box, the lid snapping shut.

They had five children, a respectable number. Peter was the third child, the oldest boy. I wasn't permitted to socialize with boys outside of Sunday school, and he held a fascination for me, with his curly brown hair and freckles, the softness of his cheeks.

I was in his room when he found me.

"What are you doing?" he asked.

"Just looking around," I said.

"You were stealing."

I couldn't deny it. There was a pin in my hand, given to him for some church boys' group accomplishment. I opened my hand, holding it out. "I just wanted to see it." It had been forgotten in the back of the drawer. It wouldn't have been missed; I would have treasured it. These were the rules I went by.

He stepped toward me, but he didn't take the pin. I dressed in loose peasant blouses and dowdy skirts, but there was no hiding that I was a young woman, and his eyes found every bit of proof of that as they wandered down my body and then up it again.

"I could get you in trouble," he said.

"Please don't," I whispered. It had been months since I got caught. Since I lost my temper or got distracted and asked a question out of turn. They were starting to relax around me.

"I've heard about you," he said. He seemed to consider. "I won't tell," he said at last. "If you lift up your shirt for me."

I considered, in turn. It was against the rules, of course, and I was well versed on the need for modesty in all things, but like most rules, it seemed to matter only if someone noticed you breaking it. Besides, wouldn't he be in just as much trouble for asking?

So we made a deal. I made him shake on it, and then I pulled my shirt out of my skirt and lifted it, a motion without an ounce of sensuality but which satisfied him, despite the very matronly bra I wore underneath. When I lowered it, he was looking at me like I was the most amazing thing he'd ever seen.

After that day in Peter's room, things escalated quickly. Deals were struck. Favors exchanged, secrets kept. My shirt came off entirely, and my bra. He was granted permission to touch and then to be touched. I could pretend that I was an innocent, manipulated by the more worldly older boy—barely older though he was—but while my education was sorely lacking, there was no point at which I didn't understand the lines I was crossing or the significance of what we were doing. I wanted him as much as he wanted me. Maybe more.

And so when Beth and Joseph were gone for the weekend, I let him in the back door and brought him to my bedroom, and for the next twelve hours while his parents thought he was with his friends, we checked off as many forbidden things as we could think of. Our imaginations weren't very expansive, but our enthusiasm made up for it. And every time he would hold me and look at me with wonder and say, *Oh god, Theodora, oh god,* and I knew that he was praying just to me.

We figured most things out. Where babies came from and how to keep them away wasn't one of them.

Bad luck for us.

I might not have known exactly the mechanics of how I got pregnant, but I'd heard enough about Beth's attempts, which hadn't stopped after I arrived, and I remember her hushed and excited whispers that she'd missed her period. Mine was regular as clockwork. So when it didn't come, I went to the library and asked for books on babies. *Like pictures of babies?* the librarian asked, and I said no, how a person gets pregnant.

I told Peter the next day. I was calm; he panicked. "We can't have a baby. I can't have a baby. My dad is going to kill us," he kept saying, and I informed him there was another way out of it, but I was going to need money, which neither I nor the Scotts had.

Peter had been saving up all his money for a new bike; he had a few hundred dollars set aside. I convinced him he could give it to me or he could use it to pay for the crib and stroller he was going to need.

I worked out everything on my own. The timing. The bus ticket. The "flu" that I'd surely caught from the Russell kids down the street, a perfectly acceptable reason to spend the week curled up in bed.

It might have even worked. But I never got the chance to find out.

Turned out Peter's father had noticed how diligently he was saving up his dollars and cents, and wanted to reward him for this sudden impulse toward delayed gratification and long-term thinking with the last fifty dollars to meet his goal. He was set to take him into town for that bike.

Peter couldn't very well say that he'd given the money to me. That would have invited too many questions about why. So he said that I'd stolen it. His father knew there was more to it. He pressed. And Peter told him what we'd done.

What *I'd* done. And what I meant to do.

He told them that it was my idea. My fault, every part of it, and they believed him, because Peter was a good boy and I—

I had always been a wicked child.

Peter's parents spoke to mine. And together they decided enough was enough.

Something had to be done.

23

Every family has its rules, most of them unwritten. The Daltons have more than most.

I can't afford to break them now. Not with this all-too-familiar feeling creeping over me—the sense that I am not safe here. That the shape of me does not fit within the boundaries that have been drawn, and I must hold myself with exquisite care to keep from straying over them.

And so when we're summoned to the lodge for dinner, I don't use my wounded hand as an excuse. I pull on my red coat and the scarf that blends into it and I follow Connor out. My body feels tender with the imprint of his touch. We haven't spoken about my past again. I haven't asked him why he's lying to me about how we met.

As we gather around the table, I consider each of the Daltons. One of them surely sent the messages on my phone, warning me away—it has to have been someone here on the mountain. The little gift left on my windowsill is proof enough.

One of these people knows about Washington. About Peter Frey and what happened after.

Connor helps himself to wine. He drinks more here. Like he's more relaxed—or like he's trying to blunt his feelings. Alexis tuts over Sebastian's refusal to eat anything but bread, trying to ply him with carrot sticks. My eyes drift across the table to Trevor.

Trevor would send those texts just to fuck with me, I reflect. Or with Connor, more accurately. I can't discount that possibility.

Trevor catches me looking. He smirks at me and raises his glass, half-full with deep red wine. Alexis catches the movement as well. Her head swivels toward him.

"Trevor," she says.

He lifts the glass toward his lips. His eyebrows raise. "Yes, dear sister?"

"You're not supposed to be drinking."

"According to who?" he asks. He takes a sip. The table has gone quiet.

"Are you sure that's a good idea?" his mother asks softly.

"Of course it isn't. Don't be an idiot, Trevor. You've gotten into enough trouble already," Nick says, half a growl.

"First-time offense. *Barely* over the legal limit. I picked up the trash and served the homeless people their soup. I'm a reformed man," Trevor says.

Alexis's body is completely rigid. Connor looks angry.

"The boy can make his own choices," Magnus says.

"Even if those choices are *fucking stupid?*" Alexis demands.

"Lex," Paloma hisses, tilting her head toward Sebastian, who seems thankfully oblivious to the drama, too busy having two of his carrot sticks wage pitched battle. I can't help but envy him. I turn my hands to fists in my lap, which sends a zip of pain through my bandaged palm.

"You can't seriously sit there and act like this is no big deal," Alexis says. "It wasn't just—"

"Alexis," Louise says, a hint of warning in her voice.

"She's not wrong," Magnus says, his silverware clinking as he continues to eat. "You know what that kind of bad behavior is? Weakness. And even weaker not to own up to it. You may not be ashamed of yourself, Trevor, but the rest of us sure as hell are."

The smile is fixed on Trevor's face. He sets down the glass slowly, without having taken a sip. "Well. Sorry to be such a disappointment to you all," he says. "Let me relieve you of the burden of my company, then." He stands.

"Trevor," Rose says, but even she doesn't seem to know whether she wants him to stay. He gives her a disgusted look and shakes his head before storming out.

"He should—" Alexis begins.

"That's enough of that kind of talk at the table," Louise says, and I feel attention tilt toward me. Meaning, whatever they have to talk about, it's not for my ears. There's obviously more going on here than a simple DUI, but I'm not about to get any more information. I glance over at Connor, but his eyes are fixed on his plate.

Louise's silverware clicks. Magnus is splashing more wine in his glass, and her lips purse. "He isn't the only one who shouldn't be drinking so much," she mutters.

Magnus's mouth quirks. "You don't need to fret about my health, dear. That's what I have the doctors for."

"And you don't listen to them, either."

He shrugs. "But at least they're getting paid for it."

The mood stays tense through the rest of the meal. When Sebastian starts squirming, Alexis seizes on the excuse to leave. "We'd better try to get him down for bed," she says. "Maybe he'll actually sleep this time."

"I doubt it," Paloma says. There are dark circles under her eyes. The two of them rise, gathering Sebastian along in their wake. Connor gives my hand a squeeze under the table, a quick assurance that we can escape momentarily.

I listen to the patter of Sebastian's footsteps down the hall, the murmur of their voices, and then—

"What the fuck?" Alexis exclaims. For a moment, no one moves. Then she says loudly, "What the hell is this?"

Connor is the first on his feet. I rise with him and follow as he heads down the hall. Chairs scrape behind us. We arrive in the foyer to discover Alexis standing in front of the Christmas tree, staring at something on it. An ornament—a resin wreath with a spot in the middle for a photograph, cheaply made and standing in sharp contrast to the coordinated silver and gold baubles that adorn the rest of the tree.

"What is it?" Connor asks, drawing closer. Alexis takes down the ornament, a frown ghosting across her lips. The photo at the center of wreath shows a car, hood crumpled, on its side several feet off the road.

It's not the only ornament. The next one over depicts Magnus at some kind of formal event, shaking hands with a broad-chested man with salt-and-pepper hair; beside it hangs some kind of legal document, snipped into a paper snowflake.

Connor walks around the tree slowly. Paloma is standing on the other side, her eyes fixed on the tree and her expression ashen. The others file in with an air of confusion and alarm.

"What . . . ?" Rose says. She drifts toward another one of the newly appeared decorations—another cheerful snowflake, the excised sections making it difficult to read the details. But the word *divorce* is unmistakable—and so is Rose Dalton's name.

Had Rose filed for divorce? Or intended to, perhaps, but never got the chance? Connor has never hinted at problems between his parents, but he was only a child, after all. He might not have known.

Paloma suddenly gives a little shake. She picks up Sebastian, holding him on her hip. "I'll be in the cabin," she says curtly, and departs with quick strides, not bothering to grab her coat.

"What *is* this?" Alexis says.

Secrets, I think. The private things we live our lives pretending no one knows.

Magnus takes the photograph from her. He looks down at it for a long moment, then says, "This is nothing."

"Nothing? Someone put these here," Alexis says in alarm.

Louise's eyes bore holes through me. I shrink back, pulse fluttering at my throat. It occurs to me that my own secrets might be hanging on that tree somewhere, but I quell the frantic urge to search. I can't give them reason to suspect.

"Call Irina. Have her clean this up," Magnus tells his wife.

"I think it's clear what happened here," Louise says, ignoring him.

"Is it?" Rose says with a swallowed laugh. "Because it isn't clear to me."

"It's her," Louise says, jabbing a finger in my direction. "She's done this."

I let out a disbelieving sound. "Me? I don't even know—" I start.

"She didn't do this," Connor says, coming around the side of the tree. "And unless you have any proof to the contrary—"

"Louise," Magnus says simply. He nods toward the doorway that leads to the living room. Standing there, hands in his pockets, is Trevor. For once he isn't smiling that smug smile. His expression is empty, and behind it is a void more dangerous than anger.

"I know what I did," he says. "But you're all acting like I'm the only one who ever did something wrong. Fuck you. All of you, but especially you, Alexis. At least I hurt someone by accident."

Alexis stares at him. And then her eyes widen and she whips around to the other side of the tree, searching. "Shit," she says. "You—" There's fury in her eyes, and she steps toward her brother—and then lets out a sound of frustration and wheels back the other way, running after Paloma.

Everyone is talking all at once. Yelling at Trevor, mostly. I walk around to see what it is that Alexis saw. That Paloma saw.

It's a photo taken in a dark room—a bar or a club. The flash washes out the faces of the two women in it. Alexis, caught mid-blink, wearing a low-cut top and perching in the lap of another woman. It looks recent. Too recent to be innocent.

Ignoring the clamor of voices, I take the ornament from the tree and turn it over, twisting the tabs that hold the back in place. I pinch the photo free and tear it into tiny pieces before tucking them into my pocket.

No one else needs to see that. Trevor's done his damage already.

My eyes scan the tree, searching for my own name, my own face. If it's here—

"Theo?" It's Connor, his hand touching my elbow lightly. "You should go back to the cabin."

I look over. Trevor is standing slumped back against the doorframe, eyes fixed on the ground, expression equal parts angry and stubborn. Tears glisten on Rose's cheeks.

This has nothing to do with me.

"I'll see you soon?" I say, but he barely manages a distracted nod. I make my escape swiftly. Part of me is glad to get away from what will follow. Part of me is stuck on thinking about what secrets there might have been nestled among those branches, if I knew how to pick them apart.

Rose, filing for divorce. A car accident. A meeting. There had been other ornaments I didn't see as well. Trevor had been planning this for a while.

I'm halfway to the cabin when I spot Alexis. She's leaning against a tree, her arms crossed, staring at nothing. She looks up at my approach. Her eyes are red and watery.

"Hey," I say softly, like you'd talk to a spooked animal. "Are you okay?"

"Paloma asked me to leave," she says.

"Leave, like—"

"Leave the cabin," she says. "For now. Did you see?"

"I got rid of it." I hesitate. "Do you want to come to White Pine? Just to warm up. Connor won't be back for a bit."

"I'm sure they're holding a family summit. That's their reaction to everything. Get everyone together and get everyone on board," she says, her voice congested with tears. "Do you have anything to drink?"

"Plenty," I promise her, and she nods. She follows me, sniffling occasionally, as we walk in awkward silence.

In the cabin I pour her a drink. She curls up on the couch, feet under her. She's a small woman, and in this pose she looks almost childlike.

"You must think we're awful," she says as I take my own drink to the other side of the couch, perching on the arm.

I take a sip. I've pilfered some of Connor's good Scotch. Not that I can particularly tell the good from the bad; the hard liquor I drink is usually smothered by fruit juice or Coke. "Honestly, I didn't understand most of what I saw." I turn the glass slowly in my hands. She takes a generous swallow of her drink. "What exactly did Trevor do?"

She grimaces. "We're not supposed to talk about it."

"I got that impression," I say as neutrally as I can. "He had a DUI, but it was more than that, wasn't it?"

"He got the DUI and got his license suspended. Community service. Granddad thought it would be a good lesson for him," she says, as if it goes without saying that otherwise Trevor would have gotten off scot-free. "Then three months ago he gets plastered and goes for a drive. Slams right into a lamppost."

"Was anyone hurt?" I ask.

She tilts her glass back and forth, watching the movement of the liquid. "A girl. Young woman. She was in the passenger seat. Her name is Kayla. Luckily, she wasn't hurt too badly. But we're in the middle of this deal. It's with—the names won't mean anything to you, but it's a Japanese company and the owner is a pretty conservative, traditional guy. He was on the fence about us in the first place. We can't have any kind of scandal right now, with—" She stops. "Granddad paid Kayla to keep quiet. And I really shouldn't be telling you this."

She drinks. I watch her. She's upset. She wants to talk. I'm inclined to let her.

"You don't exactly seem happy about that arrangement."

"He could have killed her. He could have gotten *himself* killed. And it wasn't the first time, or the second, or the third. He thinks that he can just call up Granddad and get out of whatever trouble he's gotten himself in."

"That's what you wanted to talk to Connor about, when we first got here."

She wets her lips. "Yeah," she says. "I just don't think he should be able to get away with it." She takes another swig. Her glass is almost empty. I rise and go to fetch the bottle. I probably shouldn't be encouraging this, but I'm not going to pass up the opportunity to loosen her tongue.

I tip more Scotch into her glass. She doesn't stop me. Her hand shakes as she brings the glass to her lips.

"It was a onetime thing, you know."

She's not talking about Trevor anymore. "You don't have to explain," I tell her, but I sink down onto the couch beside her, my own glass, barely touched, cradled in both hands.

"It was a business trip. And I didn't—we didn't," she says firmly, and looks at me as if she can prove the truth of it if she stares hard enough. "I didn't know someone took the photo until they emailed it to Paloma. I don't know how Trevor got his hands on it. He must have gone through our phones or something."

"She already knew?" I ask, surprised.

"It was a few weeks ago. We're . . . working through it," she says. "God, it was so fucking stupid. I was drunk and stressed and it was Dad's birthday, which is always *weird*, and I don't know what I was thinking. That's not who I am. It's not who I want to be. I promised myself I would never do that to someone, not like . . ." She trails off.

"Like your father."

"You know about that?" she asks with a note of surprise.

"Trevor told me."

She snorts. "Of course he did. He probably wants you to be worried Connor would do the same," she says. "But Connor's not like that."

"I'm not worried about Connor cheating on me," I assure her. There are other things to worry about.

She's slowed down. Her eyes have an unfocused look like the alcohol's started hitting her. "I thought my parents had this perfect marriage," she says. "I know plenty of kids think that, and then their parents get divorced or whatever, but it really seemed like they did. And I keep telling myself that I won't make the same mistakes. That I'll be a better spouse and a better parent and everything will turn out okay, but how am I supposed to know what to do if I have no idea what went wrong? I can't ask him. I can never ask him why he would do that to Mom. To us. How he could leave us like that."

She stops. Her hand grips the glass so tightly I'm almost afraid it will shatter. She has the fearful look of someone who has said something she shouldn't have, and I hate the satisfaction that slithers through me.

Alexis needs a friend right now. I can't afford to be one.

"Your father was going to leave," I say slowly, carefully. She wets her lips again, a compulsive gesture. I'm not quite right. But what could she mean?

"My father," she says. Stops. Then, "You can't tell Connor I said that. Or Mom. They don't know."

"They know about the affair," I say. "Except that's not what you meant."

My heartbeat is perfectly steady. My voice is soft and gentle. *You can tell me. You can trust me.*

But her expression shutters. "It was a long time ago," she says. "Whatever he did doesn't matter anymore."

There are deep shadows under her eyes, almost bruise-like. Her entire body tells a story of deprivation—deprived of food, of sleep, of slowing down for even a moment.

That kind of control craves release.

"I can't imagine how hard it must have been. Especially being the oldest," I say. "You were old enough to understand what was going on."

"Understand? No, I didn't understand. I never understood how he could do that," she says. "And we couldn't talk about it. None of us. Had to keep it quiet. We wouldn't want to embarrass the family. To humiliate Mom. So just carry it and don't tell anyone and just live with the fact that . . ." Her face screws up.

"Alexis?" I say softly, so gently that I hate myself for it. I tell her with my words and the way I lean toward her and the hand I put out to touch her knee lightly that she's safe with me.

"He didn't fall," she whispers. And then all at once she pulls inward—shoulders retracting, head coming up sharply, teeth clicking together.

My lips part, beginning to shape a question.

The door opens, and she jerks, guilt flashing over her face as Connor steps in.

"Alexis," he says, startled.

What does she mean, he didn't fall?

"Connor, hey." She stands, setting her drink on the table beside her, smoothing down her clothes. "Summit already done?"

"I just stuck around long enough to make sure Mom was okay," Connor says. I watch Alexis.

Does she mean he was pushed?

Mallory, I think. She did something to him. She had to run. It makes sense.

Except that Alexis was talking about something *Liam* did. Said that he left them.

My mother was hurt. And then—what? I hid; Liam Dalton found me; he died. I ended up somewhere else entirely. But what happened to my mother?

What happened to Liam?

He didn't fall.

Meaning, his death wasn't an accident.

So Mallory is hurt, but she gets up and—

How he could leave us like that.

I've been avoiding putting the pieces together, following the logic. My mother was afraid. We tried to run, but it was too late. She was hurt. *Killed,* I force myself to think, because nothing else makes sense. And I hid, but I was found. By Liam Dalton, a man whose face still haunts my nightmares.

Whatever happened, it was a scandal big enough that the Daltons would want to cover it up. To tell a story about a storm and a roof and a fall, a good man taken too soon. A story that made no mention of an affair, a vanished girl, a woman who seemed to not exist at all anymore, as far as the world was concerned.

"What the fuck was Trevor thinking?" Connor asks. I blink, startled at how few seconds have passed.

"He's always been one for dramatics," Alexis says. She pats her hair into place. In control once again. I rise slowly.

Liam Dalton didn't fall.

And Mallory—if she had killed him, Alexis wouldn't keep that secret, would she?

He killed himself. It's the only explanation that makes sense. It's the kind of secret Alexis *would* keep—from her brother, from her mother. It's a secret that would wear on her. That she might let slip to someone at last. A near stranger. The one person who wouldn't be wounded by it.

But how did she find out?

"Do you need to crash here tonight?" I ask.

"No. No, I don't think so," she says, avoiding my eyes. "Paloma just needed a little bit to—you know. I'll go back to Red Fox. Thank you, Theo. I should go." She gives me one quick look, eyes bright, hands gripping her upper arms tight enough to bruise. *Don't tell him,* she seems to be asking me. I give her the slightest nod, and a measure of relief breaks across her expression as she allows Connor to usher her out the door.

Connor sees her out, then picks up the bottle of Scotch from the coffee table and eyes the level. "She all right?" he asks.

"I don't know her well enough to say for sure. But I think she will be," I tell him, her words still echoing in my mind.

"Do you know what . . . ?" he says.

For an instant my mind goes blank. I wet my lips. "She should tell you, if she decides she wants to," I say. "As far as I'm concerned, none of that was any of my business. She did tell me about Trevor. About Kayla."

Connor sighs, shoulders slumped. "It's a shit show. Not exactly our finest moment."

I hesitate. "I saw some photos in Alexis's things," I say. At his sharp look, I add, "I was looking for a book for Sebastian, and I came across them. There was a woman. Covered in bruises. Was that Kayla?" The bruises I'd assumed were from a beating could be from an accident, the marks on her shoulder from the bite of a seat belt.

He's quiet for a long moment. Then he drags both hands down his face, sighs. "Yes. I guess she took them in case she changed her mind. Or, I don't know, if she wanted more money. Which, good for her, I guess." He looks past me at nothing as he speaks, his voice dull.

Alexis's anger makes a lot of sense, if she'd seen the evidence of the damage Trevor's actions had caused directly like that. And I get her wanting to talk to Connor about it in private. Suddenly the conversation I overheard in the kitchen makes more sense as well—when Louise asked if Connor had told me anything, it must be about this. About avoiding the whiff of scandal. They need to secure the Japan deal, and Alexis seemed on the verge of telling me something else as well. Some reason the deal is so important.

"Are you—is the family in some kind of financial trouble?" I ask. It's hard to imagine.

Connor sighs. "No. Not exactly. Granddad is selling the company."

"Oh," I say, startled and unsure how to react. "Is that . . . good?"

Connor shrugs. "Alexis is the only one still working there, and she's been wanting to move on for a long time. And Granddad should have retired properly years ago. If the new deal goes through, the company's value will be a lot higher, and he's got a buyer waiting in the wings if all the pieces fall into place. If things don't work out . . ."

"The family loses out on millions," I say.

"Try billions," Connor replies.

"I try not to make myself contemplate numbers that big, it makes my tiny peasant brain overheat," I tell him, deadpan, and he cracks a weary smile. "I'm not supposed to know any of this."

"Not yet," he acknowledges.

"Don't worry. I'm good at keeping secrets," I tell him.

"Yeah, I've noticed," he says darkly. He reaches into his pocket. He takes out an ornament, the same as the rest, and sets it on the coffee table, then regards me.

It's a photo of me. Sixteen years old. My hair a rat's nest. Even shrunk down to fit in the frame, the photo shows the shadows of bruises on my ribs, my stomach. The random patterns of dull brown on my cheek, neck, hands where the blood has dried and not yet been washed off.

"What is this?" Connor asks.

I pick up the ornament. A strange blend of feelings churns through me—the urge to protect that girl, to tell her it wasn't her fault, and at the same time a vicious sense of disdain. *You should have been smarter. You should have been more careful.*

It was Trevor, then. He's the one who found out. Who sent me those taunting messages and left that gift on the windowsill.

"Theo," Connor says. His voice is worryingly level. "Trevor told us he looked into you. He said that you were lying to us. That your parents are still alive. That you have a history of criminal behavior. That you were institutionalized."

"Institutionalized?" I echo, confused.

"Locked up for your own good, he said," Connor clarifies, and I give a choked sound of amusement.

"That's one way to put it."

"I told Granddad and Grandma Louise that I would talk to you," he says. "I told them that there would be an explanation. And I'm really hoping that's true."

"Trevor's right," I say, still staring at that photograph, at that foolish, broken girl. "My adoptive parents are still alive. And when I lived with them, I lied and I stole. And they did lock me up, Connor, but it wasn't what you think."

It was worse.

24

Peter's parents arrived without him. His part in this drama was done, after all, and his sin was so much less than mine. They came to the door. Grim faces, low voices. I watched from the top of the stairs. Emily Frey turned her pale moon face up toward me and I swear she looked afraid.

The Scotts' church didn't have a name. Preferred to call itself a fellowship or a group rather than a church most of the time. They came from a stew of fundamentalist backgrounds crossed heavily and perhaps inevitably with a strong anti-government, anti-establishment ethos. They did things their own way, and so there was no official name for what happened to me next: prayers for deliverance—from evil, from wicked forces. I'd been brought up before the congregation for prayers like these more times than I could count, but this time was different. This time was going to be private and it was meant to be permanent, because someone had to step in, and it was clear that there were evil forces resident within my soul.

Years ago, Joseph had turned the attic into a play space for me. I'd outgrown it long since, and now between the dollhouse and the toy chest, cardboard boxes were stacked, and dust had infiltrated every surface. It was there that Pastor Frey and Joseph brought me. Beth stood in the middle of the room, hands clasped together so tightly her fingers were white. The expression on her face terrified me.

It looked like triumph.

I turned to flee, but the stairway was full, Pastor Frey and Joseph blocking my way.

"This is for your own good," Pastor Frey said in the baritone voice that filled the room of the meeting hall where we held our services. He didn't touch me, but pointed, and it was like a punch to the solar plexus. It took the breath out of me entirely.

Pastor Frey had good intentions, I think; his faith was genuine, as was his belief that there was something in me that could be corrected with prayer and with divine mercy. He never intended violence.

They sat and prayed and put their hands on me. They asked me to explain the things I'd done. To confess to them and to the influences that I had allowed to creep into my life and my heart.

I clamped my lips shut and refused to speak. I stared at Beth the whole time, hate burning in my gut. I thought of every time she'd struck me, called me a little demon, told me it was no wonder my parents had wanted to get rid of me.

And as far as she was concerned, I *was* a demon. What else do you call a child who flies into rages, who steals, who lies, who tempts good young boys into sin? That's not a normal girl. That's something else.

Something that has to be gotten rid of.

I could feel their frustration building as I refused to speak, refused to cooperate, refused to fight. Beth stalked back and forth in front of me, reciting a litany of the horrible things I'd done. The bite marks I'd left on their arms when I was four years old, the closet door I'd broken trying to get out when she had to lock me in there to protect her from my wild rages.

The sun set and I hadn't spoken a word. I thought they would give up.

Instead, they left me there. Locked in that attic room, alone, with nothing to sleep on but the hard floor.

And in the morning, we started again.

The hours blurred together. As their frustration grew, so did their ardor—Pastor Frey's and Beth's, most of all. While Joseph and Emily Frey lingered at the edges, the other two gripped my shoulders and spoke directly to the evil inside me, as if it was a thing that might be ordered to leave.

I kept my mouth shut. I said nothing.

I don't remember every detail of how it ended. It was like something came over me. Like maybe I was truly possessed. I couldn't stand the feeling of their hands on me, the sound of their voices. It was too loud, too hot, too *much*. And then they were leaving—Pastor Frey and Joseph. Emily had left by then, had gone home to her poor misled boy, and this left me alone with Beth, who lingered after the men had gone downstairs.

Beth grabbed me by the face. Tenderness in her eyes and enough force in her grip to hurt.

"This is for your own good," she said, and I spoke my first words since I'd stepped foot in that attic.

I called her a cunt.

I don't even know where I'd heard that word, only that I knew it was the worst thing I could think of. I stepped toward her and maybe I did mean to hit her, to hurt her, I don't know, but she reached out and hit me hard across the face before I could.

Beth called me a demon. A slut. She called me a curse sent to taunt her. And something broke in me, too. I threw back every abuse. Bared my teeth at her. And each time, she slapped me across the face, until that whole side was lit up with throbbing pain, until her hand was bright red.

It was a kind of frenzy, a kind of ecstasy. Holy words wound their way through it, but it was pure punishment. It was like something had been set on fire in Beth's soul and decades of being a demure and submissive wife became nothing but kindling for her rage.

I hadn't eaten more than the smallest portion of food, had hardly had any water to drink in that sweltering attic, and when she brought her fist into my stomach I folded over, fell to the ground. It didn't stop her. The fire was still raging inside of Beth Scott. Her foot lashed out. Again and again as I curled over on myself, twisting to try to get out of her way. Her hard-soled shoes connected with my stomach, my back, clipped my temple, and then all of a sudden Pastor Frey and Joseph were there, pulling her away.

Enough. That's enough for now.

They left me there on the floor, curled around my middle. There was a sharp, strange pain somewhere deep inside me.

The bleeding started a few hours later.

Beth returned in the evening, carrying a tray of food. I think she may have felt guilty, or maybe she only wanted to spit more venom at me. I remember the rattle of the doorknob. The way my skirt clung to my thighs as I forced myself upright, swaying and lightheaded.

The laugh that bubbled out of me when she screamed.

The tray dropped. She fled. And she didn't close the door behind her.

As soon as I heard the front door slam, I hurried downstairs, lifting my sodden skirts, to find the house empty. I peeled the fabric from my wet skin and threw the dress in the fireplace. I washed my legs with cold water and dressed in fresh clothing. The bleeding was still coming, and I thought I might be dying, but I wasn't going to die there.

I packed a bag. Clothing. What little money I had. The treasures hidden in the back of my closet—a silver dollar, a pink shell, a tiny crystal dolphin.

Joseph Scott's hunting knife.

I was on my way to the door when Joseph came home.

I begged him to help me. I begged him to let me go, take me away from there, do *something.*

He hadn't seen the blood upstairs; I wasn't making any sense. Give him that much grace, at least. Allow him the fear of a man whose world is collapsing, whose wife has babbled a tale that is half confession and half accusation; remember that his daughter is a liar and a thief, that her teeth have left scars on his wrist before, that she is a wicked child. And yet. The cut at my hairline, the bruise I could already feel on my cheek, the tender way I moved, bent inward as if to protect myself (*too late for that*). He saw enough. He should have known.

He should have helped.

I think he said, *I'm sorry*. I think he said, *I can't let you go*. I know that he stood in the doorway. I know that he reached for me, that he grabbed my arm, that he was going to take me back to that place.

The only other thing I remember clearly is the panic—blind fear that gave way swiftly to rage.

Elemental anger crashed through me and over me and drove me against the back of my own skull because there was no room for anything but fury.

I remember, too, the sensation of the knife punching through skin, though I don't remember how it got to be in my hand. I remember it scraping across bone. I hit his sternum with that one. I must have been aiming for his heart. Three times I raised the knife and three times I swung it wildly, and I swear, I swear he didn't even try to stop me.

The thing that's clearest in my memory, though, is the sounds after. His cry of pain and shock. The thump as he fell, scrabbling backward away from me. The clatter of the knife falling from my numb fingers.

I remember that I ran.

25

Joseph used to tell stories—Noah and Daniel and David, now and then the Brothers Grimm. I loved the rhythm of the storytelling. The music of it. I could sit for hours and listen. That rhythm infects my words even now, as brutal and unlovely as they are. *Once upon a time, there was a girl locked away in a tower,* I think.

"Shit," Connor says. He's pale-faced. He sinks into the chair near me. "*That's* what happened? That's what this photo is from?"

I feel oddly focused on my own extremities. The feeling of my fingers against each other, the flex of my toes. The sensation of my teeth in my mouth, each individually defined. It's like I am being separated into my component parts, the sense of the whole of me dissolving.

Connor stares at me. "You said your parents are still alive. So Joseph . . ."

I shrug. "It turns out that a sixteen-year-old girl with serious blood loss isn't terrifically strong. I did some damage. He needed a lot of stitches, lost a lot of blood, nothing worse. But I thought I'd killed him. I ran. Didn't get far. I was lucky. The cop who found me believed me. He took me to the hospital. They took photos. And he offered my parents and the Freys a . . . a deal."

As in, the report got filed, but it didn't go farther than that. The Freys and the Scotts were spared legal scrutiny, and so was I. I went to live with Joseph's sister, a woman who didn't love me but provided what I needed—a safe place, an education, time to heal.

And no one ever spoke of it again. That was the agreement, and it's held this long.

Connor listens to me explain all this with rapt attention. When I'm done, he rubs a hand over his face.

"Why didn't you tell me any of this?"

"I've never told anyone," I say.

"I'm not anyone. I'm your fiancé. You told me your parents were dead," he says, voice raw.

"It's what I tell everyone. I didn't think it would matter."

"How could it not matter?" Connor is incredulous.

"Because you weren't supposed to be real," I say.

I didn't want to tell him, because then he would look at me like he is now. With pity and disgust. With horror at the wounded thing in front of him.

"You had to know my family would look into you," Connor says.

"I was going to tell you," I say.

"When?" he demands.

I look up at him. He's angry. Maybe he's right to be. But I don't have space for guilt right now. "You lied, too," I say.

His face goes still. "What?"

"You lied about how we met. You lied about being friends with Harper. You knew who I was and you asked her to introduce us, and then you lied about that and made her lie, too. Why?"

He draws in a long breath through his nose. Then he lets it out, turning his face away. "I can't do this right now," he says. "I can't . . ." He stands. He steps toward the bedroom, then halts. For a moment I think he's going to turn, to say something, but instead he moves again, striding into the bedroom. He slams the door shut behind him.

I sit alone on the couch, feeling the pieces of myself slowly cohering again into something approaching human.

All those stories that Joseph told were meant to impart a lesson. Mine is no different. I didn't always understand the morals that Joseph wanted me to learn, and I don't think Connor has understood this one, either. The story isn't about what happened in the attic. It's about what happened after—what happens when I feel trapped.

It is dangerous to corner a wild animal. Even a wounded one.

You brought me here, Connor. I still don't understand why.

But I'm going to find out.

26

I am not surprised to find Dragonfly empty—Trevor and Olena surely won't be out here tonight. Tonight it belongs to me.

This time I don't go upstairs. I sit against the wall on the ground floor, letting my eyes drift around the space. There is a faint pale splotch high up on the wall, where a trophy might have been hung, long since cleared away; no beast from my nightmares will loom out of the darkness tonight.

Connor brought me here. To a place completely controlled by his family—people who will do anything to protect their secrets. I am cut off here, isolated. He's never asked about my past before, but now it's all he seems to want to talk about. Who I am. Where I came from.

What I remember.

I think of the way he set that photo down, turning the conversation on me. He wanted a confession, but is that the confession he wanted?

Surely he didn't know.

Surely we just happened to meet. We just happened to fall in love, and he just happened to bring me here, and I just happen to be the little girl holding his father's hand in the snow.

Liam Dalton, the antlered man. His face is no longer indistinct in my mind. I can see it, looming above me. Half-light, half-dark, the way it is in my dream. They covered up his affair. What else did he do that no one can be allowed to know about?

I can see myself approaching the car. I can see those feet sticking out from behind the door. But I don't want to go forward. I don't want to see what's waiting for that little girl.

Run, I think. And I did run, didn't I? Cold air stinging my throat.

I ran and I hid, but he found me. A hand around my wrist. A scream. Dragging me out, away from this place of safety. I've risen to my feet without realizing it.

Come with me, Liam Dalton says, and so I do. I walk to the door and stand there in the dark, the snow silvery before me, and I can almost see the shape of two figures—one large, one small—lurching away.

I follow the ghost of Liam Dalton into the woods.

"Keep up," Liam snaps. He keeps a hard grip around her wrist, and she tries to keep up, she does, but her legs are too short. Every few steps he yanks her along, a rough jerk that makes her shoulder ache. She doesn't know where they're going. She's never been this way before. "Goddamn it," he growls.

"Where's Mama?" she asks, plaintive.

He doesn't answer.

Something moves among the trees, scaring loose a shower of snow and startling me from my recollection.

That girl—she isn't Dora Scott. She isn't Theo, either. Like me, she doesn't have a name. And without a name, she's no one.

Who are you? I ask her silently. *Who am I?*

But of course no answer comes.

There's a light among the trees, coming toward me. I'm not surprised to recognize Mr. Vance's sturdy build or the inky shadow trotting alongside him. Duchess comes straight over to me and inserts her muzzle into my gloved hand. I might not be a dog person, but I know how to follow orders. I scratch her below the chin and she gives a water buffalo grunt of appreciation.

"She's decided she likes you," Mr. Vance observes. "You're out late."

"I brought a flashlight this time," I say helpfully.

"All the same. Probably best you head back to your cabin," he replies.

I look over my shoulder. I'm not even certain which way I came from. Where I am. I find myself searching the shadows for two sets of tracks—one large, one small.

"You don't want to go back," Mr. Vance says. Duchess's dark eyes watch me, like she's waiting for my answer. I crouch down, roughing the fur behind her ears, buying myself a few seconds to answer. She looks at Vance and huffs. He scratches the tip of his nose thoughtfully. "Tell you what. Why don't you come on by my place? I can make you a cup of coffee and get you back when you're ready."

"That's not necessary," I say. "I'm fine."

"I wouldn't feel right leaving a young lady out here alone," Mr. Vance says, and I suddenly wonder if there was another woman he extended his concern to. He's been working for the Daltons for decades. He must have been here when she was.

"Okay," I say, with the slightest nod. Mr. Vance clicks his tongue, and Duchess trots over to him.

"It's not far," he says.

His definition and mine might be different. He brings us on a route between the pines, our flashlights making shadows gyre around us, and then to a road—rougher than the one we took up here, only wide enough for a single vehicle.

"I didn't realize there was another road up here," I say.

"Not much of one. It's the long way around, and there's not much reason to use it," Mr. Vance says. "It's more to get at the trails around the other side of the mountain, but it will take you down to Datura if you follow it far enough."

We walk for a good quarter mile, and here a small cabin comes into view, three vehicles parked in front of it—a Jeep, a four-wheeler, and a Sno-Cat. The heavy-duty option for getting down the mountain in the snow.

Vance unlocks the door and ushers me inside, where I'm immediately hit with the stultifying warmth of a woodstove. The snow melts rapidly from Duchess's flanks as she shoulders past me, and she leaves perfect damp paw prints as she walks over to the stove, stretches mightily, and flumps down with a contented groan.

Vance chuckles. "Feel free to make yourself comfortable, but I'm afraid Duchess has the best seat in the house," he says.

It's not much of a house and the seating is limited. There's a bed shoved up against one corner and a single armchair, seams worn through and stuffing poking out of the holes. A tiny kitchen table and a pair of chipped white chairs are the only other option. There's no kitchen, not even a fridge. The only light comes from oil lamps hung on the walls. No electricity either, then. Vance grabs a pot from a cupboard and steps outside. When he returns, the pot is full of snow; he sets it on the stove. I ease myself into the armchair. It creaks under me.

"You live here?" I ask.

"Only during this particular stretch, and now and again when I'm too bushed to make it down the mountain," he says. "Magnus likes me to be on hand during the winter, particularly if there's snow like this, though that isn't often—it's usually later in the winter it starts getting this bad."

"Are you from the area?"

"I grew up in Datura," Vance says. He collects one of the chairs from the "kitchen" and brings it over, settling into it with a sigh. "Wandered away for a few years, but I never found anything worth sticking around for anywhere else. What about you?"

I can't tell exactly what he's asking. "I haven't been many places," I say. "But I haven't found one I've cared to stay in, either."

"Not a big traveler?"

"That takes money," I tell him.

"That handsome boy of yours doesn't take you on fancy trips?" Mr. Vance's eyebrows raise.

"He tried to take me to Paris for our two-month anniversary, but I didn't have a passport," I admit. Instead he'd taken me to the desert, where the sun baked the earth and made the air shimmer, and he slid an ice cube along the inside of my elbow to keep me cool. I had never seen a sky that full of stars. We stayed in an enormous house made of white stone with a pool that ran the whole length of it, and I didn't see another human being for eight days.

I've had a rapid education in how people—including me—react to the level of wealth that Connor and the Daltons represent. There are the fawners, the sneerers, the stammerers. My own reaction has been something akin to relief. Like a fist around my throat has eased off for the first time. Maybe money can't buy happiness, but it buys peace of mind. Security. Safety.

Comfort. Pleasure. The sure knowledge that I'll never have to live in a place like the room I'm sitting in now.

Mr. Vance, for his part, seems utterly untroubled one way or another by the vast resources commanded by his employer—unbothered by the fact that he's sleeping in this cabin while the Daltons rest in comfort up the road. He stands up to check on the progress of the water now steaming on the stove.

"You've worked for the Daltons for a very long time," I remark.

"Thirty years or so," Mr. Vance acknowledges.

"Then you were here . . ." I swallow. "You mentioned being here when Liam Dalton died. Connor's father." As if I have to specify.

Mr. Vance scratches his chin. His beard rasps under his dirt-packed nails. Their tips are yellowed, and the smell of tobacco clings thickly to him. "Like I said, I wasn't actually here when it happened. Might have been able to do something if I had been." His voice is tinged with regret.

"What exactly happened?" I ask. "I thought from what you said that the damage was to Dragonfly, but T—someone said it was the main lodge."

"Oh. Yeah, that's right. Guess I can see how you got that impression. No, Dragonfly was just . . ." He trails off, and for the first time since I encountered him in the woods hunting that deer, he looks nervous.

"He had a woman living there," I say. Letting him know he doesn't have to break that confidence. He visibly relaxes.

"That's right. Mallory Cahill. Sweet woman."

Cahill. I have a last name now. "You knew her."

"Sure. You can hide from just about anyone up here, but not me," he says. "Mr. Dalton—Liam, that is—let me know that someone would be staying here and that I wasn't to ask questions or tell anyone about it, including his family. I can't say it was something I was comfortable with, but, well . . ." He shifts.

"He paid you," I guess.

"I didn't see how it would cause any harm. The lodge was locked up tight, and there wasn't anything in the cabins worth stealing. I saw her now and again, just to check if she needed anything. Her and the girl."

"So you met her daughter, too?" I ask. My mouth is dry and my heart is pounding.

"Sure. Cute kid," he says. "Of course, any kid's cute at that age. She could talk your ear off. About everything. I had a big old hound back then—Bishop. She was scared to death of him, but if I came up on my own, she'd follow me around while I was working, making me tell her what every plant and bird was. Wouldn't accept that I didn't always know, either, so sometimes I had to make things up." He chuckles.

I was the little girl with a vocabulary you could track on one hand for almost the first year I was with the Scotts. Moody. Wouldn't go near anyone I didn't know, and not even the ones I did. Sometime after, that insatiable curiosity appeared—the need to know things, collect names and meanings. I thought it was a consequence of not knowing my own name. The peculiar shape my scar tissue took. But it was part of me all along.

"What happened to them?" I ask. "Mallory and the girl."

The water has started to boil. He hauls himself to his feet again and gets out a coffee maker, spooning out grounds from a giant container of Folgers. "They were gone by the time I got up here to help with Mr. Dalton. The body, I mean."

He's lying, I think. I don't know what about, but the way he won't look at me, the way his eyes fix on his task and his normally steady hand shakes—there's something he's hiding from me.

"I suppose," I say delicately, "that she wouldn't have wanted to stick around after that. It might lead to awkward questions. About why she was here."

"I try not to judge," he says uncomfortably. The coffee is done. He takes down two mugs, blowing dust off one before he fills them both halfway with coffee that smells like it may melt my molars. He carries them over, hands one to me before taking a seat. He adjusts the mug in his hands, fidgety. "She was a sweet woman. A real sweet woman."

"Mr. Vance," I say. Hesitate. He looks at me, expectant. I blow ripples across the surface of my coffee to buy myself time. "Is there any chance—is it possible there was something more going on that day? The day that Liam died, I mean."

"What exactly are you asking?" he asks, sitting up straight.

"Honestly, I'm not sure," I say. I don't know how to explain this without explaining too much.

"I know it was a tragedy," Vance says. "A terrible thing."

"And you're sure you have no idea where Mallory and her daughter went?" I ask.

"She took off without a word. And in a hurry," Vance says. "Can't blame her for not sticking around."

"Did she leave anything?" I ask. "Something that might give any hint—"

His face clouds with suspicion. "Why are you so interested?"

"I don't know," I say. I have no good explanation. "I just . . . I'm just curious. I've always been curious. One of my faults."

He grips the mug, but he hasn't taken a sip in a long time. "You know," he says slowly, "I kept a few of her things. In case the girl—in case they came back for them."

My heart gives a hard thump in my chest. "Are they here? Can I . . . ?"

There's another beat, his eyes dark and bright. And then he stands. He goes to the wardrobe that sits against one wall and opens the bottom drawer. He pulls out a plastic bag—just a grocery bag, gone thin as tissue paper from age. He carries it over and hands it to me without ceremony.

At the top of the bag is something large and soft. I lift the bear out gingerly. Its fur is slightly dingy, its black eyes dulled.

I blink. There are tears in my eyes, but I don't dare wipe them away; Vance will see.

"It was her favorite," Vance says. I can't look at him. I focus all my will on keeping my breathing steady. "The little girl."

"I don't even know her name," I say.

"Her mother called her Teddy," Vance says, and I nod. It has to be enough, I suppose. "But her real name was Rowan."

The breath goes out of me, and I can't get it back. Rowan. The name is like a blow to my chest. I know that name. I know it. She called me Teddy when she was happy and laughing, when she was sad and brushing the hair away from my face, but Rowan—

Rowan, run.

She called me Rowan the day she was afraid.

My hands are gripping the teddy bear tight.

"Why don't you hold on to that?" Vance says quietly. "Don't know why I've bothered to keep it all this time. Guess I was still hoping she'd come back for it someday. But she'd be all grown up now, of course." I can't read his expression. There's something hard in his eyes. Something grim.

I turn my attention back to the bag to break eye contact. I draw out a rich blue scarf. It smells musty, like the bear, but it's still soft.

Blue. It was blue, I think, but still something in my memory rebels.

There's one more thing in the bag. It's a framed photograph, facing down. I pick it up gingerly, turn it over, and there she is. Smiling, a little girl's face pressed up next to hers. The woman in the photo has freckles over her nose and a birthmark right at the corner of her left eye. Her eyes are brown and so is her hair, a honeyed brown that falls in soft waves around her long face. A face that holds traces of my own—the large eyes, the prominent cheekbones, the way it's not pretty, not exactly, but it catches your eye and holds it.

"She was a lovely woman," Vance says, and I know he's not talking about her looks.

I stare at the photo and don't answer. I've seen this woman before.

Not in my memory. In a photograph—several, actually.

The photographs hidden in Alexis's suitcase.

27

I have to go," I say. I'm already on my feet.

"Are you sure?" Mr. Vance asks. "You haven't touched your coffee."

It takes all my focus to turn the words into meaning and understand what he's saying.

"I'd like you to take me back now," I say firmly.

For a moment I'm afraid he will refuse. My paranoid mind flashes images of him blocking the door, of Duchess baring her teeth. But he only nods.

The UTV sits two people side by side. I climb into the passenger seat. Mr. Vance takes the driver's side wordlessly. I grip the edge of the seat as it rumbles up the road and then onto the grounds, jouncing unevenly.

"This is fine," I tell Mr. Vance when we're close to the cabin, but not yet in view.

"Are you sure?" he asks.

"I don't want to wake Connor," I say. He doesn't point out that out here, there is nothing to compete with the rumble of the engine. That everyone will have heard it.

"If you insist."

I climb down. He stays there with the UTV running, the headlights laying down a broad path for me to follow. For just a moment, I think that he's going to call after me. But he only sits there, watching.

I'm beyond the lights now. The sound of the engine moves away. I'm alone in the dark, in the cold. I move forward, feeling as if I'm still being watched.

Mallory Cahill. Rowan Cahill.

Rowan, run.

I can almost hear her voice. I can almost see—

The girl runs. Back to the cabin. Back through the door with the dragonfly. *Are there dragonflies here?*

Maybe in the summer.

Will we see them then?

We can't be here in the summer, Teddy Bear.

She runs up the stairs. Teddy Too is wedged between the bed and the wall, tucked down in the folds of the daisy bedspread. She has to be quick. Mama's waiting.

She gets back to the car and she's afraid Mama will be mad, but Mama isn't there at all. There's only the car and the open door.

The feet, sticking out. Mama is here. She's sitting on the ground. That's silly. The girl walks around the side of the car, ready to say *boo* or make a joke, because then Mama will laugh maybe and she doesn't laugh very much anymore.

She is sitting in a funny way. Her back is against the car but she's too far away from it, so she's leaning. The red scarf is around her neck—

No. The scarf is blue.

The scarf is blue, and it's in the girl's hand. It's being caught by the wind, floating down to the ground.

Red coats Mama's neck, her throat. Not fabric, but blood. Her hand grabs at her neck.

"You have to run, Teddy," she says. Her voice is strange. Like gargling. "You have to hide."

The girl steps forward, shaking. Her teddy bear dangles from her hand.

Mama lets out a sob. "Rowan, *run,*" she says, and flings out an arm like she's pushing the girl away.

This is our castle. Nothing can hurt us here, Mama said when they came to the cabin. *We'll be safe there.*

And so that's where the girl runs. She'll be safe there, like Mama promised.

Everything will be all right.

The breeze stirs a few stray hairs against my throat. It almost feels like the drip of liquid. I can see it now. The blood a wash across her neck. The panic in her eyes.

I move in a daze back to White Pine. I stand just inside the door, my breath a cacophony in my own ears. The memory is like a dream.

No, this place is the dream, and the memory is the only real thing.

Rowan, Rowan, Rowan, the woman's voice says, but the name doesn't fit any better than the others I've tried.

"I remember," I whisper. It's almost the truth.

The cabin is silent. If Connor woke at the sound of the engine, it wasn't enough to get him up. I undress in the dark and walk to the bedroom. The door has no lock. I step in on quiet feet and he's sprawled out on the bed, peaceful in his sleep. I slide under the blanket, lying with my back to him. He stirs. He reaches out with one arm, drawing me to him.

"I love you," he mumbles against my neck. I'm not sure if he's even awake.

"I love you, too," I whisper, and it isn't a lie. It's a heat inside my chest, a blinding light that hasn't dimmed. I love Connor Dalton the way I have since I first looked into his eyes, and that frightens me more than anything.

I'm not safe here. I should be smart. I should run. But if I do, I will never know what happened to me or to my mother.

And I will never know whether Connor truly loves me or if he is like his father in this way, too—

If he, too, is a monster.

28

The morning brings a pale light that seems unable to pierce even the scattered clouds. The air feels thinner, and we don't waste it talking. We move around each other with quiet steps as if afraid to be noticed, and when Olena arrives with a summons for me, it's almost a relief.

"Mrs. Dalton would like you to come join her in the lodge," she says, eyes fixed on my chest.

Behind me, Connor stands from his spot at the kitchen table. Her cheeks turn pink.

"Just Miss Scott," she says. Connor doesn't sit back down right away. Our eyes meet, and for a moment I think he's going to insist on accompanying me. But then he nods. He lowers himself into his seat, eyes tracking away from mine.

I grab my coat and follow Olena outside. She walks with her hands deep in her pockets. In our identical jackets, with our hair under knit hats—hers white, mine gray—we look like a matched set.

"Any way I could convince you to break my leg and get me out of this?" I ask her. Her cheeks go bright red, and she gives a nervous giggle. She's so young, I think, and then I remember that I am, too. It doesn't feel that way. It never has. "Just kidding. Mostly."

"Thank you. For not telling," she says. She doesn't share her mother's lingering accent, but they have the same quality to their voice, a softness contradicted by a faint burr. She really is gorgeous, with those doe eyes and dark hair.

"You know you deserve better than Trevor," I say.

"Trevor's not . . . I know he doesn't make the best impression," she says. "You have to get to know him."

"And what is he like when you get to know him?" I ask.

Her mouth opens. Shuts. "He's good to me," she says.

I would have said the same about Peter. Though maybe I'm being unfair to the boy. He was in the same church as me, had the same messed-up stew of ideas about sex and gender and desire, and he was a teenage boy. What was he supposed to do when it all started?

Tell them it wasn't my fault, I think. But even now I can't be sure that's true.

I am not the sort of girl that parents allow around their sons, their grandsons. I am a threat to their future, and a thing that needs to be sacrificed to protect it.

Olena leaves me at the door to the lodge; I find Louise in the kitchen. There's a pot of water boiling on the stove. She's in the midst of rubbing a mixture of herbs onto the purplish meat of a skinned rabbit, massaging it in. She barely looks up as I enter.

"You can peel and chop the potatoes," she says. "If it's not too hard with your hand."

"No problem," I tell her, though my fingers pulse with pain when I stretch and grip. At least it was my left hand. At least the fingers haven't swollen, so the ring isn't biting in.

I expect her to start in on me right away, but instead we're silent for a good while, except for the bubbling of the water and the snick-snick-snick of the peeler across the potatoes. She sets the rabbit aside to rest and grabs another from a cooler at her feet.

"Are those from Idlewood?" I ask, unable to bear the silence any longer.

"In a sense. Mr. Vance raises them," she says. "Magnus always prefers to know the source of his food. Sometimes I think he would be happier running a homestead than a Fortune 500 company—but then, he does have expensive tastes. Harder to keep up with on a farmer's income."

"Was your family wealthy as well?" I ask, unsure if this is too forward a question.

"Yes, at the time when we married. Shortly after, my father made a series of abysmal investment decisions and lost everything. He came to us hat in hand and begged to be bailed out. Offered to let Magnus buy the company for pennies, anything that would save his legacy."

"What did Magnus do?" I ask.

She flips the rabbit carcass over. Its spindly ribs are threaded through the meat. "He said no. He was right to. No sense throwing good money after bad. My father never spoke to either of us again. But Magnus was correct to do what he did, and I never blamed him for it. You must look after your own family first, no matter the cost."

My mouth is dry. I carefully excise an eye from the potato, trim off a black spot. The discards are piling up. They smell of damp earth.

I straighten my shoulders. Take a breath. "I realize that I'm probably not who you imagined your grandson ending up with. I'm poor as dirt, I'm adopted, I have no idea what my heritage is. I didn't go to the best private schools or get lessons in—in etiquette and comportment—"

"I'm not concerned about etiquette and comportment," Louise says. "I am much more concerned with who you are and what you are capable of."

She is done with the second rabbit. She lines it up before the first and moves over to the sink set into the kitchen island to wash her hands. When she's done, she dries her hands with a slate gray towel.

"And who am I, exactly?" I ask her.

"A girl who seduced the son of her pastor and then stole his savings. Who attacked her father with a hunting knife. Or are you going to claim that didn't happen?"

"No. I did attack Joseph," I say. I wonder if she thinks I might hurt her. I wonder if she's starting to realize that she's an old woman, alone, confronting a girl who knows less savory uses for the knives stored only eighteen inches from where I sit. The cold of fear is gone, chased by the quick tongues of anger that make my skin feel tight and hot. "Who told you that story?" I ask. "Because it wasn't Joseph Scott. Or Peter Frey. They don't want anyone to know about what happened."

"It doesn't matter," she says, which might mean she doesn't know. She's operating on secondhand information—from Trevor, presumably. "What matters is that I know what you did."

"You don't know anything," I say. "You don't know what happened."

"I see. Is there something that excuses attempted homicide, then?" she asks.

"I wasn't trying to kill him," I say. "And beyond that, I don't owe you a damn thing."

Her mouth purses. She reaches into the pocket of her cardigan, a black drapey thing that obscures her shape. She slaps down a piece of paper—a check. I stare at it. "Go on," she says.

I reach out tentatively, like it might be hiding a thorn—or a needle laced with cyanide, maybe. A check made out to Theodora Scott, in the amount of seventy-five thousand dollars. I look from the check to her, my mouth in a thin, unamused line. "What is this, a test? To see if I care more about Connor than a quick buck?"

"It is not a test," Louise says, her voice hard as granite. "I promise you that I have entirely made up my mind about you. You are never going to win me over. You are never going to be part of this family. And you will not get to keep Connor. Either way, you will be leaving here, and you will not be returning. This, Miss Scott, is your last chance not to walk away empty-handed. Call it a gesture of goodwill. Or a consolation prize. Believe me, it is for your own good."

I look again at those numbers, neatly printed in black ink. Seventy-five thousand dollars. To her, it's nothing. To me, it's money that could change my life. Three days ago I wouldn't even have considered it for an instant, but now?

Is he really worth it?

Is it safe to stay?

For a moment I consider tearing up the check and throwing it at her. Instead I only stand. "I'm afraid I've entirely made up my mind as well," I say sweetly, and march out of the room before she can reply.

I manage not to start shaking until I reach the hallway.

I could have guessed she would do something like this. But those last words keep echoing. *For your own good.* Maybe she's right. Maybe I would be better off far from here with more money in my account than I've ever made in a year, but no—I can't go. Not without Connor.

Not without answers.

I almost scream when Magnus steps out into the hall just ahead of me. I manage to turn it into a high-pitched yip of surprise instead, reeling back a step. He stands there, hands in his pockets.

"Theo," he says. His gaze tracks past me. I half turn and see Louise in the kitchen doorway, her arms crossed. He frowns. "Everything all right?" he asks.

"Just fine," I say tightly.

"Well," he says. "I'll see you in the morning, then? To go hunting."

"Hunting. Right." I had forgotten—lost track of the slow progression of days, of where I am in time altogether. "I'll be here," I say firmly, knowing that Louise hears. Magnus steps aside, and I walk past him.

I can feel both of them watching me all the way to the door.

29

When I get to the cabin, Connor is gone. When he returns, he doesn't ask me what Louise wanted, and I don't ask him where he's been. He's in a strange mood the whole day, one moment seemingly unable to speak to me, the next reaching out as I pass to seize my hand and hold it, not meeting my eyes, for long seconds before he relinquishes his grip.

No invitation comes for dinner. We eat what's left in the fridge instead, making only tepid conversation.

The next morning, I wake up alone. I sit up, hand reaching for the empty space beside me. I never sleep longer than Connor. He's never managed to get out of bed without rousing me, but he's gone. I get out of bed quickly, combing my hair with my fingers as I walk out into the main room. Connor is there. He's dressed already in warm clothes, drinking a mug of coffee. His boots are by the door, his coat over the back of the kitchen chair beside him. He's getting ready to go out.

"What time is it?" I ask, shaking off the shadows of strange dreams.

"We have a few minutes. I set your stuff out." He nods over to the bench, where my boots and coat are waiting. I tense. "You should get dressed and grab something to eat." He sounds normal; he doesn't meet my eyes.

"I talked to Granddad yesterday," he says. "I told him. Some of it. I told him it wasn't your fault, everything that happened."

"Is that what you really think?" I ask.

"I think . . . I think I have no idea what you've been through," Connor says. It sounds too much like *I don't actually know you* to bring any relief.

"I didn't set out to lie to you."

A tendon at his jaw flares. I stand in the tortured silence wishing he would just say the words—*it's okay, I forgive you, I understand, I love you, it doesn't matter.* But of course it matters. A thing like this, it needs time. The one thing we've never bothered with, in this relationship.

Connor holds out my coat. I slide my arms into the sleeves, one by one, and when I turn, he zips it up until his fingers bump the underside of my chin.

"Better get moving," he says, and so we do.

Magnus and Nick are waiting for us. They have a pair of four-wheelers with them, built for the snow, with gear packed on the back. Nick carries a metal thermos that steams, the smell of coffee wafting out of it. He holds it out to offer me a swig. I shake my head; he shrugs. This qualifies as a conversation, this early in the morning.

"We'll be splitting up," Magnus says without preamble when we arrive. "Connor, you'll go with Nick. Been a while since you were out so do what he says. Miss Scott, you'll be with me."

Unpleasant surprise twists in my gut, but I nod.

"This many people tramping through the woods, we're not likely to get anything. More of a hike with weapons than a hunt," Magnus says. He doesn't sound too upset about it. "Could get lucky, though. If you don't just yammer the whole time and scare off everything within a mile radius."

I'm provided with a vest—bright orange and reflective. Magnus lets me get settled on the four-wheeler before he starts it up. I look over my shoulder at Connor. He's watching me, but as soon as I catch his eye, he turns to examine the gear on the back of the other vehicle.

For a while, the sound of the motor drowns out any need for conversation. Magnus takes us well away from the cabins. The guys trail behind for a stretch before they break off. Not long after that, Magnus stops and cuts the engine.

"You said you've used rifles in the past, is that right?" Magnus asks.

"Only a handful of times," I confess.

He grunts. "A bow's trickier. Which is why some folks don't bother with them. This time of year we get poachers up here. Mr. Vance does the rounds, tries to scare them off, but I'm pretty sure there have been a few lurking around." I give him an alarmed look and he chuckles. "Don't worry. They might be skirting the law, but they're still only hunting deer. Now, I'm not too worried about bagging anything today. Plenty of opportunity for you to practice," he tells me. He looks around at the clearing we've come to. "Good enough spot. We can waste a few arrows teaching you how to shoot straight."

With dawn only beginning to nudge the horizon, I sink about twenty arrows into trees, bushes, and snowdrifts, few of them the ones I was aiming at. Each draw makes the burn on my hand twinge, but I refuse to complain. Magnus criticizes my stance, the angle of my arms, the direction of my gaze. He stands five feet away at all times, never draws close, never touches me, but the weight of his scrutiny is claustrophobic.

I find I most enjoy the moment when I've pulled the arrow back. The smooth glide of the string through the pulleys hardly registers as effort, but in that ease the entire violence of the release is concealed.

At last Magnus declares me good enough for the time being—or else is simply out of patience. He directs us along a snow-laden track. I don't imagine I'll be shooting at anything living in any case.

Magnus is a man of few words. He moves carefully, quietly. I go where he directs me.

What must be an hour since we left, he looks up from where he's crouched down, deer tracks scattered out in front of him. They're not fresh, last night's dusting cupped in each depression, yet he's lingered here. "Connor told me a bit about what happened to you," he says.

I shift uncomfortably. "It's not really something I like to talk about."

"I imagine not." He flicks his thumb across his chin. "Do you regret it?"

My lips part, but no answer comes. It should be an easy question, shouldn't it? "I wish it hadn't happened."

"We can't regret the things we couldn't control," he says. "Do you regret your part in it? Your choices?"

I think of that girl in Peter Frey's room. She should have kept her head down. She should have been obedient, patient. She should have stayed quiet in her cage.

"No," I say. "It got me out of there."

"And the man you hurt?" He doesn't call him my father. I'm grateful for that.

"I'm glad he didn't die," I say. It's not the same thing as regret.

He grunts. "Sometimes terrible things happen, and they require terrible choices. In the end I suppose the difference between regretting those choices and finding peace with them is a matter of the outcome," Magnus says. "You did what you had to. I understand that. The failure wasn't yours. You should've been taken care of." He stands. He checks over his gear, but it has the air of something to do while he thinks. "Why are you really marrying Connor?"

I blink. It's not the question I was expecting. "I love him," I say. It sounds stupid now, after everything I've learned.

It's no less true.

He gives me a skeptical look. "Smart girls like you don't get married this fast without a reason."

I search his face for a hint of what it is he wants from me. He offers none. "When I'm with Connor, I feel like I belong to someone," I say quietly. "I've never felt that before. But it's not just that. It's—I need that. The idea of losing it is terrible."

The idea that it was a lie all along is terrifying.

"You're giving him a hell of a lot of power," he says. My mouth shuts so quickly my teeth click. "Nobody can be your savior. Sets you up for disaster and puts them in an impossible position. What happens if he turns out to just be human?"

"That's not what I mean," I say.

"Rose was like that," he says. "Besotted, that's the word. The whole world revolved around Liam, as far as she was concerned. He was like air and water and food to her. Then . . ." He paused.

I can tell from the way his words feel caged, carefully contained, that there is a great deal he is leaving unsaid. "You said Liam was soft. Nick said he was . . . charming." It isn't exactly what Nick had said, had implied, but it's close enough.

"He wanted to be everyone's hero." Magnus sets off again. His voice is still quiet, and I have to stay close not to lose the syllables. "He lived for the way people looked at him. He lived to make other people smile."

"That's lovely," I say.

A sound of disagreement. "He would shine, but only if there was someone there to notice it. He wasn't a bad man. But he was desperate for it. He made some bad decisions because he needed that adoration. Needed to be that hero."

"You think Connor's like that?"

"I think you are," he says.

I laugh a little. "I'm no one's hero."

"Maybe not. But you want to be the one who makes Connor smile. You want to be looked at, not seen. That's what it is, not belonging. That's what you're feeling."

"You have no idea what I'm feeling. You don't know anything about my relationship," I say. "You don't know me."

"I know exactly who you are," Magnus says. He looks back at me. I count to three in my head before he even blinks, longer before I breathe. I expect him to say it now—to confront me with the truth. *Do you really know? Then tell me,* I think, willing him to say it. *Tell me who the hell I am, because I don't know.*

"When they realize you aren't perfect, it doesn't end well," Magnus says. "You're young. You're pretty. You're a smart girl. This isn't your only chance. Connor isn't the only man who would worship you."

"Why are you all so determined to drive me away?" My voice is so soft it barely bruises the air.

"I like you, girl," Magnus says. "And that's why I'm bothering to tell you. It isn't worth it. You should leave before you get hurt."

"That's like telling me to cut my arm off to avoid getting hurt," I say, strangely calm.

He watches me for the space of a breath, two. Then, seeming to come to some kind of decision, he gives an almost-imperceptible nod. "There's a buck close by," he says. "I'm going to go around. You head that way." A gloved finger points. "There's a flat-topped boulder that way. Wait there. I'll come collect you."

He doesn't wait for me to confirm. He strides off. So this is why he asked me out here. Not to get the measure of me—he already had that. To tell me to leave.

I follow his directions. It isn't far, but the trek seems slowed by the flurry of thoughts in my mind. Everything he said about knowing me—does he? Has he guessed who I am, or did he know all along?

Why did you bring me here, Connor?

Up ahead, I spot the gray hump of the rock that Magnus told me about. It sits in a small clearing, but the clearing isn't empty. A buck grazes there, indifferent to my approach. It raises its head without particular purpose, nose testing the air. Its ears flick, twitch, like it's heard something—me, probably.

My bow hangs by my side. I make no effort to lift it, all urge to prove myself evaporating at the sight of its breath fogging the air, its dark eyes glistening with animal intelligence. I creep toward it, pressing myself close to the trunk of a tree and staying low, out of sight.

The buck moves forward a single step. You might mistake it for relaxed, the way it's standing. You might think that it feels safe. But a creature like that knows that it is never safe. That there is always something waiting for it to slow, to take a wrong step. Something like me.

Suddenly the buck's head jerks, ears swiveling toward some sound I didn't catch. It looks toward the trees ahead of it, frozen in sudden alarm, and my gaze follows. For an instant, I think I see something—the barest hint of movement. A gray glint of metal. And then the deer bursts forward in violent motion, bounding for the other side of the clearing.

The brown flank passes me. In that instant I see what is directly on the other side of the clearing. A figure in an orange vest stands among the trees.

Connor, with an arrow drawn back, aiming directly for where the deer just was. Where I still am, directly beyond it.

Connor, releasing the arrow.

30

There's blood on the snow. *Clean as a bullet,* Magnus said, and he wasn't wrong. It's a straight slash through the fabric of my coat, the shirt beneath it, the skin now slit apart and gaping.

I reach up and touch my throat. It's wet. No, my fingers are wet, but the skin of my throat is whole.

I see again the brown flank of the deer. The orange vest. Connor, seeing me. The arrow releasing, so fast my eye barely registered it before the tug at my arm. No. No, he released the arrow before he saw me. Didn't he? It was an accident.

Wasn't it?

Connor is shouting and charging toward me, and I'm still standing here waiting to feel the pain.

"Theo! Theo, are you all right?"

The deer. Connor, loosing the arrow. Connor, eyes widening as he sees me.

He catches my hand.

"Theo?" he says. "Talk to me."

The deer. Connor, eyes widening as he sees me.

Connor, loosing the arrow.

"She's in shock," someone says. "Put pressure on that. Sit her down." Nick.

Connor wraps a hand around my upper arm, and suddenly the pain is there, lancing hot as a brand, and with it comes searing panic. I shove away from Connor, stumbling back. *He saw me, he let go, he let go, he saw me—*

"Theo—I'm sorry, I didn't mean to—" Connor is stammering. I feel woozy. I start to sway.

"For fuck's sake," Nick says. He steps past Connor and catches me under my good arm. "Sit down before you pass out."

His voice is cold and firm—almost angry. I let my legs fold and practically fall to the ground. The impact jars my arm. I let out a hiss of pain, which Nick ignores, kneeling down to peel apart the shredded edges of my sleeve to look at the wound.

"Nasty, but it didn't get muscle," he says. "You need stitches." Up close, I can see every detail of his face. The scruff of his beard. The tiny scar under his left eye. "Come on. Let's get you to the UTV."

Connor moves toward me. To help, probably, but I shy away. Connor flinches. Hurt. *He's not allowed to be the one who's hurt,* I think, and I cling to Nick's offered arm instead. He hauls me upright. I'm still woozy. Blood loss or shock, I can't tell, but my whole body is shivering.

"Are you going to take her to the hospital?" Connor asks.

"The nearest hospital is over an hour away, and then you're sitting around for god knows how long," Nick says.

"Datura," I say through chattering teeth. *Get me out of here.*

"No sense in going down the mountain and trying to scare up a doctor when you've got one right here. I'll get her stitched up. We've got the supplies," he says, hustling me along.

They won't let you leave, I think, and fear flushes through me.

"Everything okay here?" a voice says. Nick pulls up short.

Mr. Vance stands between the trees, a dark gray cap jammed over his unruly hair. For once, he doesn't have Duchess with him. Nor does he have a bow—he's carrying a rifle, the strap over his shoulder. He grips the strap with one hand. They have trouble with poachers, I remember. Mr. Vance tries to scare them off.

"Theo decided to impersonate a deer," Nick says. I can't say I particularly appreciate the attempt at humor. "We're taking her up to the lodge."

Mr. Vance rubs his chin. "Well. Lucky it wasn't worse, I suppose."

"We'd better get moving," Nick says pointedly.

"Does Mr. Dalton know?" Mr. Vance asks, obviously speaking about Magnus. There's something odd in his expression. What is he doing out here?

"Why don't you go find him?" Nick suggests tightly.

"I could take the girl up the mountain for you," Mr. Vance says.

"She needs medical care. Unless you're a doctor, you're not much use," Nick snaps, and then he moves, ushering me along. He keeps a hand on my elbow—on the uninjured side—and though I don't actually need help walking, I'm not sure I would remember to keep moving forward without it.

We leave Mr. Vance behind. He stands there, watching, not moving. Connor follows us, but he's lagging, his face blanched with shock.

Images play through my head on repeat. I keep picturing the hole in the side of the deer we dressed, imagining it transposed on my rib cage. Remembering that flash of gray metal among the trees and the image of myself reflected for an instant in the dark of the deer's wild eye.

It was an accident, I tell myself. But part of me refuses to believe it—the part that knows what the deer knows. That I am prey. And prey is never safe.

31

There isn't room for Connor on the UTV. I ride back with Nick. At the lodge, he removes the makeshift bandage, along with my coat, then slices my sleeve up to the shoulder and flushes out the wound—a process that is almost as painful as getting shot in the first place, though I try not to show it.

Instead of leaving me in the kitchen with Olena lurking curiously by the door, he takes me to Magnus's office before going to fetch more supplies. For privacy, ostensibly. Or maybe it's more about containing me.

Magnus's office is how I would have imagined it. Deep wood tones and navy, a gold fountain pen on the desk, a trio of mounted antler trophies on the wall. Bookcases that would kill an elephant in an earthquake. I spot *Dubliners* among them but can't manage to be amused.

I sit in a leather armchair that has the softness of old age and high quality, my shoes off and my knees tucked up, feeling like a small girl—lost and vulnerable.

The clock on the wall of the study ticks steadily, a hollow sound. Without it, I wouldn't be sure that time is passing at all. Nick left me here, the chair protected by several towels. It wouldn't do for my wounds to stain the good furniture. The study is private. A room away from the plate glass windows and flowing light.

I keep trying to picture Connor's face, the instant the arrow came toward me. But every time I shut my eyes, I see not Connor but Liam.

The door opens. I shrink against the chair, still subject to the startled animal living inside of me, but it's only Nick. He's come in with a large leather satchel, which he unzips to reveal a first aid kit—though calling it that seems reductive, given how extensive it is.

"Let's get a look at that," he says. He pulls the office chair over to me and unwraps my arm. I hiss with pain and force myself to look. The edges of the wound are clean. The skin is split, gaping, and I don't particularly want to think about what I can see underneath. "You're lucky," he says, voice gruff with barely restrained anger. "And Connor's an idiot."

"I wasn't where I was supposed to be," I say. I backtracked. He didn't expect me there; it couldn't have been some kind of plan to stage an accident. *Except that Magnus told me where to go.*

Nick leans back. "I'm going to give you a local anesthetic to numb it up before I suture it."

"I forgot to ask what kind of doctor you are," I say idly.

"Endocrinologist," he says. "But don't worry, I know how to stitch up a cut." He takes a syringe from the tray beside him, filling it from a tiny bottle. I look away when he brings it to my arm, biting the inside of my cheek at the pinch. The pain recedes, fading into cold and absence.

Images play through my mind in an endless loop. My blood, speckling the snow. The antlers of the deer. Connor's face, replaced by his father's.

Nick works in silence. He leans close as he pushes the needle through my skin. I feel minuscule next to him, swamped in this armchair. I watch the clock on the wall. It's not even lunchtime.

"Nick, can I ask you something?" I say when he's almost done. He doesn't pause in his work but ticks his chin in a nod. "Was Liam ever violent?"

He pulls the needle free of my arm slowly. The suture draws shut, bringing the edges of my skin together. With his other hand he presses a gauze pad to the edge of the wound, dabbing up the blood that still oozes from it.

"You worried about Connor?" he asks at last.

"No," I say. I look away. "I don't know."

"This was an accident," Nick says.

"I know." But everything is too strange. That flash of metal in the woods. Mr. Vance, appearing out of nowhere. Magnus directing me to a clearing alone. Stories of poachers in the woods: a perfectly plausible explanation, if the worst were to happen.

I cannot help but feel hunted.

We're silent again. The needle glides through my flesh once, twice. "Liam had a temper. But he never hit the kids, if that's what you're asking." He says it carefully.

"Did he hurt someone else?"

He's on the last stitch. He finishes it. Clips the thread. "What is it you're asking?"

I wait until he looks at me. "Mallory Cahill," I say. "You knew her. Didn't you."

He pauses. His eyes flick to me—and then down, and there he stops. I'm not wearing a turtleneck today, but a scoop-neck, and his gaze has frozen on the two dark birthmarks just above my collarbone. He looks at me again, and his face is pale.

I go still, instinct telling me not to make a sound, not to twitch. I don't even breathe.

He jerks. Looks away. He sets his tools down on the tray, cleans blood from his fingers with the gauze. "You'll need to keep that clean and dry, but it can stay uncovered. The stitches should dissolve on their own in a couple of weeks, and of course I'll check it for you. You'll have a scar."

He stands, gathering his things. When the door closes behind him, tension floods out of me. Relief doesn't come in its place, only a scraping emptiness as the pain in my arm begins to leach back, and suddenly I'm biting back tears.

I don't want to cry. Crying is useless. The feeling in my chest, in my gut, in my throat is useless. I don't have time for sorrow or self-pity; I never have.

So I won't feel them. I knuckle the tears from my eyes, but I can't seem to get a proper breath.

These people knew me. They know that something happened here. And the Daltons don't do scandal. They don't let the misdeeds of their sons become known. What happened here, what Liam did, was covered up. I'm a threat to that.

And Nick recognized me. I know he did.

I blink the tears from my eyes, trying to steady my breathing. I need to think.

My gaze catches on a scrap of green, slotted between the heavy bookshelf and the side table opposite me. A curl of paper, fallen into the gap and forgotten. I stare at it a moment, not quite sure why it's caught my eye, and then I realize with a jolt that I've seen it before.

It's wrapping paper. The same wrapping paper from the gift that was left so lovingly on my windowsill just days before.

My fingers dig into the chair's arms, fingernails scraping against leather. That scrap of paper might have blown in from anywhere. But it's here, in Magnus's study.

So Trevor wrapped that little present in here—but no. Why would he cart it all the way here to the lodge, the place he was most likely to be spotted? Trevor's angry. Lashing out without particular direction or intent. Those messages, though, that warning? They had purpose, and it wasn't to wound. It was to drive me away.

Louise gave me that check so I would go. Magnus tried to talk me into it, directly. And when I didn't . . .

I check the door quickly—closed, and no sound of anyone approaching. I'm sure they're off discussing what happened. Planning how to keep it all under control. Keep the story straight.

I rise. I don't know how much time I have or what I'm looking for, but I know how to dissect a room, to slit open its secret places. I go to the side table first. It has a set of drawers, but these don't offer much—a heavy set of scissors, a blank legal pad, a set of inks. I snatch the scrap of paper from the floor and shove it into my pocket, and then I go to the desk.

The top of the desk is spartan: a closed laptop, which I don't bother with—it will certainly be password protected—and a black-and-gold Montblanc pen on a wooden stand. The top drawer is locked, as I expected, but the second slides open. Inside is a well-thumbed appointment book, which at a glance is from four years ago, and a random assortment of office supplies.

I'm about to close it when I stop. There's something else, chucked into the back of the drawer like an afterthought. It's a phone—a cheap flip phone.

Probably ancient. Left here and forgotten. I pick it up and flip it open.

The screen lights up, asking for a passcode.

I catch my breath. Not an ancient phone—a disposable one.

The murmur of voices jerks my attention back toward the door. I quickly slide the drawer shut with my foot, slipping the phone into my pocket, and scurry back to the chair. I lean back just as footsteps approach, and a moment later the door opens.

It's Connor, and he's a mess. His hair is disheveled, his clothes damp, and he hasn't taken off his boots, a fact that his grandmother, standing behind him, looks horrified about.

"You're all right," Connor says with evident relief.

"She's fine," Louise says. She could at least try to sound a little happier about it. "As I told you. What, did you think we were going to have her put down like a lame horse?"

Connor turns to her. "Can we have a moment?" he asks.

She purses her lips. And then she turns, walking with a clipped gait back down the hall. Connor shuts the door, closing the two of us inside alone. The lump of the phone digs into my thigh. I watch him, mouth dry.

"I'm so sorry," Connor says. His head is bowed, his hand still on the knob. "I didn't see you." He turns then, and I see the glistening moisture in his eyes. My first thought is to wonder if those tears are real or if it's the cold.

He walks to me slowly and then bends, kneeling to put his hands on my knees. My whole body thrums with fear. It tells me to run. It tells me that the hunter is here, and I am prey. I have always been prey.

I don't want to feel this way. Like a knife has slit its way up to the notch of my rib cage, and even that is cracking open. It would be easy if I didn't love him. I wish that what I knew would blot out how I feel, but it hasn't. It can't.

"Please," Connor whispers, his voice a raw ache. "I don't know what's going on with us. With anything. But I need you, Theo."

I cover one of his hands with my uninjured one. I lean forward. He puts a hand around the back of my neck and presses his brow against mine, shutting his eyes.

There's only him. Only Connor.

Connor, who lied to me. Who sought me out and brought me here to dangle in front of his family. Who had to have known. Who saw me—maybe—standing there in the woods. Every fearful part of me is screaming that he is dangerous. Telling me that I need to get away from him, that it's a matter of survival.

But I don't know how to lose him and still survive.

"We need to leave," I say. It's a plea. It's a test.

He sits back. "All right," he says. The ache in my ribs eases. "You're right. We need to get out of here, if there's any chance . . ." He doesn't finish the thought. *If there's any chance of us making it through this. If there's any chance to keep us from falling apart.*

"Can we leave today?"

He runs a hand through his hair. "Tomorrow," he says. "First thing in the morning. Give me today to try to smooth things over. Make it about . . ." He gestures at my arm.

Make it seem like I fled because I was hurt and wanted to go recuperate, not that they'd scared me off. Not that anyone would be fooled.

They won't let you leave. The thought squirms through my mind. I silence it.

"Come on. Let's get back to the cabin," Connor says, putting out a hand, and I fit mine to it. He helps me to my feet and walks me toward the door.

I tell myself that it was an accident. That in the morning he will take me home, as promised, and I'll be safe. I'll be gone from here and never have to return.

The animal inside me bares its teeth.

She never got away from here, either, it whispers, and Connor slides his arm around my waist.

32

Connor tells me I don't have to go to dinner. Everyone will understand. But I have to. I have to be able to look into their faces. I dress in the clothes Connor bought me—wool trousers, a cowl-neck sweater in sage green, the same red coat, hastily washed, because I don't have another.

Olena takes my jacket. Irina walks us to the dining room. The doors open and faces turn toward us. Rose rises from her seat. "Theo, shouldn't you be resting?" she asks. Is that only concern in her voice, or is there displeasure, too?

"I'd rather have some company," I say. Connor pulls my seat out for me; I lower myself into it. My left arm is bulky with the bandage underneath, and it twinges every time I move.

Louise and Magnus exchange a glance. It's not the only one being traded down the table. Trevor sits back with a smile, a glass of sparkling water in hand.

"Glad to see Connor's attempt to get out of the wedding wasn't a success," he says.

"Trevor," Alexis chides.

"What? I'm just glad I'm not the only Dalton who almost killed someone," Trevor tosses off.

"Shut the fuck up, Trevor," Alexis snaps.

"Lex," Paloma says, looking pointedly at Sebastian. "Please."

"That's enough of that kind of talk," Magnus cuts in. He shakes out his napkin. "We're glad you could join us, Theo."

Connor's hand rests on my back, between my shoulder blades. "Well, it's going to be our last dinner here, so we wanted to make sure to at least stop by," he says.

Louise's eyebrows raise. Alexis gives a twitch of surprise.

"Your last dinner?" Rose says, with the air of someone trying not to fret. "You're leaving?"

"I think if I stick around any longer, I might lose an arm next," I say, trying for humor. Instead it sounds like prophecy.

"You'll miss Christmas," Alexis says. "We've literally never missed a Christmas together."

I wish I could shrug Connor's hand from my back without being obvious. I'd thought we weren't going to make a big announcement. I wanted to leave quietly. Explain things when it was already too late to argue.

"Are you seriously surprised she wants to run?" Trevor asks.

"It's perfectly reasonable, after what happened," Paloma says.

"Perfectly," Magnus agrees, voice neutral. He raises his glass in my direction. "I'm sorry that the mountain treated you poorly. I hope when you've recovered, you'll give it another chance."

The wrapping paper was in Magnus's room. This is what Magnus wanted. Me, leaving. But not with Connor.

Nick says nothing, but stares at me. A needle of cold goes through me, and I hear the rush of my own blood in my ears. Nick's gaze doesn't relent. He holds his glass, a single drop of red wine balanced at the rim, but doesn't drink.

He knows me. He didn't before, I think. But now he's seen.

"Theo?" Connor is saying, and I startle. Irina has already arrived with the first course; I've been drifting.

"Yes, thank you," I say, not sure what was being asked, but it appears to be the right answer as Irina adds a generous helping of Parmesan to the top of my salad. Thick, dark slices of beet are arranged on top. They're cold against my teeth and taste faintly of rich soil. When I dab my lips on the white napkin it comes away with pink stains. Sebastian has made a mess of his hands with them, setting Paloma tutting.

No one talks. They all pretend to focus on their food.

"Theo," Connor says softly. "Are you okay?"

I flinch. Now everyone is looking at me again. This was a mistake. I should have hidden away in the cabin like Connor told me to.

"You know, I'm actually feeling a bit tired," I say. "I think I'm going to turn in for the night. I'm sorry to bail."

"It's quite all right," Rose assures me, and Alexis and Paloma murmur agreement.

"I'll come with you," Connor says. I almost let him. But then I smile, shake my head.

"No, you stay. Enjoy your time with your family," I say.

He makes another protest, but then he lets me go. As soon as the doors are closed behind me, I start to shake.

I don't want to wait until morning. I want to get out of here *now*.

But I have another twelve hours in this place, and so I need to think. Be strategic. They're all in there, which means they aren't out here. They aren't watching me. This might be my last—my only—chance to look around unobserved.

Run, my mother's voice tells me, and I am trying to listen to her warnings, but I only just learned her name, and there is so much more than that I need.

I head out, grabbing my coat as I go.

The cloud cover blankets the sky and chokes out the light of stars, but there are the beaming lights of the lodge to glance off the snow and illuminate my way.

Wildflower is tucked out of sight of the lodge. I don't have to worry about anyone glancing out those big picture windows and seeing me.

If it's locked, I'm skunked. My curious habits never extended to breaking and entering; a simple dead bolt is more than enough to put an end to my snooping career. But Trevor is in and out of here all the time, and he has a careless nature. Impulsive.

The door is unlocked. I slip inside, intruder and thief, and mindful of how easily light shines between the trees, I leave them off and use my flashlight instead. I haven't been inside this cabin before. It's homier than the others. Framed pictures of flowers and birds on the walls; a rug with a pattern of roses; quilts instead of expensive white wool blankets folded on the back of the couch. Someone has gone to deliberate effort to preserve the past here.

I start with Trevor's room. Like his sister, he hasn't unpacked. Unlike her, he's flung his clothes around the room with abandon. I move swiftly, atrophied skills coming back to me. I open drawers. Slide my fingers along the tops and bottoms to check for things hidden. Peer inside shoes. Dip my hands into the pockets of coats and pants. I find condoms. An empty baggie with a few white grains sticking to it—predictable. A bottle of vodka, surprisingly full. Trevor might not be as clean and sober as he insists, but he isn't wasted, either.

The things he's done, he's done clear-eyed, I think. Is that worse?

His phone is on top of the dresser. It unlocks with his mother's birthday—how sweet. His texts are full of him wheedling racy pictures from an impressive array of young women. They arch their backs and pile their hair on top of their heads and pout their lips. At least he's not a dick-pic guy; his selfies are of the shirtless variety, nothing below the belt.

I'm about to set the phone aside as uninteresting when I see a message a few months old.

I'm so sorry, it reads. *I know I'm not supposed to be talking to you. But for what it's worth, if it's worth anything, I wish it had been me. If you want to take the money, do it, but if you don't, I'll*

It ends there. It's a draft. Never sent. The number is saved under *Kayla.*

The girl he hurt. So Trevor felt contrite. Or he was playing an angle. And apparently decided against pursuing it, either way.

I doubt Trevor will notice anything out of place in this mess, but still I rearrange it all to my mental snapshot before I cut through the living room to the other bedroom. Here I hesitate. Rose hasn't been warm to me, but Connor loves her. I wanted to love her, too.

Entering her room is a violation; there is no way around it. I push inward against good sense and morals and I invade her sanctum. Everything I touch, I imagine stained—my fingerprints on the pill case that rests on the dresser, the oils of my hands on the temples of the reading glasses at the bedside.

There is nothing to find. No damning photographs; no convenient diary detailing a campaign against me or laying out what happened years ago. There are only the things you bring on a vacation like this. The only photograph is the one on the wall: Connor, Trevor, and Alexis in the middle, young and smiling, the too-bright light of summer making them squint. On one side of them stands Rose—only a few gray hairs, the faintest wrinkles at the corners of her eyes. On the other side, Nick has his arm around Alexis's shoulder. He's beaming; so is she.

No photos of Liam. There was one in the main room of the cabin, but here in her private space she is allowed to cut him away from herself. She's allowed to be angry.

Angry people do unpredictable things. We all have violence inside of us. It needs only the right fuel.

I retreat. There's nothing to find here.

I could go to Nick's cabin next, but I think of the photographs in Alexis's bag. They're proof that something happened to my mother. I can't leave them behind.

The path to Red Fox, recently cleared, has begun to fill up again. Powder spills from the shoulders of my coat as I walk. I catch a snowflake on my tongue, and a memory comes to me—arms outflung, spinning, the sensation of my momentum pulling at my in all directions like I might fly apart as I tipped my face up to the falling snow.

I reach the cabin. I never gave Olena's key back to Alexis; it's still in my pocket. Half of me expects the key not to work this time, but of course it does, and then I am standing in the interior where embers still smolder in the woodstove and Sebastian's stuffed animals are strewn around the room like a great zoo breakout.

I head straight into the bedroom, to Alexis's suitcase. For an instant I think the photographs are gone and panic closes my throat, but then

I claw aside her clothes and find the envelope jammed in the bottom, a halfhearted attempt to hide it better.

There she is—Mallory. My mother. Not the girl from Trevor's accident after all, and I can't believe I ever thought she might be. There are darker marks inside the shape of the bruise on the small of her back: knuckles. That bruise on her shoulder—not a seat belt, but a palm, a stretched-out thumb, digging in. Her face untouched, because it wouldn't do to leave marks where they could be seen.

Liam Dalton had a temper. He never hurt his own flesh and blood, no, and never touched the respectable girl he married, the one who could stand up to him and his family, but Mallory Cahill, the girl from nowhere at all, she was fair game.

She looks frightened. And she looks resigned. Why did you take these photos, Mallory? Did you think they might save you? Did you plan to run?

Did you try?

I can see her. Honey-brown hair. Hand clapped against the side of her neck, trying in vain to stop the blood. She reaches out as if to grab me but pushes me away again.

Hide.

My memories swirl around each other in impossible combinations, tainted and warped by the images from my dreams. I can't be sure of them. I try to reorient myself, stick to what I know.

Alexis has photos of my mother. Her father was having an affair with my mother. My mother was beaten.

Alexis was fifteen years old when her father died. Just a kid, really. Could she have known about Mallory? About what her father was doing? Maybe not.

The sound of a key scraping in a lock startles me. I jump to my feet, the photographs clutched in my hands. There's nowhere to run. Nowhere to hide, unless I want to try to shove my way under the bed and get found in an even more compromising position than I already am.

Indecision paralyzes me, and so I'm standing there, clearly visible in the doorway, when Paloma enters.

She freezes, keys in hand, her face flushed. "What the fuck are you doing?" she demands.

"I—I can explain," I say, which is what you say when you have no idea how to explain yourself.

She says something rapidly under her breath and strides forward. "You had better start, then," she says. She's holding the key in her fist like a weapon. Her eyes are red-rimmed; she's been crying. "What are those?" she demands.

I hold them out, opting for honesty—it's not like I have a better idea. "I found them earlier, when I was looking for Sebastian's book," I say.

She takes them from me slowly, stares at them. "What the fuck are these?" she says. She swears with the condensed intensity of someone who does not get many chances to do it.

"Do you know who she is?" I ask.

"No," she says, voice clipped. "What are you doing, digging around for dirt on the family?"

"No. Not exactly," I say. "I'm just trying to figure some things out."

She snorts. She walks over to the kitchen, tossing the photographs onto the table, and opens a cabinet. She takes down a glass and a bottle of whiskey, pouring herself a sloppy portion.

I hesitate. "I talked to Alexis, about the ornament."

"She mentioned."

"You already knew, she said."

"Trevor's a pretty shitty blackmailer. Or he would be, if the point was to get anything out of it, not just piss us all off." She puts a hand to her forehead. "I'm so tired of pretending like all this is normal. Like having this many fucking secrets is anything but diseased." She looks at me over the rim of her drink. "Do you know who that is, in the pictures?"

"Her name was Mallory Cahill," I tell her. "She was . . . involved. With Liam Dalton."

Her eyes widen. "That's her?" she says.

"You know about her?"

"Everyone knows," she says. "I mean, everyone in the family." She walks back over, picks them up. "God. He did this to her?"

"I don't know. Do you have any idea what Alexis would be doing with these?"

Paloma blows out a breath. "No. But . . . she's been helping her mom clear some things out of the old house. Maybe she found them there?" She sets them down. "Did Connor tell you about her?"

"No. Trevor," I say.

"Shit-stirrer," she notes. She crosses her arms. "I cannot tell you how much I hate that man."

"Trevor?"

"Liam," she says. My eyebrows go up. "It's not my best quality. I know I shouldn't, given the way—but it destroyed her, you know? She was my best friend. I saw what it did to her. She almost didn't survive it herself."

"He killed himself, didn't he?" I say, and now she does look shocked.

"Alexis said that?"

"Not in so many words."

"Fuck." She takes a drink, then tips it toward me. "Want some?"

I shouldn't. But I nod. She marches back over, discovers there are no more clean glasses, and pours a measure into a mug decorated with mistletoe. "Happy holidays. Anyway. Yes. But I'm surprised Alexis told you. I don't think she's told anyone but me."

"How does she know?" I ask.

She leans back against the counter. "He talked to her. Right before it happened. So when she found out he was dead, she guessed. But they told her not to say anything. Secrets and the Daltons, you know how it is."

"Who told her? Rose?"

She shakes her head. "The old man, probably. He was the one who came up after Mr. Vance found the body. All I know for sure is that Alexis was sworn to secrecy. Rose and Connor have no idea. Trevor either, obviously. It's messed up. They deserve to know. But it's not my place." She gives me a look that makes it very clear that she doesn't think it's my place, either.

Alexis was fifteen years old. Fifteen and her father killed himself and she couldn't tell a soul. It's monstrous.

"She blames herself, you know," Paloma says. "She thinks she should have known, figured out what to say. And instead of talking about it and fucking *dealing* with it, she did what she was told and she's kept it secret all this time, no matter how much it hurts her. That's what you're getting into, Theo. And I swear, most of the time I think it's worth it, but sometimes . . ." She swigs the rest of her drink. Slams it down. "Sometimes I wish I could go back and tell myself to fucking run."

33

I walk as quickly as I can in the direction of the cars, scuttling around the south end of the lake to get to the road. Soon enough I have the gate in view, and then I'm over it, not breaking stride until I reach the same spot where that first bit of signal appeared like a fern frond poking up out of late spring snow.

When I left White Pine, I made sure to slip the phone I found in Magnus's office into my pocket. I'm still wearing the same red coat, despite the slit in the arm, despite the blood. I don't have a second one.

I take the phone out. I can't access its contents, but maybe I don't need to. I take out my own phone. Open the messages.

Stay away from Connor Dalton.

Maybe I should have listened.

I press the button to call the sender. I wait and wait—and then the flip phone lights up. Incoming call.

I end it quickly. Magnus *is* the one sending the messages. I wrote him off as an old-school guy, but of course he's tech-savvy. He runs multiple companies, deals with big international deals, and he's not a figurehead or a hands-off kind of manager. And the gift? A dramatic gesture, to be sure. And also a way to drive home a sense that someone here wanted me gone.

I still have my phone in my hand. Seizing onto the thin thread of signal, it offers up my notifications faithfully. Three missed calls from Harper.

Two from that unknown number. Joseph.

I'm about to swipe the notifications away, but at that moment, the screen lights up, and it begins to buzz. Joseph is calling again.

I freeze in indecision as it rings once, twice. I never wanted to talk to him again. The thought of hearing his voice makes me shake. But Joseph might have answers. He might remember things that I didn't know to ask about, before now.

I accept the call.

"Hello?" I say. My voice shakes, despite my best efforts. I decide to blame the cold.

"Dora, I didn't think you'd answer," Joseph says, and he sounds exactly the same as he did eight years ago.

"My name is Theo."

"Theo, then," he says. I was wrong. He sounds older. "Theo—it's so grown-up."

"Don't," I say. I shut my eyes. I'm not grown up. I'm shrinking inside myself with every word he says. Becoming the girl who wept and begged and pleaded with him to help her. "You said we need to talk. So talk."

"Dora—Theo—I'm sorry for what happened. You have no idea how often I've wished I could go back to that moment," Joseph says.

I give a choked laugh. "Yeah, it didn't turn out too well for you."

"That's not what I mean. I pretty much got what I deserved," he says. He sounds genuine. I think of the last time I saw him, soaked in blood, the knife on the ground between us. The way he looked at me, like I was a wild animal, like someone ought to put me down. Maybe he wasn't wrong.

"I don't want to talk about what happened," I say in a deadened voice. "But someone has been talking. About the things we all agreed we wouldn't." It feels like swallowing down something rancid, using that word: *we*. Like I'm making myself one of them, the way I used to be—the way I never was.

"I know," Joseph says. "I'm sorry, Dora."

"It's Theo," I snap. "I always hated that name."

"Theo," he repeats, like he's reminding himself, training himself into it. He doesn't need to. We won't speak to each other again. "You know why they gave you that name?"

"Because I was a gift from God," I say bitterly.

"It's because it's the only thing you would say. 'Teddy.' It was the only word you spoke for the first solid month. So: Theodora." He says it like it's sweet. Like he has no idea there might be something terrible wrapped inside that story. "Things have changed, you know. For me. Beth and I—we split. Not long after you left. I'm living in Colorado now. I'm actually getting married, next year."

"Felicitations," I say flatly.

"Bradley's great. I think you'd like him," Joseph says. My stomach gives a flip.

"You . . ." I try to fit this piece of information into my recollections. Joseph and Beth. The way they never touched. The way she said so many times how she saved him. How his sister would purse her lips and shake her head whenever she mentioned her brother's religious turn. Those moments when Beth would spit out blame at him for her infertility, in her lowest moments, true acid and hatred in her voice.

"You don't need to say anything," Joseph continues. "It doesn't make up for what I did. What I didn't do. I was supposed to take care of you. But I was too afraid. Of a lot of things. God-fearing, that's what we're supposed to be, right? But I'll tell you. I've only ever felt God since I stopped being afraid."

"Then I'm happy for you," I say. I'm surprised to discover it's even true. I can't forgive him. But I can be glad that he found his way to being someone new.

"That's not really why I called." Joseph clears his throat. In that sound I can hear the fracturing of hope. He must have known this wouldn't be some joyous reunion, a mending of all our wounds, but some part of us always holds on to those fantasies. *This will be the day they finally love me. This will be the day I am finally good enough.*

"Someone contacted you, didn't they? About me. About what happened."

"Yes," Joseph says.

"And what did you tell them?"

"I wasn't going to tell them anything," Joseph says. "But I'm not the only one they called. I guess some folks figure it's been enough time. Chief Monroe retired; he's down in Boca Raton now. His threats don't carry so much weight anymore."

"I hadn't heard." There was a time I'd fantasized about Chief Monroe taking me in, adopting me. But his interest in me extended only as far as getting me the hell out of there. It saved my life. I couldn't have asked for more, not really.

But the heart hopes.

"This guy, he already knew most of it, only it was all the worst version."

"The version Beth would tell, you mean," I say. Or Peter.

A grunt. "That's the one. So I . . . I sent him those photos. So he'd see. So he'd know why you did it. I told him I didn't blame you. Because I don't. I deserve these scars. Every inch of them."

My breath is labored. The cold air makes my eyes water, but there are no tears, not now. "Do you know who it was?" I ask. My voice is so calm. I don't understand how it can be so calm. "The person asking, I mean."

"There was more than one," Joseph tells me. "First time it was a guy who wouldn't give me his name. Frankly, he seemed like a dumbass. Second time it was a private investigator. I looked him up—it seemed like a real slick firm. What kind of people are you tangling with, D—Theo?"

"It's not important," I say. "Thanks for the heads-up."

"The thing is . . ." He pauses. I can hear the sound of his weight shifting, a chair creaking. I wonder what the stars look like in Colorado right now, whether he's far enough outside the city to see them spread out overhead. Here, there's nothing but the dark blanket of clouds. "That second time around, they weren't just asking about what happened. They were asking about where we got you from. About if you'd told us anything, about before."

I watch the path of a single snowflake as it drifts down inches from my face. "And what did you tell them?"

"Nothing," Joseph says, voice gruff. "It's no one's business but yours."

"But there was something to tell."

The silence is a long one. I wait. "You didn't talk much, back then," he begins at last. "For the longest time, you'd say only that one word. *Teddy*. Bought you a million teddy bears, too, but you always just shoved them away, shook your head like they were wrong."

Because the right one was here all the while, with its soft brown fur and red ribbon. I shut my eyes.

"But then you started talking, little by little. Just at night, when I would read you stories. You'd snuggle up in the crook of my arm. It was the one time you were ever calm. And one night out of nowhere you told me a story. You said that you used to live in a castle on a mountain. I asked if that made you a princess, and you said no, the princess was dead. You said that a terrible ogre had come to the mountain. You told me . . ." He takes a deep breath. "You told me that you knew what it felt like to be dead. That it was very, very cold. But you weren't alone, because the princess was there with you. You woke up. She didn't. And then the fairies took you away to find a new family."

"Where did I come from, Joseph?" I ask. "You always said someone in the church . . ."

"That was a lie," Joseph tells me, and I wish I was surprised. "Or, not entirely. Someone in the church did approach us. They knew we'd been trying, and we were getting desperate. He said that there was a kid who needed a family, but it wasn't . . . official. He said we'd have to do it quietly. And there'd be some money. We didn't ask questions. We were just grateful to have you. But I always knew there was something wrong about it."

"Wrong about me, you mean."

"It was never anything wrong with you. You were traumatized. I know that now. Hell, I knew it then, but I thought that loving you would be enough."

"Maybe it would have been, if you were better at it," I say, and the bitterness oozes through my words.

"Theo, I—" Joseph begins.

I end the call. And then I block his number. Tears drag tracks down my cheeks. I don't want his apology. It won't do any good, not now.

A princess in a castle. An ogre. It makes as much sense as the rest.

I can almost see it. I can almost hear her voice. I sink down into the snow, wrapping my arms around my knees. I stare out down the silvery road as snow falls. It is eerily silent. I cannot even hear myself.

Mallory Cahill. No, *Mama.* I picture the woman in the photos, the bruises on her body, and for an instant she's there.

Mama. Her back bare. Her head turned to look over her shoulder. I can just see her through the crack in the door.

I'm not supposed to go in.

The numbing cold bites through my clothes. I should be shivering, but I'm not. My body is gone; all sound is gone, and there is only the eerie pale unlight of the snow and the night, and in this space I don't exist; *here* doesn't exist. The warmth and the light are all gone, and I follow it back, and there she is.

The girl watches her mother piling clothes in a suitcase. "Are we going on a trip?"

"For a little while."

The girl traces shapes in the condensation of the car window. Her mother adjusts the rearview mirror to look at her, smiles. The girl smiles, too, but she feels like crying. Outside the window, snow begins to fall.

The girl spins and laughs, topples into the snow. She pops back up again, eager for the approval of her audience. The boy rolls his eyes, but he's smiling. She's pleased. She wants to impress him. She thinks they'll always be friends.

She looks up into the face of the antlered man, and she screams, but she's frozen in place, and he grabs her by the arm—

The snow is still falling. It comes thick and fast and it covers her. She burrows beneath it like a blanket. She was so cold before, but now she's beginning to feel warm again. She thinks she would like to sleep now.

The sun has vanished. She can't feel her feet or her right hand, though she knows it's there because it's resting on top of the snow right in front of her nose.

Clouds cover the sky. Occlude the moon. But there's one star still shining in the night. Sometimes it's amber, and sometimes it glows a duller red. It moves from time to time. She thought at first it was a wishing star, but she has been wishing for one thing and it hasn't come.

Help.

She tries to say it, but her voice doesn't work. The star flares. It illuminates a face, the dark shine of eyes that watch her with patient disinterest.

She's not so cold anymore, she thinks. She feels very warm now. She shuts her eyes. Maybe help came after all, and her mother has bundled her up in a blanket in front of the fire, and soon she will tell her a story about the princesses in the forest and all the places that they will go next.

The memories shiver. In the dark they are almost physical things. I could reach out and touch them.

"You look so cold," my mother says. She crouches down in front of me, wraps a red scarf around my neck. Her smile is warm and unafraid. "What are you doing out here, Teddy?"

"Looking for you," I whisper. I blink my eyes. They feel gummy. My limbs are heavy. "Mama?"

I'm alone. I'm alone and my mother is dead, has been dead for years, and I am here and now, and she isn't. How long have I been out here? Too long, sitting here with the snow piling up around me.

I don't know how much of the memory is real. It's scraps, fragments. I'm drawing lines between them, around them. Making a story. And

I can't tell anymore what's my invention and what is truth. Maybe I never could.

I have to move. I don't want to. Here, where my body ceases to be real, my memories have room to blossom. The cold and the memory—they are linked. As if I left them behind in the cold, and I've returned for them.

Rowan, my mother's voice says, tight with fear. I want to stay with her. I want to remember.

I know what it feels like to be dead. It's cold, so cold.

The answers are there. In the cold. In the dark. If I stay, I'll find them. If I stay, I'll never leave.

I push to my feet shakily, almost fall. My feet have gone completely numb; so have my hands, my face. I crook my fingers. They're slow to bend.

You have to run. You have to hide. I was so good at hiding. But he found me, didn't he? The man with antlers. Liam Dalton. *The ogre.*

Movement begins to warm me. I shove my hands under my armpits to try to hoard my body heat. My footsteps are muted. The story pieces itself together in my mind.

Liam brought us here. I don't know what promises he lured her with—money, safety, love—but she followed. Then things turned sour, once she was isolated and alone. So we had to flee.

But he must have found out she was going to leave him. He returned. He was angry. He hurt her.

Killed her.

And then—?

Maybe he realized what he'd done, and the guilt overcame him. One way or another, he killed himself.

And where does that leave me?

I was a witness. A loose end. A threat to the story the Daltons would tell.

It's here. In the cold. All of it. The pieces of me that have been frozen in winter's ice all this time and are thawing now.

The red scarf—*blood, drying dark*—the bitter cold, the star glowing red—*amber, the end of a cigarette*—the antlered man with his face half-black—*there you are*—and we have to go, love, we have to go now.

Pieces. They don't connect up. It's a kind of madness, trying to lay them out in the proper order, find the lines between them.

I reach the top of the road. My heart is racing so quick I can barely feel the space between each beat. The windows of the lodge are lit up. The Christmas tree shines, red lights and green and white. A figure stands near the window. From this far, I can't tell who it is.

I hold still, afraid that even at this distance, they might spot me. I don't know what time it is. I'm afraid to get my phone out to check, in case the light is visible. I know I've been gone a long while.

A sound splits the silence of the night—muffled, distant. It sounds like a bird, or maybe a rabbit caught in a predator's teeth. The person at the window seems to turn toward it as well, but the curtain of quiet falls again quickly. The figure turns away and begins to walk out of the room, and I recognize the gait—Louise Dalton.

I strain my ears for the sound to come again, but it doesn't. My teeth are chattering. I see the light of White Pine up ahead. It doesn't feel safe to go inside. I can't stay out here.

I walk to the door. My hand fumbles with the knob, and then the door opens and Connor is standing there, staring at me. His eyes travel up and down my body, and he lets out a breath between his teeth.

He reaches out, pulling me inside, wordless. My hands are too numb to strip off my snow-packed gloves, get off my boots, and so he does it for me. As if I'm a child.

He wraps me in a blanket and guides me over to the end of the couch nearest the woodstove, which gives off a wall of heat. I shrink back from it; it makes my skin hurt. He wraps his hands around mine, breathing on them to warn them.

"What were you doing out there?" he asks.

"I went to where I could get a signal."

"Who did you call?"

"Magnus," I say, my lips twisting mirthlessly, but he only looks confused. "I've been getting text messages, telling me to stay away from you. I found a phone in Magnus's office and I went to try the number. The texts came from him."

"That doesn't make any sense," Connor says. "Why would he do that? It was probably Trevor. Being an ass, like always."

He's still rubbing my hands between his. They prickle, pins and needles as feeling returns.

"I saw a photo of you," he says, without looking up. "I was at Harper's show. We'd never met—it was a friend-of-a-friend thing. I was on a date, actually." He gives a low laugh. "A bad one. I saw the photo of you, and I saw the tattoo. It reminded me of the other cabin—Dragonfly. Dad picked the name for it, you know. He bought the ornament for the door. It reminded me of him. It made me think of . . ." He lets out a breath and bends his head over my hands, resting his brow against my knuckles. Then he looks up, meeting my eyes. "I don't really know how to describe it. The way things were when he died, they were . . . complicated. I've never been able to be angry with him like everyone else was. When I saw that photo, saw the tattoo—saw you—I felt like it was somehow a sign. That's why I asked Harper to introduce us."

"Why didn't you tell me? Why did you pretend to be her friend?" I ask.

He makes a sound of dark amusement. "Because I didn't think 'Hey, you make me think about my cheating dad and I find that weirdly compelling' was a great pickup line."

I choke. "Yeah, I can see that," I allow.

"I told myself it was fate. Which I guess is a fancy way of saying a coincidence with staying power," he says. He rises, moving to sit next to me on the couch. He settles so that he's not quite touching me, both of us facing in the same direction. "I'm sorry. I should have told you right away. I shouldn't have lied."

I look over at him. His face is open and vulnerable, those blue eyes bright. But a confession doesn't mean much when you've already been caught.

"Those photos. In Alexis's room," I say. "You said they were of Kayla."

He doesn't answer, guilt flashing briefly over his features. I unzip my coat. The photo I stole is still there, pressed against my body, its edges curved by the shape of my ribs. I set it on the coffee table between us, and his fingertips graze the edge.

"That's not Kayla," I say. "It's Mallory Cahill."

"How do you know that?" he asks, his voice rough. "How do you know her name?"

"Did your father do that to her?" I ask.

His breath hisses between his teeth. "No. He wouldn't."

"Then why—"

"Alexis found them at the house. In some of Dad's old things," Connor says. "She wanted to know the same thing. Did I think Dad did it. But he wouldn't."

"Is he really the person you thought you knew? He stashed a woman here," I point out. "Did he ever hit your mother? Or you?" I ask.

His head whips toward me, fury in his eyes. "No. Never," he says. "And he wouldn't have hurt Mallory, either."

"Then where did those photos come from?"

"I don't know," he says. "I have no idea. He was cheating on my mother, okay. That's awful. But he wasn't violent."

"Okay," I say quietly, relenting. He looks back at the photograph. He picks it up, eyes lingering on each bruise.

"I met her once, you know," he says. "Mallory. My father drove me up here. He didn't tell me—he just said she was a friend. I mostly remember the little girl. We were almost the same age. Spent the afternoon playing together. It was a fun day."

"Same age?" I echo.

"I mean, not really. I was seven. She was five," he says.

"Are you sure?"

He gives me an odd look. "Yeah, actually. You know kids at that age. They make a big deal out of it. She found out my birthday was exactly a week before hers, so she kept telling me, like, 'When you're twelve, I'll be ten. When you're seventeen, I'll be fifteen.' And she'd make up the things we'd do together. It was actually . . . really sweet."

Two years and one week. And all of a sudden, I know my birthday. I'm a year older than I thought. I sit back in the chair. Connor is still watching me.

"I don't think he planned to bring me up there," he says. There's a touch of defensiveness in his voice. "Mom was sick. He got stuck with me for the day unexpectedly. I had no idea why they were here."

The feeling of spinning comes back to me, the touch of snowflakes on my tongue. The boy who laughed and grabbed my hand, pulling me along. *Let's go.*

The image morphs. The antlered man, hand on my wrist, those same words echoing, anger in his voice—or—

"Theo?" Connor reaches up. I flinch, but he only presses the pad of his thumb to my face, wiping away a tear. He looks at me, a line between his brows. "He was a good man, you know. He was always so patient with us. Gentle. He never even raised his voice, and he taught me to help people. He said that's the point of being in the world. To help each other. He wouldn't have done that."

"Then who did?" I ask, but Connor is staring at me, doesn't seem to hear. His lips part.

I reach for him. "Connor—"

"Oh my god," he says. "Teddy. Her name was Teddy." He stands up abruptly, hand over his mouth, and my hand falls back to my lap. He looks at the photo on the table, then back to me. I sit with my elbows on my thighs, body pinched together.

"I didn't know," I say.

"It's true?" He has one hand on his hip, the other running through his hair, a look of utter bewilderment on his face. "You're her. How—but—did you arrange this whole thing?"

"How could I? You're the one who tracked me down, remember?" I point out.

"You said I looked familiar. The day we met, you said you thought you knew me. Because—"

"Because we'd met before," I tell him. My voice cracks. "And because you look so much like your father."

He shakes his head. "But you had to have known who I was. You must have—wait. You said you were adopted when you were four. That doesn't make sense."

"I was small for my age. They were guessing. Connor, I didn't remember anything about my life before the Scotts until I came here with you. I didn't remember you or your father or my own fucking name. Rowan Cahill. My mother called me Teddy. And I was here."

I was here. It was real. I came from somewhere, and I was someone.

There are tears running down my face. Useless things, but I can't stop them. I scrub at my cheeks with the heels of my hands, and the bandage still wrapping my palm scrapes my skin.

Connor watches me, silent. Then he sits slowly, lowering himself to the edge of the coffee table. He leans forward, elbows on his knees, gaze to the side. "Explain it to me," he says. He looks directly at me. Anger simmers behind his eyes.

No, not anger.

Fear.

"I know only bits and pieces," I say slowly, deliberately. I have just one chance to explain this so that he'll believe me. "It started with the cabin—Dragonfly. I remembered being there. And then I found a photo of myself." I get up and walk to the bedroom, returning with the photo, which he holds in both hands, studying it intently. "Trevor told me about Mallory. That your dad had her here, that she had a daughter. I started to remember things. Nothing *solid*. But I remember . . ." I trail off. I ball my hands into fists. "My mother didn't run off after your dad died. She was killed. Murdered, I think. And then I somehow wound up on the other side of the country, and the Scotts got paid a bunch of money to take me in and not ask questions."

"You think my father did it," Connor says hollowly. "You think he hurt her."

"The man in my dream. It's him," I say, and I don't have to tell him which dream I'm talking about. "Connor, Alexis told me that your father didn't die from a fall. He killed himself."

He recoils, his face contorting in shock. "What?"

"Paloma confirmed it. She said Alexis knew but someone—presumably your grandparents—made her promise not to tell you or your mom," I say, as gently as I can.

Connor is shaking his head. "That doesn't make sense."

"I know it's hard to hear—"

"No, I mean it genuinely does not make sense," Connor snaps. "When I was eighteen, I got a copy of the autopsy report. I thought it would bring me closure, or something like that. The cause of death was listed as hypothermia and an epidural hematoma—a blow to the temple. He would have lost consciousness briefly, and probably woken up and thought he was all right. That would last a few minutes. But the blood would have been building up in his skull. Eventually, he'd collapse again. They couldn't definitively state if it was the cold or the bleeding in the skull that was the definitive cause of death. He fell and hit his head. That's what happened."

"He could have jumped," I suggest.

"Even the lodge is only two stories," Connor points out. "Shitty way to kill yourself. Good way to break a leg."

"Mr. Vance . . . he said it was a broken neck," I remember. "But wouldn't he have known? He's the one who brought the body down. What did they tell you back then?"

"Nothing. An accident. He fell," Connor says.

"There was blood on his face," I say. Connor looks confused. I raise a hand, gesture in a vain attempt to explain as I fumble for words. "I went to find my mom, and she—she was dying," I say. Hand to my throat, fingers tracing the path of the blood. "She told me to hide. So I did. But he found me. He came in the door and I screamed, because he looked like a monster. The antlers behind him and his face—"

Half of it dark. With shadow and with blood. Not hers. His own.

So she'd fought back, before he hurt her. And then he came for me, and when he found me, he grabbed my hand and he was so angry—

But it wasn't anger. I'd made the same mistake with Connor. It wasn't anger, but fear.

I'm not supposed to go in.

I can see that door again. See it swinging open, just enough to peer through.

The girl opens the door two inches, no more. She knows she's not meant to be here. She knows she's not meant to see.

"Is that enough?" her mother asks.

"We need to get all of it," a voice replies.

"It won't matter."

"It might."

"You don't know what he's like. You don't know how these things work."

"So you're just going to give up?"

"I have nowhere to go."

"Let me help you, Mallory," Liam says. And then he looks up and sees her, and smiles. "Hey, Teddy."

"It wasn't him," I whisper, my gaze unfocused. "It wasn't him at all. He was trying to help." I got it wrong. I was afraid, but not of Liam Dalton.

"Theo," Connor says slowly, "what Mallory and my father did was awful, but it wasn't just because he was cheating on Mom. I didn't find it out until much later. It was part of why Nick and Mom—why they got so close, after. Commiserating."

"Nick," I repeat, stunned.

"Mallory was living with him when she and Dad got together," Connor says.

Nick. He'd known her, too. Known me. I thought it was odd, but I didn't think it through. And Trevor—his cracks about disloyalty running in the family. He wasn't just talking about his father cheating on his mother. He was talking about Liam betraying Nick.

Nick, who saw that photo in my pocket. Who saw the birthmarks on my neck and knows exactly who I am. Knows that I've been asking all the questions that I shouldn't.

Connor is still talking. "When Alexis showed me those photos, I thought it didn't make any sense. Why would Dad have had them if those bruises were his fault? Unless he was holding on to them for her. Nick's always had anger issues. Mom used to think I butted heads with him because I didn't want him replacing Dad, but I swear I always felt like he hated me."

I feel numb. I touch the tips of my fingertips to my face, chasing any sensation at all.

"What *exactly* do you remember?" Connor asks.

I close my eyes. And I tell him.

34

The girl knows how to hide. She knows how to stay quiet. When the monster is angry, you do not run; you do not make a sound.

The door bursts open. A beast steps into the room—a beast with the shape of a man, and antlers springing from his temples—and she screams—

But it's only Liam. Not the monster at all.

"There you are, love. Come on. We have to go," Liam says, but she's too scared to move. He looks terrifying, half his face masked with fresh blood that flows from a gash at his temple. He leans down, grabs her wrist, and hauls her upright. He starts to pull her toward the door. She flings herself back and he stops, panting for breath. His eyes are filled with worry, but he drops to one knee and puts his hands on her shoulders.

"Listen to me, Teddy. I need you to trust me. Do you trust me?" he asks. The girl nods. "We have to run. We have to run and not stop until I say so. Don't look back and don't slow down. Can you do that?"

"Yes," she whispers. Then, "Where's Mama?"

His hand rises from her arm, lowers again, a helpless gesture. "Let's go" is all he says, and then he's drawing her out into the snow. *I don't have my coat,* she wants to tell him, but she sees the look on his face and swallows down the words.

The snow is deep enough to catch at her legs. She has to take three strides to every one of his, and his grip on her wrist yanks her along, but she presses her lips together and doesn't make a sound. His head swivels constantly. "This way," he mutters sometimes.

The girl is getting tired—but it's his steps that slow first. He stumbles, catches himself against a tree. He shakes his head, straightens up.

"Have to keep moving," he says, and takes two steps.

And then he falls.

He tries to rise once, pushing himself up on one arm only to collapse again. He lies in the snow, face down, head turned to the side so she can see his eye, open only to a slit.

"Mr. Liam?" the girl says. "Mr. Liam. We can't slow down." She grabs his arm. She tugs on it. Tugs again. He isn't getting up. She sinks down, kneeling beside him. She looks around. There's no one else here. No one to tell her what to do, where to go.

The sun is almost gone. The woods are getting dark. Dark, and oh so cold.

She lies down beside him and waits for him to wake.

35

He fell," I whisper. The scraps have stitched themselves together. I was never afraid of him. Not really. He was the knight, not the ogre. We tried to get away. "Nick hurt her. Liam—he must have tried to help. That's why he brought her here, to get away. But Nick found out where she was. He was there. I remember him standing there."

Watching me die.

Connor's hands are shaking. I still can't seem to feel warm. "I told Mom about meeting you," he says. "Dad told me to keep it a secret, but I slipped up. She must have told Nick. If he went up there—if Nick hit him and then Dad got away and got you, but then . . ."

A sound escapes me, like a cry of pain. Connor startles. I look at him, my vision blurring. "You believe me," I say.

He pauses, but it's not because it isn't true. I can see him thinking it through—because he wants to be deliberate. He wants to be certain. And he wants both of us to know that he means it when he says, "I believe you."

"And you didn't know who I was," I say.

"No, I had no idea."

"And bringing me here wasn't some kind of trap? To find out what I knew? If I was going to cause trouble?" I demand.

"No, of course not. I wasn't even sure about bringing you, but Mom convinced me," he says. "Not that I didn't want you to come," he adds quickly. "It's just, my family can be a lot. Even without . . . all this."

"But you found me. On the other side of the country. If you didn't know . . ." How could it be a coincidence?

"Fate?" Connor suggests.

"I don't believe in fate," I say flatly.

He regards me, and for all the horror, there's something like wonder in his eyes. "That day, all those years ago. We spent hours together, in the snow. You told me that you didn't like the cold. That you wanted to go where it was always warm. I said you should live in Los Angeles. It's where my mom is from, and it's warm there all year long. You said you were going to move there and go to school for books—you said it like that, go to school for books because books are where they keep all the interesting stuff."

I make a skeptical noise. "You think I moved to Los Angeles because you told me to?"

"Maybe," Connor says.

"Los Angeles is a big place."

"And I found you. Stumbled in off the street and there you were in black-and-white," Connor says.

"So we're back to fate."

"It's enough for me," he says.

A strained laugh forces itself between my lips. "We should have just eloped."

"Still could," Connor says. He puts his hand in mine. I stare down at our fingers.

He could still be lying. Maybe this *is* a ploy to discover what I remember and what I'm planning to do.

Maybe he saw me and then released the arrow.

But I know that I was never afraid of Liam Dalton. And I am not afraid of Connor now.

I lean in toward him and press my lips against his. The lightest touch, a question and nothing more, until he answers it. His hand cups my face as he deepens the kiss and then he's shifting from the table to the couch. His hands run over my leg, brush my neck, slide my coat gently from my shoulders. I wince as his palm brushes against my arm, but the pain is fleeting.

It isn't delicate. It isn't demanding. When his palm skims under my shirt, he pauses; I press against him. When I wrap my legs around his waist, I put a hand against his chest and look him in the eye, and I don't move again until he does, bringing his body to mine.

Every movement now is a question. We could put words to them, but there is only one answer that matters in this moment.

The parts of me that are wounded still hurt, but having him like this is worth the pain, because I'm sure now. I'm sure of nothing else, but I'm sure of him.

36

I wake with a cry, my skin slick with sweat despite the chill. Morning light slants weakly through the window. I remember Connor nudging me awake, helping me into the bed. And I remember sheer exhaustion carrying me back into sleep. Connor isn't here now, and the blankets are undisturbed on his side of the bed. He never joined me.

I put on my slippers and head into the main room. Connor is already up and dressed, standing in the kitchen with a mug of coffee. I glance toward the door; his boots are there, caked in snow. He's been out already.

"Did you sleep at all?" I ask. He shakes his head, and I can't help but smile a little. "We should get packed." But something in his face makes my stomach twist.

"We can't leave," he says. Fear closes up my throat. He nods toward the door. "Look outside."

I go to the window, lifting aside the curtain, and my heart sinks. The world is blanketed in white—a deep, relentless layer of snow.

"The car can't make it down the mountain safely in that, not today," Connor says. "Vance'll work on clearing things, but it won't be today, and probably not tomorrow."

"Then we take the Sno-Cat," I say.

Connor hesitates. Then, "I'll ask."

"Connor—" I give him a warning look. He puts his hands on my arms soothingly, rubbing them up and down.

"I will figure it out. I promised you we'd leave, and we will. But I don't know how to operate the Sno-Cat, and if we act like this is an emergency, it's going to raise some eyebrows. Although . . ."

"What?" I prompt.

"We could tell people," he says. "Talk to Granddad. To my mom. If they know what's going on, Nick can't—"

"Magnus is the one who sent me those messages, remember?" I ask. "Why would he do that unless he knew who he was? Whatever happened, Nick didn't cover it up all on his own. We don't know who else is involved." I don't add that this includes his mother.

His shoulders cave. "Okay. You're right." He kisses my forehead. "I'm sorry. I wish I could whisk you away from here right now. But Nick can't do anything as long as you're with me."

"We'll go to breakfast," I say. "Smile and hold hands and pretend everything is fine. And we'll take the first ride out of here."

"Hey," Connor says. He rests his thumb on my chin, just beneath my lower lip. "Theo, listen. I don't know exactly what happened all those years ago, or what's going on now. But I know what's going to happen."

"You do?" I ask, skeptical.

"I do. We're going to get away from here. We're going to find the truth. And we're going to be together," Connor says. "We're going to get married and travel the world and get a cat and have kids, if we want them—we're going to do all the things we planned. All the things we promised."

"Your family—"

"You are my family," he tells me. "That's the way it works. That's what the ring means. Whatever happens, whatever we find out—we chose each other. That hasn't changed."

I put my hand on his chest, feel the quickened pace of his heart. The edge of my tattoo peeks out from under my sleeve. I never knew if it was a warning or a guide. Now I see that it's both. It brought me here. Brought me to my past, to my memories. But first, it brought me to Connor.

"Let's go," I say. I take his hand, and we leave together.

It's quiet in the lodge when we arrive; we're up early, though already the scent of coffee and something spiced with nutmeg reaches my nose, and I imagine Irina has been up earlier still.

Irina appears almost as quickly as that thought, and waves us in. "I'm sorry, I am a bit behind," she says as she shows us into the dining room, already set up with coffee on the sideboard and an array of tiny breakfast pastries. Her definition of *behind* isn't the same as mine. "Olena is supposed to be helping, but she is—" She pauses, a frown creasing her face.

"It's no problem," Connor assures her.

"I believe your grandmother will be here shortly," she says, and exits, muttering something about "that boy" under her breath. Three guesses as to who Olena is dawdling with.

I'm pouring my coffee—or, as Connor teases, my cream and sugar with a splash of coffee—when Louise arrives as promised, steps clicking on the hardwood. In the doorway she pauses, eyes on me, displeasure evident.

"Connor. Miss Scott," she says.

My cup scrapes against its saucer. I walk to the table, setting it down at my place and offering her a gracious "good morning." Play the part. Don't let the cup rattle, even if your hands are shaking.

"I was under the impression that you would be departing," she says thinly.

"Oh, I don't think anyone's leaving with all this snow," I say lightly, not quite answering the question. "Can I get you some coffee, Louise?"

"Black," she says, and takes her seat beside the head of the table, a good distance from me.

"I've got it," Connor says, perhaps sensing that I might decide to pour it over her lap.

He's setting it down beside her hand as the dining room door opens again, and Trevor comes slouching in. He's a mess—collar undone and hair disheveled, eyes gluey from lack of sleep or drink or both. He yawns openly as he meanders over to the sideboard, plucking up a wheel of puff pastry filled with some kind of cinnamon-nut mix and popping it into his mouth right there, dusting the crumbs off his fingers and onto the floor.

"Quite the storm last night," he says as he drops into the chair immediately next to me.

"It felt like an Arctic trek just to get here from the cabin." My voice is bright. My fingers dig into my thigh. Every nerve in me is telling me to run, but there's nowhere to go.

Voices in the hall. ". . . at some point they start sleeping in past dawn, right?" Alexis is saying, and then she and Paloma bustle in, Sebastian in Paloma's arms. He's carrying a pair of dinosaur toys and is smashing them together, growling like a feral beast. Paloma plops him unceremoniously in a chair and heads for the coffee, leaving Alexis unwinding a scarf from around her neck as she hovers awkwardly near the door.

"Hope everyone got a decent night's sleep, because we sure didn't," she says with forceful cheer.

"Anything wrong?" Connor asks.

"Oh, just something woke up Bastian in the middle of the night and he wouldn't go back down. Kept getting freaked out by every little noise." Alexis tracks Paloma as she speaks. Paloma loads up a plate with treats and sets it beside Sebastian, taking her seat without ever making eye contact. "Which you would think would mean he'd sleep in, but . . ."

Rose arrives then, and Magnus. Rose is put together as always—with that way of moving and speaking like she's considering every twitch of her facial expression around her in-laws. As we all take our seats, Louise watches me, not bothering to hide her unhappiness at my presence.

Irina comes in, carrying a tray with a steaming scramble of egg and mushroom. She sets it down in the middle of the table and wipes her hands on her apron, obviously frazzled. "A moment, please, I'll be right back with the rest," she says.

"Where's that daughter of yours? Not helping you?" Magnus asks.

Irina's eyes cut to Trevor. "She's running a bit late. Haven't seen her yet today."

"We need to discuss you distracting the help," Magnus says.

Trevor's expression is blank. "She's probably just sleeping in," he says, and then Irina is out the door and the food takes the focus.

I reach for the serving spoon. I can feel Louise's eyes on me as I finish loading up my plate and go to take a bite. Finally she sets her silverware on her plate with a sharp sound and says, "I'm sorry. I cannot do this."

I freeze, fork in midair, laden with eggs.

"Do what?" Alexis asks.

"I will not sit here and share a meal with this woman as if we don't know what's going on," Louise replies, all genteel offense.

"I don't know what you mean," I say through my teeth.

"Grandma, I already explained," Connor cuts in.

"Yes, yes, you told us about this so-called explanation. This perfectly tragic tale," Louise says acidly. "But it's not as if we can verify any of it. And she's already lied repeatedly, by her own admission. *Now* we're meant to believe her?"

I put my fork down with a soft clink. "I'd be quite happy to leave," I say, enough syrup in my voice to drown out the fear. "If we had a vehicle that could get down the mountain."

"I'm sure Mr. Vance can oblige you with an escort," Louise says.

I don't know what Mr. Vance knows or suspects. What he's been told. But he was here when Liam died, and he's loyal to the Daltons, and that means he can't be trusted. But Connor will be with me.

"If Mr. Vance can give us a lift, then we'll go," Connor says.

I manage a nod. "Thank you all for your hospitality." I stand, and Connor follows suit. He reaches a hand as if to take mine, but Louise's voice pulls him up short.

"Connor, a word," she says.

I press my lips together but give him a tight nod. "I'll wait in the foyer," I say. Play nice. As long as he comes with me, they can pour whatever poison in his ear they want. Soon we'll be away from here.

I stride out, resisting the temptation to linger and try to catch what they're saying. Connor will tell me what's going on. I walk steadily, keeping my breathing constant, and I almost succeed in keeping my fear in check.

Nick is in the foyer. His back is to me, but at the sound of my footsteps, he turns, as he did the night we arrived, and as it did that night, his expression freezes in place. "Theo," he says. "What are you doing here?"

"Getting breakfast," I say. "Or getting kicked out of breakfast." I keep my chin tipped up and tell myself I have no reason to be afraid, here in the lodge with witnesses only a hallway away. It doesn't help.

He moves toward me, so quickly I don't have time to react before his hand is closing around my upper arm, inches from the wound he stitched up only yesterday. The pain makes me cry out, but his grip doesn't relent as he stares at me, searching my face for—what? His teeth are clenched, his breathing suddenly ragged, and I freeze.

Don't move.

Don't make a sound.

Don't make the ogre angry.

"What's going on here?" Trevor's voice comes from behind me, lazy and unbothered. He slinks around into view, hands in his pockets. "Did the peasant girl steal the good silver?"

Nick lets go. He steps back. And without a word, he walks past us both, down the hall toward the dining room.

"What the fuck was that about?" Trevor mutters, sidling another step closer to me as he watches his uncle go.

"I don't know," I say, voice shaking. It's only half a lie. Trevor gives me a curious look.

"He's an asshole, you know," he says.

"I know," I say.

"No, I mean—he's a serious asshole. His wife filed for a restraining order. He's not allowed near her or the kids. That's why they're not here," he says. "Would've put that one on the tree, but he'd probably shoot me." He still stands with that casual, no-shits-to-give posture, but there's an old wound behind those words, ridges of scar tissue running through them.

"You're kind of an asshole, too," I remind him.

"Yeah," he says. And to my surprise, he looks guilty. "I'm sorry about your hand."

"Are you?"

He pulls his hands from his pockets at last, and almost delicately he rolls up his left sleeve, one fold at a time. My breath hisses between my teeth. His inner forearm is dotted with a dozen circular burns near the elbow, all in various stages of healing, from scar tissue to fresh scab. "Sometimes I get the urge, and it's like the only thing my brain can hear. Only I've never hurt someone else. So, sorry. That was fucked."

"No shit," I manage. He rolls his sleeve back down. "Thank you for apologizing, I guess." I'm not going to stand here feeling sorry for this little psycho.

"Listen," he says. "Olena and I were out at the cabin last night, but she left on her own. She should have been back in her own bed, only it sounds like she wasn't."

Dread curdles in my stomach. "Then where is she?"

"I don't know. But I don't want to freak everyone out or get her in trouble if she's like—ditching work somewhere," Trevor says. He swallows. "Can you help me look for her?"

"Why are you asking me?"

"Because if you rat us out, no one's going to believe you," he says with a shrug.

Olena isn't back. There was a fucking storm last night and Olena isn't back. But I'm not about to go off on my own.

"Trevor," I start to say, and then I glance toward the hall. Nick hasn't disappeared into the dining room. He's only retreated a ways, and Magnus is with him, the two of them exchanging quiet words as Nick's gaze fixes on me. Cold fear floods me at the look in his eyes.

I'm not safe here.

"Fine. Suit yourself," Trevor says, and starts to leave.

"Wait," I say quickly. "I'll come with you." Better out there with him than in here with them. Trevor may be an asshole, but he's one of the few people I'm completely certain isn't involved.

They'd never trust him enough.

We walk out together. Trevor holds the door open for me, a show of chivalry that feels more like mockery. I glance once behind myself and see Nick and Magnus still watching us. I pick up my pace, following Trevor out toward the trees.

"She should have come straight back here," Trevor says.

"What's the fastest way to Dragonfly?" I ask. He points, but lets me take the lead, forcing me to put him at my back. My nerves prickle, on high alert. Trevor was a toddler when his father died. And he's clearly not invested in protecting the family's good name. That doesn't mean he's not a potential threat.

"Your family seems to have gotten over your little stunt pretty fast," I say, mostly to get him talking, make it easier to track his position when I can't see him.

"There will be consequences," he says in a gruff imitation of his grandfather. "Like it matters. They don't even have control over my trust fund anymore, so they can't keep dangling that over my head."

"Oh, thank goodness for that," I say, and can't restrain myself from rolling my eyes.

"I'm a spoiled little brat, I know," he says, and I can hear the grin.

"Don't you have any loftier ambitions for your life? Or are you just here for a good time, not a long time?" I ask, not bothering to keep the disdain from the words.

He actually falls silent for a moment, our footsteps keeping up the conversation for us. "Do you know what *anhedonia* means?"

"It's an inability to feel pleasure or joy," I say. I've always thought the word was oddly lovely, for such a depressing thing.

"I think maybe I was born with it," he says. "Can't remember feeling happy. And if the best I can aim for is not quite as fucking terrible, what's the point in trying at all?"

"Are you telling me this because it's true, or because you want me to feel sorry for you?" I say, turning to look at him.

He stares at me a beat. And then the corners of his mouth hook up, one crooked tooth showing. "You could fix me."

I start to turn back around, about to tell him to go fuck himself when something catches my eye. Everything in the woods is gray and white, the occasional green of pine needles prickling through. And in the midst of it all, a brief flicker of red.

Red—like a cardinal in the snow, but I haven't seen any of them here, and then my mind fills with other things. *Red scarf.* I turn my head back toward it, but the contours of the landscape have hidden it from me if it was there at all. Still, I take a step in the direction where I think it was, and then—yes, a spot of red. Not blood red; brighter than that. The red of the coat I'm wearing now, and I take another step, and another.

"Theo?" Trevor says.

Vance warned me it wasn't safe to walk out here in the dark at night. There are places that drop off suddenly, depressions and gullies. Easy to trip. Twist an ankle. Break a leg.

She lies at the bottom of a steep depression, face down. One hand is out in front of her, resting on top of the snow; the other is twisted under her body. Her dark hair spills out, the white wool cap lost. Snow has fallen thickly, covering her shoulders, covering the blood that pooled beside her head, but it's seeped up, making a pattern of pink across the snow like creeping mildew.

"Theo, what—" Trevor says, and then he's caught up to me. He makes a garbled sound of horror, lurching. "Oh *fuck*."

I ignore him, scrambling down the short slope toward her. I grab her shoulder, forgetting everything I know about stabilizing the neck, securing the airway, just frantic to get her turned over, certain she's suffocating—

Her eyes are open. Her skin has a bluish cast, and she's dead, she's been dead for hours, there was nothing I could do, and the first thing I feel, the very first thing, is a wash of relief, a release to know that I cannot save her and so I am spared the agony of trying, and I know that for the rest of my life I will remember that moment and be ashamed. And just as quickly, the feeling is gone. It collapses into sorrow, into horror and confusion.

"Olena!" Trevor says, falling to one knee beside me. "We need to get help. Get her warm. We have to . . ."

I look at him, waiting. He's panting, frantic. And then his mouth closes, the air going out of him all at once.

I turn my gaze back to Olena, though it's the last place I want to look. Her hair is frozen to the side of her face with a mixture of blood and snow, and the ragged lip of a wound protrudes beneath it. I look back, farther down the slope. There's a rock there, the size of two fists pressed together, one edge sharp. It's dark with what might be blood.

I think of the sound I heard last night, stumbling back to White Pine in the dark. Like a bird or a rabbit crying out in pain.

I brush hair from Olena's face with my fingertips. Her empty eyes stare into mine, and I feel like I've been here before.

Here, in the cold.

Here, with a body that has long since lost its warmth.

With eyes staring into mine.

I've been coming and going from Dragonfly—Mr. Vance saw me. He told people. Told Nick. And this path—we've veered off course, farther south than the direct path Olena would have taken if she was going the shortest route. With all the snow, Olena must have been cutting over to the cars and the lake, to get to the easier path around the lake edge.

She was walking in the direction of White Pine. In her red coat, the same color as mine.

We looked the same in the dark, Olena and I.

"What happened?" Trevor asks, as if I know. As if I can explain it.

I look up at him, voice perfectly level, and say, "She fell."

37

What do we do?" Trevor asks. He looks at me helplessly. "What do we do?"

You would think that I was utterly calm, to look at me. "Stay here," I tell him, firm and assured. "I'll get help."

I walk away before he can object. My mind charts the path back to White Pine. To the keys, to the car, down the mountain through drifts of snow. I might make it.

Not without Connor.

I follow my own footprints. Back up the steps of the lodge, inside, not bothering to remove my shoes. I'll track snow all over the gleaming hardwoods, but so what? Let it seep in. Let it warp the wood and let the Daltons tear it all up and start over again.

Connor's voice floats toward me. He's in the living room. I follow the sound, that calm that is not calm at all keeping me steady. I expect to find him with Louise, but it's Rose in there with him, the two of them standing close together. Her arms are crossed lightly, her head bent, everything about her pose emanating discomfort and defeat. Connor has one hand on his hip, the other at the back of his neck, no happier than she is. My winter boots thump gracelessly as I enter, and he turns.

"Theo?" he says, brow creasing. "Where did you go?"

"I need to talk to you."

The line between his eyebrows deepens. He touches his mother's shoulder once, a *just a moment* gesture, and then hurries over to me, dropping his voice. "What is it? You look—"

"We need to leave," I say under my breath, quietly enough Rose won't hear. "Now."

"We will," Connor says. "We need to talk to Mr. Vance and then—"

"Not Vance. Just the two of us, and we need to do it right away," I say. "Listen to me carefully and do not make a scene. Olena is dead."

His face goes blank with shock. I take hold of his hand, squeeze hard. He can't freak out.

"Connor, we need to leave *now,*" I say again, but at that moment the front door slams. Heavy footsteps stagger into the foyer, and I curse under my breath as a voice calls out.

"Mom? Mom!"

"Trevor?" Rose calls back, startled, and glances at me with a frightened expression, and then Trevor is staggering into the room. His face is bloodless, eyes wild.

"Mom, she's—Olena—she's dead," he says.

Rose gives a cry, her hand going to her mouth and her eyes still flicking from Trevor to me, back to Trevor, trying to fit the pieces together. I'm still holding Connor's hand. We could go. Walk out the door and leave. But it's already too late. Louise appears at the other doorway—"What is going on?"—and then more footsteps, people flocking to the sound, and there's no escape now.

"Olena's dead," Trevor says again, his voice a wreck. "She's just—she was just lying there, and—" He chokes, gestures desperately in the general direction of the woods. "I don't know what happened. She was with me, and then . . ."

"Oh god," Rose says softly, but she isn't looking at Trevor, she's looking past him, and all of us turn.

Irina stands in the hall. Her hands are in front of her face, as if she is trying to hide, to cover her eyes, to blot it all out. Her whole body trembles. And then she begins to scream.

Louise is the first to move. She covers the distance with surprising speed and gathers Irina against her. Irina's cries draw anyone who wasn't already here. Confusion and fear thicken the air. Alexis grabs Paloma's hand; Paloma lifts Sebastian up as if getting ready to flee, and Nick looms behind them.

Irina's screams taper off. She sags against Louise, murmuring something raggedly. "It isn't true," I hear. "It isn't true."

"What is going on?" Magnus asks. He stands in the hallway that leads to the bathroom and the study.

"It seems there was some kind of accident. Olena is dead," Louise says. Every time the words are spoken out loud, it somehow seems less real.

Trevor, haltingly, explains. Alexis and Paloma draw together, hands interlaced. Irina weeps quietly in Louise's arms.

When Trevor is done, Magnus looks at the ground for three solid seconds. And then he nods. "Louise, take Irina upstairs."

Louise nods. Gently, with an expression of practicality and focus, she guides the other woman to the stairs. Magnus waits until the sound of a door closing on the second floor before he continues.

"Trevor, take Connor and Nick to Olena. We'll be told not to move anything, but find something to cover her with, at least. I'll call the sheriff and the coroner and see what they want us to do. Alexis, Paloma—you should take Sebastian back to Red Fox. Rose, see Theo to the study; she can rest there."

"I can go back to White Pine," I say immediately.

"You've had a shock. You shouldn't be off on your own," Magnus says briskly, not inviting disagreement. "And as you were with Trevor when Olena was discovered, the sheriff may have questions."

The sheriff—if the sheriff is coming here, surely that will be its own form of protection. And a possible ride out of this place.

Rose takes my arm, her grip kind and unyielding. I glance at Connor; he looks helpless. There's no reasonable way to object. Nowhere to go, if I did. And so I surrender.

The seconds tick by on the clock above Magnus's desk. It's been an hour since Rose left me here. I have no idea what's going on. No one has come to get me. No one has spoken to me at all. I stare at the door and wonder if it's locked. I don't see a reason yet to try, but I take a mental catalog of the objects in the room that are heavy enough to serve as a weapon.

Olena is dead. Someone killed her. Because they thought she was me.

It isn't the only explanation. But the way I figure it, it's the only one that matters. Because if it is true, then I cannot afford to disbelieve it. It explains Nick's shock at seeing me in the foyer.

There's a polite knock on the door, and it opens before I can respond. Rose again. She has a mug in her hands. "I thought you could probably use some tea," she says. Her eyes have that shiny, trying-not-to-cry look.

"Thank you," I manage. Everyone has been speaking to me like I'm made of spun sugar. Maybe it's useful, to let them think that my silence is me falling apart, instead of trying to make a plan.

I accept the mug and take a sip. It's overly sweetened, but I bend my lips in a grateful smile. The heat, at least, is welcome.

"I thought about bringing you something stronger," Rose says. Instead of leaving, she moves farther into the room. She half sits against the desk, hands cupping her elbows. "I'm sorry that we sort of forgot you in here. We're all in shock, obviously."

I wet my lips, trying to think of how to respond. "You shouldn't be worried about me. Irina must be an absolute wreck."

"She's being taken care of. Louise gave her some kind of sedative, to help her calm down," Rose says. "I can't imagine."

"You don't have to imagine, though," I reflect. Slowly I sip the tea. The sweetness is growing on me.

She frowns, as if she hadn't thought of this. "Because of Liam? I suppose. Though at the time I was so angry with him, it was . . . complicated."

"You were filing for divorce," I say.

Her lips thin. "Trevor," she begins, and stops. "But yes. I had the papers drawn up a few days before he died. I had discovered he was cheating on me, which I think you know." She says it matter-of-factly, folding her hands. I flush.

"I'd heard."

"He'd been distant for a while. Going off on trips. The thing that I was angriest about, though, is that he involved Connor. He brought him up here. It's how I found out. Seven-year-olds aren't famous for being able to keep secrets," she says dryly, and my heart gives a squeeze. She's spent all these years thinking her husband had betrayed her. "You don't involve your kids in that kind of thing. When I say that I can't imagine what Irina is going through—it's hard to understand until you actually have them that it isn't just . . . Oh, love plus. Like it's better or more than. It isn't that. It's animal. Feral. The need to protect them . . . You'd do anything."

I take another sip, rather than tell her that in my experience, the instinct she describes is faulty in a distressingly high portion of the population.

"But sometimes . . ." Rose sighs. "I don't know. I think the flaw of the Daltons is being too protective. I know that I was with Trevor."

I think of Nick, saying how he tried to get through to him. The scars on his arms. How tired he is of keeping quiet about things. "I don't think Trevor was protected when he actually needed it," I say.

"What are you talking about?" Rose asks.

"Rose," I say carefully. "When Connor told you about Mallory Cahill, did you tell anyone else?"

"I—well, yes, I suppose. I told Nick." She laughs grimly. "And then I told Liam. Told him that I was filing for divorce. And you know, that's the first thing he asked me, too. Who else knows. Like the biggest worry was people knowing what he'd been up to. He asked who I'd told and then he took off. He went straight to her, and—" She stops. She takes a sharp breath, realizing how much she's said. "I'm sorry, I think I'm not thinking straight, with everything."

"He came to Idlewood after you told him," I say. He must have gotten word to Mallory, warned her that Nick knew where she was. Then he headed up himself, not stopping to explain things to Rose. "And that's when he died, wasn't it?"

"Why are you asking about all of this?" Rose says, suddenly defensive. "It was years ago."

The dregs swirl in the bottom of my tea. "Has the sheriff come?" I ask, avoiding the question.

Rose frowns at me. "No. He can't make it out today," Rose says. "But Connor and Mr. Vance went to fetch the coroner."

"What?" I say, alarmed.

"His vehicle can't make it up the mountain, so they'll have to bring him," Rose says.

My pulse thuds in my temples. Connor left? He can't have. Not without telling me. He wouldn't leave me up here. He wouldn't leave me with them.

"When did he leave?" I demand.

"Only a few minutes ago, I think," she says, brow furrowing. "I'm sorry, I thought he would have stopped by to tell you."

"I have to go," I say. She isn't sorry to let me go; she's uncomfortable, embarrassed by what she's shared. I walk out the door, a buzzing in my ears, and she doesn't stop me. I have to get out of here. I have to catch up with Connor. I can't do it on foot, but the UTVs—there's one parked out back, by the shed. I can take that.

My boots are in the hall. I don't know where my coat is, but the thought of putting it on makes me shudder. I can't stop picturing that moment. The red at the edge of my vision. That keening cry—*a rabbit, it was only a rabbit*—echoes in my ears. She wasn't supposed to die.

It takes my eyes a moment to focus on the laces of my boots as I do them up. The lights of the Christmas tree stretch into long-pointed stars.

I walk around the side of the lodge. My steps feel heavy. I jump at every noise. Wind dumping snow from a branch; the flurry of a bird's wings. I feel a hand wrapped around my wrist, dragging me forward.

Hurry, Liam tells me.

Hurry, because he's coming. Because he's here.

I weave past the trash cans, hoping the concrete wall will help block me from view if anyone glances out a window. The trees provide another screen. I hold my breath until the shed comes into view—the shed, and the four-wheeler parked outside.

I check the UTV. No key. I vaguely remember Magnus hanging them on a hook inside the shed—which is, luckily, unlocked. I haul open the door.

A corpse greets me. The deer carcass hangs, skinned and gutted, aging in the cold air. A few white strips of fat marble the deep pink flesh. The chest cavity gapes. The head has been removed. The air in here feels thick, faintly scented with blood. This deer isn't the one that I helped dress days ago. Magnus must have stayed out, the day Connor almost killed me. He must have caught his quarry after all.

I cross to the workbench. The keys are there, dangling on a hook in a pegboard. I pocket them—and then look down. Sitting on the table is the knife Magnus handed me earlier: handle hand-carved from an antler, the blade folded neatly within it. I pocket that, too, and I've begun to turn when the slash of light coming through the door vanishes.

Nick Dalton is standing in the doorway. His hands are relaxed, loose at his sides. There is no malice at all in his expression. My stomach tightens with dread, but he only sighs.

"Hello, Teddy."

38

Nick," I say. My voice comes out strained. My legs wobble. "I told you. I've never gone by Teddy. It's just Theo."

He takes a half step forward, still filling the doorway, still blocking my way out. I could shout, I think. How far would my voice carry? Would anyone who heard it come to help?

"It was such a cutesy nickname. Mallory's little teddy bear. Rowan—your name is Rowan Cahill," he says. He shakes his head. "I thought it was a coincidence. I thought it couldn't possibly be you, and I told myself not to be paranoid. Rowan Cahill's dead, I told myself. I can't believe how long it took me to see."

"I don't know what you're talking about," I say, but it's only a whisper. The walls feel close. The smell of the hanging meat is suddenly overpowering, and my stomach lurches.

"Why did you come here? Why go after Connor?" he asks, giving me a puzzled, inquiring look. "Did you just want to mess with us? Did you think you could get something from us?"

"I don't want anything from you." My hand drifts toward my pocket. My arm feels heavy. So does the rest of me. My mouth is cotton-ball dry, and my heartbeat is slow, very slow. My fear feels like a voice calling in the distance. I can't quite make it out.

"You should never have come back here," he tells me, and takes another step forward—or is it two? He's right in front of me now, and it's like I've lost the seconds in between.

Gave her a sedative, to help her calm down, I think. The tea. Stupid. Should have been more careful.

"Whoa there," he says, under his breath, reaching out to grab my arm. I try to pull away but my knees half collapse instead, and I pitch forward, brace myself against his chest with one hand. He looks down at me. It's too dark in the shed to read his expression.

"What did you do to my mother?" I whisper.

"I did what I had to," Nick says, and there is not an ounce of regret in his voice.

I open my mouth to scream—but he claps a hand over my face, muffling the sound. My limbs are weak, the air like Jell-O. He shoves me to the ground. I don't have the strength to resist. I finally make a sound, a bark of pain as my back hits the ground, and then his knee is digging into my stomach, his weight on my chest, and I can't get a breath to scream as he grabs my arms. The wound he stitched up less than a day ago flares with pain, but even that feels muted.

It's like I'm a doll, limp-limbed, his to manipulate. He grabs my wrist. I try to pull free, but it's barely a tug, and then he has the other one and something thin and hard is tightening around them both—a zip tie. I shove upward, trying to buck him off me, but he doesn't even seem to notice.

His weight lifts for an instant—I draw a breath to scream—and he crams a foul-tasting rag into my mouth. He seizes my hair at the root, right at my hairline, pulls my head back to look at him. "Enough," he says, like he's chastising a dog. "I'm not going to hurt you."

Not yet, he means. He uses a cord to tie the makeshift gag into place, and then he shoves up to his feet.

"That should do," he says. It takes me a moment in my sluggish state to realize he isn't speaking to me. Someone else. Right outside.

"Move her. You have a few minutes. Put her in Dragonfly, I'll be by shortly." It's Magnus's voice.

Nick's shadow moves toward me again, blocking out the light, and as the darkness falls over me, whatever sedative they've given me pulls me under—not all the way, but enough that I can't stop my eyes from drifting shut. Enough that moments become unglued from each other, and I'm reduced to sensations—

A shoulder digging into my chest. A hand rummaging in my pocket—not the one that holds the knife, not that, at least—and the shudder of a motor starting up. It takes me far too long to fit together the pieces of a coherent thought, *I'm on the sledge on the back of the UTV*, and then all I can think of is that Magnus uses this thing to drag the bodies of deer to where they'll be butchered, and then time skips and I'm not outside anymore, I'm being carried up a set of stairs. Dumped out on a wooden floor.

I'm in the main bedroom of Dragonfly. I lie on my side, facing the vanity. Nick is framed in the mirror.

"You really shouldn't have come back." He says it like this is my fault. Something inevitable, a regrettable thing he will not in fact regret. He crouches down. I turn my head, every movement requiring careful, conscious thought, and squint up at him. "You were supposed to be dead. This shouldn't have happened at all."

I'm so tired. So unbearably tired. I try to keep my eyes open, but they drift shut, and my ears fill with a sound like buzzing—like the droning wings of an insect, and it's the last thing I hear as I slip away from consciousness.

The girl lies on the floor, her cheek pressed against the wood. It's cold in here, but not as cold as it was before. She can't feel her fingers. It's hard to open her eyes, but she does, and when they focus, her mother is lying across from her. Her neck is a dark red; the red is cracked like river mud. There's a strange furrow in the skin at her throat, and more blood soaking her sweater, all that crimson blooming from the hole in the middle of her chest. Her eyes are open. She doesn't see the girl.

The girl tries to speak, but her voice doesn't come. She tries to reach out, but she's still so cold, and her arms won't lift, and the girl knows with deep certainty that this is what it feels like to be dead, because dead is when your body doesn't work anymore and they bury you in a hole and cover you up with dirt and she doesn't want to be buried, she doesn't want to be covered in dirt, and she starts to cry, a thin little breathy sound—

"What the hell?" Footsteps. A new face appears in her vision. A man crouching down. "You alive, little one?"

A foot jostles my shoulder. I try to open my eyes, then curl inward instinctively against the onslaught of the light.

"Welcome back," Nick says. He crouches down. "You dipped out for quite a stretch there. I was worried she gave you too much."

I flex my hands. The zip ties bite into my skin. At least they're in the front, not twisted around the back. He watches me, chewing on his lip.

"I want to ask you something," he says. "I'm going to take off that gag. Don't yell. No one would hear you, and it'll just make things unpleasant for you. Got it?"

I nod. Anything to get this thing out of my mouth. He grunts and reaches around, fumbling with the cord. He gets it undone and pulls the rag out of my mouth. He sits back, leaning against the wall with one knee up.

"Why'd you come here?" he asks me.

"What do you mean?" My mouth is so dry the words come out broken.

He waves a hand. "Connor. This trip. What was the plan?"

My breath is ragged. I wish I could sit up, but my muscles feel like taffy. "No plan."

"Seems reckless."

"I didn't know who I was. I didn't know any of it. There was no plan."

"Then it's what, it's fate?" he says. He laughs, tips his head back against the wall. "Well, that's a fucking head trip."

"No kidding," I rasp out.

He slams the side of his fist against the wall. "Bad fucking luck. That's it?" he says, looking at me like I've got answers. "You really didn't know."

I shake my head, which sets it pounding.

"So if you and Connor don't meet, if he doesn't fall head over heels like an idiot, none of this happens," he says. "I bet you wish you'd never laid eyes on him."

I should. Olena is dead. I'm sure I'm about to follow. But I can't wish Connor out of my life. It's not because of Connor that I'm here, with my hands tied in front of me. It's because of Nick.

"What are you going to do to me?" I ask.

He lets out a breath, looking off to the side with an expression of consideration. "That's the question, isn't it? We can't exactly let you go."

"You could."

"No. We really can't." He has the gall to look regretful.

I try to draw enough spit to swallow, get rid of the taste of the rag, but the combination of the gag and the drugs have left my mouth feeling gummy. "You killed Olena, didn't you."

"That was an accident," he says at once.

I scoff. "Meaning she fell? Or meaning it was supposed to be me?" I ask. I flex my wrists subtly, testing the restraints. They're far too sturdy for me to snap. I hunch, pressing my elbow against my torso, and feel the hard lump of the knife in my pocket. Good. I'm not out of options yet.

His head cocks. "I convinced myself I was going crazy. I really did. Up until I was stitching you up, and you were still asking those questions. But it was impossible. I saw you die."

"I remember." The face in the glow of the cigarette as the cold closed in—it was Nick. Standing in the dark. Just waiting for me to die.

"He never told me, you know," Nick goes on. "That you weren't really dead. That he spirited you away. Thought he could handle the whole thing by himself and we wouldn't find out what he'd done."

"Your father, you mean," I say.

He makes a noise in the back of his throat. "I get it. Save the cute little kid. Who wouldn't want to? So he bundles you off and finds you a new home and that's that. Problem solved, conscience clear. But then you came back."

Did Magnus recognize me right away when Connor called, said he'd be bringing his fiancée, sent pictures? He must have known that if I came here, everything would come to light. What I saw. What he'd done, sparing me. So he tried to warn me off.

"Of course, you're not a cute little kid anymore," Nick is saying. "He did finally come to his senses. You're lucky your fiancé is such a shit hunter, you know. He saved your life with that fuck-up."

The flash of metal in the woods. Mr. Vance with his rifle. And Magnus, giving me one last chance to leave before he told me where to go. Where to wait. "Trouble with poachers," I say.

"It would have been easy enough to pin the blame on some trespassing hunter. I'll give him credit for the plan. But he should have fucking *told* me. He should have trusted me, but he was too worried about me finding out about his little moment of conscience. If I'd known, I could have kept Connor well away, but no. Instead my genius nephew blunders into the middle of it. It spooked you. You were going to leave, and it was obvious you weren't just going to slink off quietly, whatever Dad had hoped. So yes, once I realized what was really going on, I decided to take care of things. She had the same coat. She was where you were supposed to be. It's unfortunate. She was a sweet girl. Not too bright, but sweet." He gives a flick of his hand, like *What can you do?*

"I can tell you feel just awful," I say.

"Would me feeling guilty bring her back? No? Then why bother," he says. "You learn being a doctor, when you make mistakes, sometimes someone dies. You can't spend the rest of your life agonizing over it. You learn your lesson and you move on."

"Murder isn't a mistake," I say.

Rage flashes in his eyes. I think suddenly of how furious he was when we found Sebastian out in the cold. I'd assumed it was on Sebastian's behalf, born of concern. I took his reaction as a sign that he was a good man. But it turns out he's just an angry one.

"Killing my mother. Was that just 'unfortunate,' too?" I ask. "Was that just an accident?"

He watches me, his fingers dangling idly. "She was infuriating, you know. She really knew how to push my buttons. But I'll admit I went too far. I was young. In love."

"That's not love," I spit out.

"And you think you know what love is?" he asks disdainfully. "I loved her. Would've done anything to hold on to her. What happened in the end—yes, it was unfortunate." He pauses. "But I didn't kill her."

My breath speeds up. He's lying. He has to be. He looks off into the distance. His hand reaches for his pocket, as if for a cigarette that isn't there anymore. And then he begins to speak.

Funny, the way a secret fights to get free. You think you've got them locked up with threats and promises and careful planning, but they'll find their way. His brother was so careful—and then a sick wife; a kid in the passenger seat; a call from the mountain that the water isn't working; a promise extracted and quickly broken.

Don't blame the boy. He doesn't understand what he did, telling his mother about the woman living at Idlewood. But now the secret is free, and it flies swiftly from ear to ear. The boy tells his mother and she does what she has always promised herself she would do: she does not make excuses, does not dwell on denial. She will give him a chance to explain, but first she will make sure she's prepared. She calls her lawyer, has papers drawn up. That day she sits waiting for him to come home. Waiting to confront him. She needs support, she needs a sympathetic ear, and so she calls her husband's brother. She tells him everything.

He listens. And then he sets out for the mountain. Only to find he's not the first one there.

The woman's already shot when he gets there. Didn't expect that, did you? Hand clapped feebly against the wound on her neck, but she's struggling to her feet. Still got life in her. She always was stubborn.

She sees him and screams. She lunges forward to grab at something—a rifle, dropped in the snow. She has to take her hand off her neck to lift it, and as fresh blood gouts from the wound, she staggers. He crosses the distance to her in two quick strides and yanks the rifle from her grasp.

"Idiot," he snarls at her. He grabs her by the throat. Only way to stop the bleeding. Shoves her into the back seat of the car. "Lie the fuck down. Who—"

"Get away from her!" It's his brother. He's sprinting across the lot. No chance to explain. They collide. His brother grabs at the rifle. They tussle, the man gets the upper hand, the rifle pulls free and then comes down hard, just once.

Just self-defense.

But his brother drops, and the woman's staring at him with horror in her eyes.

"We're getting out of here," he says. "Where's the girl?"

But she shakes her head. Always an unhelpful bitch, that one. Wildflower. They'll be in Wildflower, surely. Girl's probably there now. He starts off across the snow.

"I never shot her," Nick says. Every word could be a lie. But why bother? "She made up stories, you know. Took every little thing and turned it into this grand operatic event. I'm not making excuses. I was a shit boyfriend. I drank too much and got too angry. But the way she made it sound, like I was this monster . . . I'm not a monster."

"Could have fooled me," I say. "I saw the photos. I saw what you did."

He drags his thumb across his lips. "You were a sweet kid. I truly wish none of this had happened."

"It didn't just *happen*. You did it. You chose it," I say.

"I didn't do anything to you."

"I remember." There are tears in my eyes, and I can't wipe them away. "You just stood there. You watched me die."

"I didn't kill you. The cold did," he says. "It would've been better if it took. Saved everyone a whole lot of suffering. You, especially. But none of this was my fault. I never shot Mallory. And Liam, that was an accident."

"If you didn't kill her, who did?" I demand.

For a moment, he looks as though he's about to answer. Then the stairs creak. Vance appears, Duchess at his heels, and my heart leaps, but of course he looks to Nick.

"Mr. Dalton?"

Nick sighs. Pushes himself to his feet. "Sorry about this," he says. Then, to Vance, "Don't talk to her. Just keep an eye on her until sunset. We'll move her then."

"Yes, sir."

Nick mutters something under his breath; the stairs creak to mark his retreat.

He says he didn't kill her.

I don't want to believe him. But why lie about that at this point?

I remember. I remember him, I think stubbornly, and I do. But I never saw him shoot her.

Someone else was there.

39

Mr. Vance goes to the window. He takes off his knit cap as he looks out, crushing it between his hands. The front door opens. Closes. Toenails click. Duchess pads into view. She sniffs at me, giving me a curious, concerned look, and then goes to sit next to Vance.

"Why are you doing this?" I ask him.

He looks down at his hands, wringing that gray hat between them. "The Daltons, they're good people. I don't want you thinking they're not. I told you I traveled a bit when I was younger. Got into a bit of trouble. A lot of it, really. Magnus, he was the only person who really believed I was worth anything after that. Gave me a chance to start over. I owe him my life, not that it's ever been of much value. Still. You owe a debt like that, it doesn't get repaid easy."

He turns those sorrowful eyes on me and I want to gouge them out.

I start to speak, but I cough, my mouth still dried out from the drugs and the horrible rag. Mr. Vance makes a sound like *tsch* and comes over, hauling me upright by the elbow and helping me scoot over to lean my back against the bed. He takes a flask from his pocket and puts it to my lips. It's warm from his body and tastes of turpentine, and I cough again, but I can talk.

"They're going to kill me."

He looks at me sadly. He already knows. "It was supposed to be quick. So you wouldn't know," he says.

"You were going to shoot me. After you told me all those things about my mother," I say. "About how much you liked her."

"Mr. Dalton did his best. He tried to protect you. Told you to leave," Mr. Vance says.

"So I've heard."

"That night you came over, that's when I saw it. I worked out who you were and I told him—about the questions you were asking. You shouldn't have asked, is the thing. And I shouldn't have told you, but I didn't—you're all grown up. I didn't recognize you properly, I didn't know. It's not my fault."

Funny, how none of this is anyone's fault.

He scratches the side of his neck with blunt fingernails. "I'm the one who figured out you weren't dead, you know. Back then. Heard you making this little noise, all whimpery. Like a little puppy. I bundled you up, got you warm. Snuck you back to my cabin. Don't know what I was thinking I was going to do after that, only couldn't stand to have anything else happen to you, poor little thing."

He doesn't seem to realize how much this contradicts his rosy view of the Daltons. The only reason he'd need to keep me secret, sneak around, is if they were a danger to me. To a five-year-old child.

"Magnus found me out, of course," he says. "He came up with the plan. A place for you to go. Didn't tell me where."

"And my mother?" I ask. *Blue scarf—she smiles, wraps me up in her arms. Red scarf—she tells me to run.*

"We buried her," he says. "Off in the woods. I made sure to find a nice spot. A really nice spot. There are wildflowers in the summer. Mallory would have liked that."

"Are you going to bury me in the same place, Mr. Vance?" I whisper, and I don't try to hide the fear snaking through the words.

"That's not my call," Vance says, but he looks uncomfortable. "You can't blame them, Miss Scott. You can't blame them wanting to protect their own. She was angry. She wasn't thinking straight."

My brow furrows in confusion. Everything still a bit sloshy from the drugs, and for a moment I think I've missed something. "She? She who?" I say. Louise?

"She just meant to talk to Mallory. The gun was for show, that's all," Vance says.

I can imagine Louise angry easily enough, but threatening someone with a rifle is harder. Louise is the kind of person who lets someone else hold the gun.

But Rose—

Rose is the one who gave me the tea. All that talk was just to draw out what I knew. Rose found out that her husband was cheating on her—or so she thought. She found out where he was stashing them.

She went to confront them.

I had assumed it was Nick. Nick in a rage, storming up here to do god knows what and Liam—Liam, I know now, was protecting me. Protecting us. But I was wrong about who he was protecting me from.

The gun was only for show. But something went wrong. Accident or anger? Does it matter? A pull of the trigger. My mother with her hand on her throat and blood gushing between her fingers, and all of a sudden an affair wasn't what the Daltons needed to cover up.

Mr. Vance sighs. "I better go downstairs. Keep an eye out and all that." He grabs the rag.

"No—" I start, but he jams the rag in, then pulls the cord back up. I make a muffled sound of protest, but it's no use.

"You just wait here," he says, as if I have any other choice.

Duchess stays. She stands, ambles over to me, and sniffs at me once again, nose prodding against my sides. She circles back around and I freeze, heart thudding, waiting for her to bare her teeth. But then she gives a sigh and settles down beside me. She lays her head over my thigh, her eyes dark and wary, ears pricked toward the doorway.

Her breaths are steady. Her body is warm. And with her head nestled in my lap, I shut my eyes and allow myself to weep.

I don't know how long it is before my tears are spent. I train my attention on the steady rise and fall of Duchess's side, calming my own breath to match it.

I have to think—to wrench my mind out of memory and out of the blind panic of my situation and try to imagine a way out of this mess. I have the knife. And I might have a minute or two before Vance comes back.

The knife is easy. It's still in the pocket of my coat, blessedly overlooked in Nick's haste to get me out of there. His urgency suggests there are people on this mountain who aren't part of this. Louise, Vance, Magnus, Rose, Nick—all of them are threats. But there might still be help here.

I have to hope.

I wriggle the knife from my pocket, awkward with my hands tied together, and manage to open it. I contort my hands to get it under the plastic zip tie and saw, but I'm not getting anywhere. Instead I twist, wedging the blade of the knife between the floorboards, and finally there's enough pressure against the tie and it snaps, my hands springing apart. I scrabble at my cheeks, pulling the cord free and spitting out the gag. As I sit up, Duchess hauls herself upward with a slightly annoyed huff, irritated at having her headrest taken away.

"Hush," I say under my breath. "Settle, girl."

She blinks at me. Gives a long stretch. Stands there, as if waiting to see what I'll do next. Warily, I get my legs under me and rise. I wait for her to growl, to bark. Instead her tail fans slightly and she paces forward to fit her blocky head under my hand. I scratch between her ears, and she pants.

"Good girl," I whisper. Now to get out of here.

There's a window next to the bed. We're on the second story—a longer drop than I'd like, but the snow looks soft. I have to hope it will cushion a fall. I unlatch the window, moving with painful slowness, and start to ease open the window.

Two inches up, it sticks. I bite my lip to stop myself from swearing. I wrap my fingers around the bottom of the window. Haul upward—

It gives all at once, scraping another four inches up before thumping as it sticks again.

"What are you doing up there?" Mr. Vance calls.

"Shit," I hiss, and tug at it again, but it won't give. It's far too narrow for me to fit through. Vance's footsteps thunder up the stairs. I strain. Crouching down, I shove my shoulder against the bottom of the window, and it wiggles but won't give.

"Stop it," Mr. Vance orders, and rough hands grab hold of me, pulling me back and spinning me around. I barely have time to flinch as he backhands me, hand cracking against my cheek.

Duchess snarls. She's a blur: black fur, white teeth, pink gums bared as she snaps the air as she launches not at me but at Mr. Vance. He stumbles back in surprise, losing his grip, and I rear back away from him.

"Duchess, down!" he hollers, but she stands between us, hackles bristling and her teeth bared. "What the hell has gotten into you?" he demands. He starts toward me. She half lunges again, teeth snapping a warning, and he skitters back.

I bolt. Past Duchess. Down the stairs. As I dash for the door, my eyes catch on a pale spot above the door—the ghost of a trophy mount, its outline permanently marked by the fading of the wood around it.

The air hits me cold and razor-sharp, and like I did so long ago, I run.

40

The sun is bright against the snow, dazzling my eyes. I can't head to the lodge. Or to White Pine—they'll look for me there first.

But there's one person here I'm certain isn't involved in all this. She might hate me for getting her involved, but I don't have a choice.

I head for Red Fox.

At every step I expect to be spotted, but the woods are empty. I reach the cabin and try the knob—unlocked—and burst inside without knocking.

Sebastian is on the floor with his dinosaurs. Paloma is at the table, hands wrapped around a mug. Alexis stands at the side of the room, a thumbnail tucked between her teeth. All of them are staring at me.

"Theo, what—" Alexis starts, and then Paloma leaps from the chair, running to gather Sebastian in her arms. I realize I'm still holding the knife, brandishing it out in front of me.

I lower it. I shut the door with my foot and hold up my other hand, palm out. "I'm sorry," I say. "I didn't mean to scare you."

"Then put that knife away," Paloma snaps, backing away to put the couch between us. Sebastian squirms in her arms.

"I can't," I say. "Look, I don't have time to explain everything. Is Connor back yet?"

"Connor? He never left," Alexis says, confused. "We thought you went to Datura with Mr. Vance."

I blink, shake my head, confusion spilling through me. I can't sort the lies from the truth anymore. "Do you know where he is?"

"At White Pine, I think," Alexis says. "What's going on?"

"I need to talk to him," I say. "I need one of you to go and get him. Don't tell anyone else that I'm here. Please."

They look at each other. Paloma's grip on Sebastian tightens. "We can go get him. You wait here," she says softly.

"No," I say, wishing I could trust them. "Only one of you goes. The other one stays with me." I don't make it a threat, but they both understand. They exchange another look.

"You go," Alexis says. "Take Bastian."

"Right," Paloma says. "Come on, honey." She walks toward me slowly, shifting Sebastian to the other side of her body.

"Here," Alexis says softly, holding out Paloma's coat. Her hand touches Paloma's briefly.

"Don't tell anyone," I remind her. "Please. It's not safe."

Paloma considers me. Then she nods. "I'll send Connor and I won't say anything to anyone else," she pledges, and I believe her. Or I want to believe her.

I open the door for her. She flinches away from my approach, and then she's striding out the door. I watch long enough to be sure that she's heading in the direction of White Pine before shutting it behind her.

Alexis closes her hands into fists, then releases them. She's such a small woman. Bird-boned. I find myself considering how easily I could overpower her.

"You're hurt," Alexis says. I don't know what she means, but she puts a hand to her cheek, near her mouth, and when I echo the gesture, my skin is tender.

"I'm sorry about this," I say. "I just need help. I didn't actually mean to come in here waving a knife."

"And yet you're still holding it," she says icily.

"I'm sorry," I repeat. "I can't take the risk."

"What risk is that?" she asks. Her voice is level. She's a woman used to dealing with crises, I'm sure. But at the edges of her hand there's a faint tremor.

"That you might tell someone where I am," I say.

"Did you do something?" It's barely above a whisper. "Did you hurt Olena?"

"No. God, no," I assure her, and step forward—only to have her stumble back. I almost want to laugh. I've been so goddamn afraid. It's at least a change of pace, someone being afraid of me. "Nick killed Olena."

"That's ridiculous. Why would he do that?" she demands.

"Because he thought it was me. Look, it's complicated. And you probably wouldn't believe me anyway," I say.

"Try me." Her chin comes up, defiant. I glance toward the door. It'll be a few minutes yet before Connor gets here.

"Did they tell you?" I ask.

"Tell me what?"

"About me. About who I am."

"That whole thing about you being a juvenile delinquent?" she asks. "You stabbed someone, right? Which is not making this look great, I'll be honest."

If I trusted her, I would put down the knife. I would assure her that I meant her no harm. We would sit down together and talk.

But I don't trust Alexis Dalton.

"No. Did they tell you that my birth mother was Mallory Cahill?" I ask. To my surprise, Alexis turns white. She staggers, putting a hand out to catch the back of a kitchen chair. "I take it that's a no."

"That's impossible," Alexis says.

"Why? Because I'm supposed to be dead?" I ask.

She gapes. "What? No. Because—because that's crazy," she says, but her voice is shaking. There's something more there.

There's a knock on the door. I peer through the crack in the curtain, keeping Alexis in view, and I let out a breath of relief when I see Connor standing on the porch. I open the door just enough to let him in, keeping myself out of sight. Immediately he wraps his arms around me.

"Thank god," he says, releasing me. "Granddad told me you'd left, but I knew you wouldn't have gone off alone. Where were you?"

"Tied up in Dragonfly," I say. "Your mother drugged me."

"She *what?*" Connor says.

I run a hand over my head. "She gave me tea, and there was something in it. She told me you were gone—she lied. And I tried to get away, but Nick found me, and he tied me up and put me in Dragonfly. They all knew about it. Magnus, Louise. Mr. Vance."

"But my mother wouldn't do that," Connor says, staring at me. "She wouldn't be involved."

"Mr. Vance told me . . . He said she had a gun. That she didn't mean to," I say, and my anger at Rose is nothing compared to how much I wish I didn't have to do this to Connor. "It was an accident."

"She . . ." His confusion gives way to understanding. The breath goes out of him, and he looks at me with dawning horror. "You think she killed Mallory? My mother isn't capable of something like that. She wouldn't hurt anyone. Vance was wrong."

"No. He wasn't," a soft voice says.

I had almost forgotten that Alexis was there. She hasn't moved from her spot by the table, but now her arms are folded tight across her torso.

"Alexis?" Connor says.

"Mr. Vance wasn't wrong. But it wasn't Mom," Alexis says. She takes a shuddering breath. "It was me. I killed Mallory Cahill."

41

She's not an idiot. She's fifteen; she knows what an affair is. She's noticed her father's disappearing act over the last few weeks. She's heard him on the phone, making arrangements for things to be paid in ways that won't show up on the credit cards. She saw him buy those expensive gifts and she knew they weren't for his kids, his wife. So when Connor tells her about the woman living on the mountain, she knows exactly what it means.

She doesn't say anything. Not at first. Not until she hears Mom on the phone.

I thought you should know, her mother says. And *I'm giving him the papers as soon as he gets home.*

The papers are at the bottom of her mother's dresser drawer. She sees them and she knows what it means. What will happen.

She has never felt like this before. Rage and despair and panic, like she's trapped and she'll do anything to claw her way out. Her parents can't divorce. They love each other. They aren't like other parents who split up—they don't fight, they laugh together, they sneak away for a private moment anytime they can. She knows their marriage is good. *Was* good.

Which means that something has to have caused this. Some*one.*

The Other Woman. She's never understood the anger the phrase provokes until now. Her father is a good man and her parents' marriage is strong, so it has to be this woman's fault, and everything will be okay if only she's gone. Her mother isn't going to do it. Rose Dalton bears hardship gracefully. She smiles; she says, *We will get through this,* as if that's the only option.

Alexis knows that sometimes you have to do more than endure.

Her dad's been teaching her how to drive. She's not old enough for a license. But she looks older, especially when she borrows her mother's clothes, wears her favorite sunglasses. Paloma always gets carded, but she hardly ever does.

She takes her mother's car. She puts the rifle in the trunk. She isn't going to use it, but it makes her feel more secure to have it. What does she know about this woman? She could be dangerous. She can't be a good person, not if she's doing this to their family. The gun will make her listen. The gun will make her understand.

The first part of the drive is easy. Cop cars pass her and don't even glance twice. She checks her reflection in the mirror. No sign of tears. Red lipstick that Paloma bought her because it makes her look like a forties movie star. She looks twenty-three, at least. She feels invincible.

She isn't expecting how difficult the drive up the mountain proves to be. The road has been partially cleared, but she's never had to drive in snow like this, and the car slews, mires, lurches. She's white-knuckled by the time she reaches the top, leaned over the steering wheel and panting, and she ditches the car by the gate rather than go farther. She can't remember the code anyway. She gets the rifle from the trunk. Hoofs it.

She sees the woman from behind first. Standing by an old brown sedan, shoving things into the back seat. She has dirty blond hair, the kind that looks like dishwater, with cheap highlights shot through it. She's skinny as a stick. Maybe that's why Dad looked at her at all, tired of Rose with her three-children body and no time for the gym, and this fills Alexis's adolescent heart with righteous fury.

And then the woman turns. That bony face, those too-big eyes, and they stare at each other for a moment of startled silence before the woman says, "Who the hell are you?" and Alexis realizes that as many times as she's planned the biting words she'll say, they don't actually add up to anything but raw hurt. She can't string them together into something sensible, so she stammers.

"I don't have time for this," the woman says, and starts to turn away, to dismiss her, to *ignore* her. Alexis raises the rifle.

"Stop," she says. The woman freezes, mouth opening in a little O of surprise, and a jolt of satisfaction goes through Alexis's belly. This feels like power. It feels like justice.

"Look, I don't know what this is about—" the woman starts, and Alexis snarls.

"You don't know what it's about? You don't know who I am? My name is Alexis Dalton. You're fucking my father."

The woman has the audacity to look puzzled. "Alexis? You're Liam's daughter," she says, realization dawning. "No. Alexis. You don't—"

"You don't get to talk," Alexis says. She is aware that there are tears streaming down her face. "You have to listen. You can't have him. You can't do this to our family. You're going to leave, okay? You're going to leave and you're never going to come back."

The woman laughs.

She *laughs*.

"What the fuck do you think I'm trying to do?" she says. "Alexis, just—" And she steps forward.

She steps forward and reaches out.

She steps forward, and the movement is sudden—

And she *laughed*—

And she's reaching for the gun—

And she's destroying *everything*—

And Alexis is startled.

It's the surprise that makes her finger spasm on the trigger.

It's the anger.

It's the way she lunged forward so suddenly.

She laughed.

The shot splits the air.

42

I didn't mean to. I swear I didn't mean to."

The buzzing is back. That drone of insect wings. I stare at Alexis, but it's like the individual features don't add up to anything. Lips, eyes, curve of a cheek, pert nose—not a face. Not a person.

She's still talking. "I should have tried to help her, but I . . . I ran. Dad was there, somehow—he asked me what had happened. I told him I'd killed her. He told me to go to Mr. Vance's cabin. He said to stay there, no matter what, until he came to get me. So I did. I stayed. But Dad never came back. It was Grandpa who came to get me. Because Dad, he—he—" She chokes on her own tears.

"Paloma told me he killed himself," I say. Told me that Alexis believed it, at least. Connor's hand tightens on my shoulder. I'm not sure if it's meant to be comfort or if it's meant to hold me back.

"It's my fault." Her voice is small, fifteen and lost all over again. She takes a steadying breath. "Granddad and Grandma told me what to do. Which was nothing, basically. Pretend it didn't happen. Go along with the story. Don't ask questions."

It was Alexis. Not Rose at all. I should have seen it. How they leapt in to cover for her. Louise, Magnus, Nick—flocking together to shield their little princess from the consequences of what she'd done. No matter the cost.

Even if that cost was me.

"Did you ever bother to ask what happened to me?" My voice is a growl. It sounds like a stranger's.

Her eyes are wide, frantic. "I didn't know about you. Not until later. And I did ask. They said you went to live with family. That you hadn't seen anything, and they were making sure you were taken care of, they said not to worry."

"I almost died out there," I say. "And when I didn't, they dumped me in the middle of nowhere with strangers. I didn't even know my own name. The only thing I remember about my mother is what she looked like when she was dying, and you—"

She was attending her private schools. Kissing her girlfriend. Getting an Ivy League degree, getting married on an island, enjoying every perk of being a Dalton. It doesn't matter what you do. It matters who you are. She's a Dalton.

I'm no one.

There's only one way this is supposed to turn out. "Did you know who I was?" I ask.

"Not until literally just now," she says.

"So you didn't know what they've been doing. Your grandparents, Nick, your mom—that they tried to kill me, to cover up what *you* did?" I demand.

"No. I swear, no, and I never would have asked them to," she babbles.

"Your grandparents promised you it would all be taken care of, didn't they? You wouldn't get in any trouble. They're not about to let that promise be broken," I say.

"But they can't—they wouldn't do anything like *that*," Alexis says. I look at her steadily. And then I turn to Connor.

"We have to get out of here," I say. He's staring at his sister. His gaze is burned hollow. "Connor."

His eyes snap to me. "Right," he says. "How?"

"One of the UTVs," I suggest. "Nick had one. I don't know where it went. But there should be another at Mr. Vance's cabin. Do you know the way? I went there once, but I don't know if I can find it again."

"Yeah. Back road. Not hard to find." Connor's losing words, losing his grip. I lace my fingers through his. *We can do this,* I try to tell him.

"Wait. What are you going to do?" Alexis asks.

"We're going to leave," Connor says, but it's clear what Alexis is asking.

"Are you going to . . . when you get back, will you . . ." She can't say it.

I step toward her. She flinches but holds her ground. "Alexis, your family is trying to kill me to protect you."

"No," she says, but it isn't a real denial. It's a child's wish.

"Olena died because Nick thought she was me," I grind out. "Do you really want to see what happens if he gets another chance?"

"Please," she whispers. I can't tell what she's asking for. For me to keep her secret—or for none of this to have happened at all? "Connor, I—"

"Don't say another fucking word," Connor growls. She shies back, her whole body shrinking in on itself. "If you can't help, stay out of the way."

There's so much pain in her eyes. She killed my mother. She took my whole life from me. Part of me wants her to hold every part of that hurt and never let it go, no matter how much it tears into her. But not all of it is hers to bear.

Connor opens the door, but I pause, looking back toward Alexis.

"Your father didn't kill himself," I tell her bluntly. "They lied about that, too."

I don't wait to see her reaction.

We leave Alexis in Red Fox and head into the woods.

43

We don't take the path. They'll be looking for us—for me. Our only advantage is that there are still people here who would ask questions if they were too obvious about it. Subtlety will slow them down.

And Connor knows this mountain.

It's beautiful out here, I think. The sun has broken through the clouds and the fresh snow glitters and gleams in every direction. The stately trees are robed in pale finery, the deep emerald of the evergreens peering through.

We lived in an enchanted forest, my mother and I. For a little while.

Connor looks back at me, and I remember it again, spinning in the snow—laughter bubbling, going faster and faster. Despite everything, despite the knowledge of what is pursuing us, I smile, and Connor's lips bend in answer, and for a brief moment it is just the two of us beneath this canopy of branches, and this place is as magical as it was meant to be.

But we can't stop. This isn't that sort of fairy tale. Not the one with the princess singing to woodland creatures and the prince who rides to her rescue, but the kind where witches dance on hot coals and farmer girls have their hands cut off by their loving fathers.

"This way," Connor says. It's the first either of us have spoken, and the sound sends a black crow into flight, croaking its discontent. Our path bends. We're heading downhill now, and the going is easier. We come to the road. It's untroubled by wheel treads, which I decide to take as a good sign. We travel parallel to a set of heavy tracks leading in a single direction—the opposite of the one we're taking. So Vance is gone, and he hasn't returned.

More good news. Which ought to be a sign that our luck can't last, but still I'm beginning to hope that we will be away and free in moments when the sound of an engine rumbles in the middle distance.

Connor pauses only long enough to look at me, both of us confirming in that moment what we heard, and then we speed up.

The engine is definitely getting closer. I almost cry out in relief as the side of Vance's cabin comes into view. We sprint for the UTV, which is sitting parked right where I saw it last.

"Keys?" Connor says.

"Inside?" I suggest. Connor runs to the door. Locked. He takes his gloved fist and without a second's hesitation punches through a window beside the door. He reaches through, ignoring the shards of glass left behind, and screws up his face as he contorts his arm to get at the lock. There.

I run past him. The keys. Where did Vance put the keys? I have a vague memory of a drawer opening, a clink of metal. I run to the tiny kitchen area and start yanking drawers open and there they are. I toss them to Connor and follow him out.

The motor is not a growl but a roar now, and still getting closer. Whoever it is must have seen our tracks and guessed where we were going.

Connor straddles the UTV. I sling a leg over behind him and wrap my arms around his middle as he starts it up. He doesn't give me any warning before the vehicle surges forward with a deafening snarl of the engine.

"Hold on!" he yells. We slew to the left and down the road.

This is not like the road we took to get up here. It's narrow and winding and it drops on one side with barely two inches to spare, and it would be terrifying even without the snow masking it and the other vehicle still getting closer. Connor jerks the handlebars to bring us around a sharp turn and I look over my shoulder and see the dark forest green of the other UTV, and Nick riding it.

"Connor," I say in a tone of warning.

"I know!" He slows as we approach another turn. Nick doesn't. The slope slices away to our left, a short, sharp drop and snow-scattered rocks at the bottom.

I twist, looking back at Nick again. He's stopped. For a moment I'm elated, and then confused—and then I watch as he takes the rifle from his shoulder. Levels it.

"Gun!" I scream as the first shot rings out. Connor's hands jerk and so does the UTV. Something pings against the rocks beside us. *Missed, he missed,* I think, and then a second shot splits the air, and Connor gives a startled grunt. He lurches forward in his seat. The UTV swerves.

Toward the edge.

Over it.

I lose my grip. First I'm falling through nothing, and then my shoulder crunches against the ground and I'm tumbling down the slope. I wrap my arms around my head just as I slam into the rocks at the bottom.

All the breath goes out of me. My vision fills with bright lights. I lie in the snow, stunned, my face pressed against the ground. I can't move. I can't think. I can't see where Connor has landed.

The sun is nearly gone. And in that near darkness, a single light shines above. Too bright to be a star, I think. It's not supposed to look like that.

And for a moment, the present slips away, and I exist only in memory.

The man hasn't moved in a long time. Not since he fell. For a while his body offered hers some warmth, but all of it is gone now. The amber glow of the star remained longer, but she can no longer keep her eyes open. She can no longer move at all.

Some part of her marks the crunch of footsteps, the voice, low and angry—

"What did you do?"

"He came at me. I was defending myself."

"And the girl? She come at you, too?"

"I didn't touch her."

"How long have you been standing there?"

Silence. A disgusted sound and then hands on her body, on her neck. Fingers pressed against her throat, and more quiet. "She's dead."

The voice is wrong, of course. There is still, deep in her chest, the faintest flicker of a heartbeat. The cold is killing her, but its work isn't done yet.

"What are we going to do?"

"We? You're the one who did this."

"Am I?"

"What are you talking about?"

"Maybe you don't give a shit about me, Dad. But what about your darling granddaughter?"

"Get Vance. We need to clean this up."

The cold sinks through me. The single star glares, so bright it's nearly blinding, and for a muddled instant I can't remember where—when—I am. The light isn't the glowing end of a cigarette but the headlight of the UTV, and the silhouette cutting through it is Nick. He has to turn to face the slope to descend safely, his back to me. Farther along the hillside, I can make out Connor's brown coat, the bulk of his body. He isn't moving.

Unconscious, I tell myself. Not dead. He can't be dead.

My hand is by my pocket. I dip my fingers inside. The knife is still there. I draw it out. My numb fingers fumble with the blade, but then it's open. Nick reaches the bottom of the slope. I let my arm lie limp, the knife itself hidden in the pocket. I keep my eyes shut to slits and I don't move. Don't breathe.

"Teddy," Nick says softly. "Teddy, can you hear me?" He steps so close I can feel him. His boots scrape as he crouches down, leans over me. "You still alive, Teddy?" he asks, and grabs my shoulder, pulling me over. I make my body stay limp. He grunts. Strips the glove from his hand. Reaches for the side of my neck.

The knife comes out of my pocket. I drive upward, shoving against the hard ground with my other hand. The blade goes in under his armpit and he howls, throwing himself backward. The knife comes free with a liquid sound, and ignoring the sharp pain in my back, my shoulder, my neck, I scrabble upright and launch myself at him.

No use going for the heart. Too many bones in the way; I learned that lesson once.

The throat will do.

He gets a hand up. Gets a blade through his palm for his trouble, and this one's harder to pull out. He's clawing for the rifle, but it's trapped under him. He's out of good hands. Closes the bloodied one around my neck anyway and squeezes hard. Instead of pulling away, I go slack. The sudden weight takes him by surprise. His elbow collapses and then we're face-to-face and there's nothing between me and the soft skin of his throat.

"Should have made sure I was dead," I tell him. And I drive the knife up beneath his jaw.

44

Don't get too close to a dying animal. Prey is not helpless and every predator can bleed.

I don't make Nick's mistake. I'm certain he's dead before I pull the knife free and push myself, legs trembling from the effort, to my feet. I look down at him, eyes bulging, tongue thrust half out of his mouth, blood a solid wash across his stubbled neck, and I feel not an ounce of regret.

He stood there. He watched me die. Waiting for the cold to do its work because he was too much of a coward to do it himself—or maybe it was only that he was smart enough to know that fewer questions would be asked about a girl dead from exposure than one with a necklace of bruises, a bullet in the back.

He watched Liam die, too.

More lies. More stories not lining up. There was no suicide. Horror and shame didn't drive Liam to his death, a blow to the head did, and Alexis got fed a story that kept her cowed. Her guilt kept her silent. But now it's over, I tell myself, and in the same instant I know it isn't remotely true.

"Theo." Connor staggers toward me. The side of his face is scraped to hell and he's holding his arm tight against his body, the opposite hand clapped over the spot where blood blooms on his arm, but he's breathing, he's upright, he's *alive*.

He stares at me, and I know what he sees. Blood on my clothes. On my hands. On my neck, where Nick grabbed it, on the knife still clutched in my hand. I brace myself for him to shy away from me.

But he only walks forward slowly. Eyes flicking to Nick, away. He reaches out, his own hand slick with crimson, and pulls me to him. He kisses me. Not rough, not tender; this kiss is needful, certain.

"You're okay," he says. And then, pulling away, looking into my eyes, "You're okay?"

I nod, a tremor of a gesture. "Your arm—"

"It's not great," he says tightly. What he means is that it's bleeding, though not so much that it seems like it hit something vital. He's wearing his gray scarf; I take it from around his neck and tie it tight around the wound, making him hiss in pain. It's makeshift, but it seems to slow the bleeding. "It went right through. I think—I think I'll be all right." He sounds queasy.

"We'll get you help," I say, trying to keep my voice from shaking and failing. I almost lost him. Almost lost everything.

"Let's get out of here," he says.

We should run. Take Nick's ATV and get down the mountain and away from here.

And they will chase us. Chase me.

Rowan, hide.

I'm not her anymore. I am done hiding. It's time to bare my teeth.

"We're going back to the lodge," I say. Connor looks at me like I've lost my mind. I touch the side of his hand. "Do you trust me?" I ask.

He thinks for a long time. I wait. I'm not offended. I want him to decide. To be sure. "I trust you," he says.

"Then help me get the gun."

45

The lodge is a beacon in the night. Every light is on, and through the vast picture windows I can make out figures in the living room. We've turned off our flashlights, but the light reflecting off the snow is enough that if they look toward us, they'll see us.

"You ready?" I ask Connor.

"Nope," he says, and keeps walking.

They're all in the living room when we enter. Everyone but Sebastian—even Paloma is here, standing in the corner of the room with one shoulder against the wall and a glass of purplish wine in her hand, her thoughts clearly a million miles away; I wonder what Alexis told her. Then Louise looks up and her eyes widen, then narrow.

"What the fuck?" Trevor says; Rose gives a cry. Alexis reaches for her drink, hand trembling, and Magnus does not move at all, sitting in his place of primacy in a wingback chair.

"Oh, good. Everyone's already here," Connor says. "Sit down, Mom."

"You're hurt." She's on her feet, reaching for him.

"Rose, sit down," Magnus says. She looks at him, back at Connor, conflicted. Then, obedient, she sinks down to the couch.

"Trevor, you too," Connor says. Trevor is standing behind the couch. With a look of indifference that almost conceals the flicker of concern in his eyes, he rounds the couch and sits between his mother and sister, crossing an ankle over his knee and winging his arms out over the back of the couch in a faux casual pose. I can see the pulse at his neck, beating fast.

"Where is Nick?" Magnus asks.

"Not here," I say. Magnus's eyes narrow, but I'm not ready to give him a conclusive answer.

"Connor, what's happening?" Rose asks.

"What's happening is that this family has been keeping too many secrets for far too long, and it's time to get them out in the open," Connor says. He looks to Paloma. "Is Sebastian okay?"

"Sleeping upstairs," she says.

"You can go, if you want," I tell her. She isn't part of this.

"I think I'd like to stay," she says. Everyone else is seated—Rose, Trevor, and Alexis on the couch, Louise and Magnus in the chairs to either side of it. Quite the tableau.

"Well?" Louise snaps.

"Okay, I'll start." I step forward. "My name is Theo Scott, but it wasn't always. I was born Rowan Cahill. Mallory Cahill was my mother." It feels important to say it out loud; it feels sacred.

"Holy shit," Trevor says, mouth dropping open. Rose lets out a noise and covers her mouth, but it might be an act. Louise and Magnus don't look surprised, and of course Alexis isn't, either.

"Mallory Cahill? That was . . ." Paloma begins, brow creased as she recalls the name.

"Liam's little mistress," Louise says, fingers tapping on the arm of the chair.

"That's a lie," Connor growls.

"Connor," Rose says softly, "I know that you have never wanted to believe it. I know that you loved him. I did, too. But good people make terrible mistakes sometimes."

"Connor's right. Liam wasn't sleeping with my mother," I say. To Alexis, I add, "Those photos you found. He helped her take them so that she'd have proof of what Nick was doing to her. He was hiding her until she could figure out where to go next."

"No. That can't—" Alexis says. Conflicting needs war within her. If her father wasn't having an affair, one kind of pain is eased. But that means that her anger that day was utterly misplaced. A senseless thing made all the more wretched.

"He didn't tell you, Rose. He didn't tell anyone. Because he was trying to keep her safe. Which you knew, didn't you." I look at Magnus. At Louise.

"I won't let you say these things about my son," Louise says. "Nick would never—"

"She'd tried to leave him before," Magnus interrupts. His head is bowed, hands laced. "He nearly killed her. Threatened to kill you." His eyes lift to mine, and something passes between us. Acknowledgment, maybe. It's time for the truth, and we both know it. "Liam was setting her up with a place to go under a new name."

"I thought it was her fault," Alexis says, almost a whisper. "I wouldn't have . . . I didn't know."

Rose turns to look at her, but it's Paloma who speaks. "Lex, what did you do?" she asks, voice hoarse.

Alexis stands. Her hands twist together. "I came—I was just going to talk to her. I didn't mean for it to happen."

"Alexis, we don't need to do this," Louise says.

"Yes, we do." I step forward. "Alexis, tell them."

She draws a ragged breath, steels herself. "I drove up here. I brought Dad's rifle. Mallory was here. We argued, and I—I shot her."

Rose lets out a moan. Paloma braces a fist against her stomach, drawing in a sharp breath.

"You understand why we didn't tell you the truth," Louise says to Rose. "Alexis made a mistake. A wretched, terrible mistake, one that we have tried to stop from causing any more suffering."

"You covered up a murder," I scoff.

"An *accident*. One that could have destroyed Alexis's life, too. Or would the world have been a better place with her sitting in a jail cell this whole time?"

"Alexis, it's really true?" Rose asks in a soft voice. Alexis nods miserably.

"You didn't know?" Connor asks, giving her a hard look.

"Of course not."

"But you drugged Theo."

"What?" She looks so genuinely startled, I have to believe her.

"Oh, don't be absurd," Louise scoffs. She brushes the air with a dismissive hand. "I made the tea. I took care of things. The way they should have been taken care of years ago."

She rises to her feet. Connor tenses, but I put a hand on his arm. The last thing we need to do is start shooting.

"Now listen. It's true. Mallory was murdered. And Liam, rest his soul, couldn't face the truth of what his daughter had done, and he killed himself. But we cannot change what happened. We can only decide what to do now. Let's consider what we have here. Theodora Scott. A young woman from a troubled background with a history of violence, promiscuity, and criminal behavior. A woman who has targeted and harassed our family, seduced Connor, invented this wild story."

"She's not—" Connor begins, but I stop him.

"No. Please, Louise. Finish," I say.

She huffs a breath. "What I am saying is that we have a choice about what story we tell here. Is it the one that lands your daughter—*your* wife," she adds, flinging a glance at Paloma, "in prison? Not to mention maybe the rest of us for covering it up. Or is it a story about a disturbed woman who infiltrated our home? Concocted a wild fantasy. Tried to blackmail us. A violent woman who went so far as to murder Olena."

"Olena fell," Trevor says, straightening up.

Louise looks smug. "The autopsy will find that she was struck multiple times. And the police will find evidence clearly linking Ms. Scott to the crime. As well as a confession."

In the form of a suicide note, no doubt. "So that was the plan?" I ask. "Tell me. Was it your idea to kill Olena, or did Nick do that all on his own?"

"He thought it was you, you little bitch," Louise snaps, and Rose gives a small gasp. Trevor is watching his grandmother intently. That pulse point at his neck is thudding away.

"Where is Nick?" Rose demands.

He stepped in to help, after Liam died. She relied on him. He was her friend. Her ally. A father to her children. I wish that I didn't have to do this.

"He's dead," I say.

"No," Louise says, a flat denial. "No. He—he isn't, he—"

Rose lets out a sob. Trevor growls. "Good."

"Trevor," Magnus says warningly.

"Didn't she just say he killed Olena? He was, what, beating that woman? Which shouldn't come as a shock to you, Grandpa, given that it's your lawyer helping him get out of doing the same fucking thing to his wife," Trevor says. "Uncle Nick, what a fucking hero. Great guy, shame about the bit where he loves to hurt women."

"You're one to talk," Alexis snarls.

"I never meant to hurt Kayla," Trevor snaps. "Olena was—she was sweet. She didn't deserve this. Nick—fuck." He jams the heels of his hands against his eyes.

"You're sure," Rose says.

"Mom, he shot me," Connor says. He gestures to his arm.

"That's a lie," Louise insists, but her voice is high and shaky. "He wouldn't have hurt you. This was to protect the family."

"He killed his own brother," I say.

"No," Louise says. "That's absurd. Liam killed himself." She looks at Magnus. Her hand grips the arm of the chair, blanching her knuckles white. "Liam killed himself, you told me that."

"Epidural hematoma," Connor says. "Dad died of a blow to the brain. I saw the report. There were no wounds that could have been suicide."

Alexis swallows. "You said they lied. But why would they—"

"They told you it was suicide to keep you quiet," I tell Alexis. "To make it all your fault. But it wasn't just the two of you up there. Nick was there, too."

Alexis's face is blank. Uncomprehending. Paloma reaches for her, but Alexis doesn't seem to register it—and then all at once her knees buckle. Paloma lunges just in time, catching her and lowering her to the floor. She holds Alexis against her chest, shushing her like a child, but Alexis isn't making any sound at all, her eyes fixed wide and her body trembling.

"Magnus," Louise says, and for the first time I see a hint of fear in her eyes, of things slipping away from her. "That isn't true. Is it?"

Magnus leans forward, wincing as if in pain. "They fought. Liam took a blow to the head. It was unintentional."

"Bullshit. He could have lived if he'd gotten help," I say. "Nick watched us. Liam fell and he wouldn't get up and I didn't know what to do, so I stayed with him in the snow. And I could see Nick standing there. Waiting for us to die."

Louise's hands flutter, as if attempting to grasp at something invisible. "Magnus," she says again, as if she's pleading with him to deny it, but he looks perfectly calm.

"It was over when I got there," Magnus says. "I did what I could to limit the damage. Including not sharing information that would only hurt people."

"But telling Alexis that her dad killed himself because of her, that was fine?" I shoot back. Magnus interlaces his fingers before him and offers no answer.

Louise lays her palms firmly on the arms of the chair. She stares into the distance for a long moment, and then she squares her shoulders. "None of this changes what we need to do," she says deliberately. "We have to protect our family. We need—"

"Oh, fuck you, Grandma," Connor says. The whole room falls to shocked silence. "Protect our family? You mean protect our reputation. Protect a killer."

"I mean that we need to protect your sister. Alexis," Louise says.

Alexis is still kneeling, but she's upright now. Paloma's arms are around her loosely. Alexis's eyes are fixed on the floor. Her jaw clenches. I can imagine what she's thinking. She's not her grandmother. She doesn't want me dead. But still, there's that voice, that instinct for self-preservation.

She killed someone. You don't just get to walk away from that.

"If we make the right decisions here, this is a tragedy, not a disaster," Louise says. "Think about the consequences if all this gets out. Or we all agree on what happened, and—"

"No," Alexis says. Her eyes look sunken, ringed with dark circles. "I'll confess. I'm not going to go along with it any longer. I never should have."

"Don't do this to yourself," Louise says. "To your family. You—"

"Lou," Magnus says. She falters. He stands up. Connor tenses, but Magnus only puts his hands in his pockets and looks around at everyone, as if taking in the scene. "I'd like to speak to Theo alone."

"Like hell," Connor says.

Magnus meets my eyes. I think part of me has always understood Magnus, the way that he has always understood me. "It's all right," I say. Connor looks bewildered, but Magnus nods. He holds out a hand, a genteel gesture to usher me out of the room.

"We can speak in the study," he says.

"Theo, what are you doing?" Connor keeps his voice low. I squeeze his hand once.

"Don't worry. I'll be right back," I tell him.

He doesn't stop me. Neither does anyone else. Behind us, the room is deathly silent as I exit, Magnus following behind.

46

Magnus says nothing as we make our way to the study. I step inside and pause; he closes the door and walks past me, to the sideboard where a decanter of Scotch sits.

"Drink?" he asks.

"Is this one drugged?"

He laughs. "A little late for that, don't you think?" He pours himself a measure, sips, and then stands tilting the glass to examine the liquid. "I used to hate Scotch, you know. I drank it only because it seemed like it was what I was supposed to do. Part of the businessman image. Somewhere along the way, I forgot that I didn't like it."

He pours another glass and holds it out to me, but I don't move. He shrugs.

"Suit yourself."

"Why are we here, Magnus?" I ask.

"I did try to save you, you know," Magnus says.

"I know. You sent me those messages. Left me that gift," I say.

"And I didn't tell a soul. The only people up here who knew you survived were myself and Mr. Vance, and I knew I could trust his silence," Magnus tells me. "Louise wouldn't have allowed it. Nick certainly wouldn't."

"Am I supposed to thank you?" I ask.

"No. But I want you to consider the fact that I am not an unreasonable man. Even when you came here, I gave you every opportunity. I took the time to ascertain whether you were aware of who you were. Whether you remembered what had happened. I waited as long as I could, but when Mr. Vance came to me and told me he'd given you

Mallory's things, I knew that my hopes were unfounded. It couldn't be avoided."

"So you tried to have me killed."

He savors a sip of his drink. "Nick worked it out that day, of course, and told Louise. I don't know if she'll ever forgive me."

"She's more ruthless than you are," I observe. "I don't know if that surprises me."

"She isn't the one who has to get her hands dirty," Magnus says. "She's never taken a life. She doesn't understand the cost. But she also isn't wrong about the consequences of what's happened here today. It will be disaster. Not just for me or for her. For the whole family, the company. Connor's trust fund, his inheritance, is largely in company shares, did you know that? Everything that funds the lifestyle of this family."

"Tragic," I say.

"Then there's the stain on the family name," Magnus goes on. "Alexis could go to prison. Sebastian would lose his mother. Connor and Trevor wouldn't escape that taint, no matter that they had nothing to do with it."

"Like that's a good enough reason to cover up murder? You heard Alexis. She wants to confess. She's done living with this secret."

"And that would be a great tragedy, given that she is not a killer," Magnus says. I lapse into startled silence. Magnus takes a deep draft of his drink. "The bullet caught Mallory in the neck. A dangerous wound, to be sure, but not an immediately fatal one."

I stare at him. The smell of his Scotch mixes with the smell of the blood drying on my clothes. "Then how did my mother die?"

This is how it starts: a phone call, Vance's worried voice.

Your girl's here. Something's wrong. Won't say anything, except she didn't mean to do it.

She won't say anything to you, either. Her father won't answer his phone; neither will your younger son. It's up to you to find out what's happening. To control the situation. You're not far from the mountain. Still, it's past nightfall when you make your way up the road, heading for the gate.

The woman appears like a specter. She's pale, staggering. There's a scarf wrapped around her neck, soaked through with blood, but she's upright. She has a phone in one hand. You get out of the car slowly. She falls to her knees at the sight of you, as if the chance of help has robbed her of her strength.

"Please," she says. "I can't find them. My daughter—" Her voice is weak. She is weak. Your mind is on that phone call.

"What happened?" you ask her.

"Alexis," she says. "She was here—I tried to tell her—she had the gun, and—" Her eyes are glassy, unfocused. She looks down at her phone. "There's a signal," she says, with a shuddering exhale of relief. She starts to put in the number.

There are decisions you make little by little. Decisions made by degrees; decisions made with consideration, weighing the options. But in moments like these, there isn't time for that. Moments like these need men who can take everything in and do what needs to be done, without hesitation.

"I've got it," you say, and she gives you the phone, because why wouldn't she? You walk away from her. You speak into the phone, play-acting. When you return, she's still kneeling, still shivering.

"My daughter," she says. "She's still up there, and Nick—"

"It will be all right," you assure her. You put a blanket down on the back seat. Put her on it. You drive up the mountain.

You need to control the situation.

You find the car. Blood in the snow; bloody tracks leading every which way. You tell her to wait, that you'll be right back. You follow the tracks to the cabin, find it empty. Then farther out. The tracks are confused, the night dark. You lose your way, backtrack, find it again.

They're already dead by the time you find your youngest son. His brother and the girl both. "What did you do?" you ask.

"I didn't do anything," he says.

Your eldest son is dead. So is this child, whoever she is.

You need to control the situation.

You walk back to the car. She's still alive. Weaker than before. Her breath is fluttery. Her eyes have trouble focusing. When she speaks, you can't hear her; you have to lean close.

"Did you find them?" she asks. "My daughter. Liam. Are they okay?"

"Everyone is fine. They're on their way here now," you tell her.

She says "Thank you" the same moment you put the knife in her chest. The same hunting knife you've kept on your belt every time you come up to this place, the talisman that tells you that you've tripped over the boundary between the outside world and the world of the mountain.

You know how to make a clean kill. She doesn't suffer. She dies thinking her child is safe, and maybe that's a mercy. So you tell yourself as you drag her body out of the car, lay it in the snow.

Control the situation.

You do what has to be done.

47

I take my hand from my pocket. The knife rests in my palm, open, the blade still stained with Nick's blood. I stare at it, my fingers tightening.

"You can kill me with that knife. There'd be a certain poetic justice in that," Magnus says. "Or you can go down off this mountain and tell everyone exactly what happened. But I'm never going to see the inside of a prison cell."

"You don't think they'll believe me? Or Alexis? Connor?" I ask.

"Oh, I'm sure you'll convince them. But the thing is, I'm dying." He quirks his eyebrows, his tone ironic. "Pancreatic cancer. I have maybe eight months or a year left to live, at most. I'd rather not spend all that time on a trial. So I'll make a deal with you. We all leave here with the same story. Nick killed Olena and tried to frame you for it. When you found out, he tried to kill you, too. His death was a matter of self-defense. Terrible, of course. We'll take a hit. But he doesn't work for the company. We'll denounce his actions thoroughly, and invite you—Theodora Scott, you understand, not Rowan Cahill—into our family. You and Connor will get married in a beautiful ceremony, and the world will see how you've forgiven us. Everyone gets their happy ending, and you get to know that I'm rotting in the ground."

My hands feel frostbitten, numb. I can feel every ridge of the knife in my hand, the texture of the antler it's carved from. Was it a deer Magnus killed himself? I wonder.

He takes another sip of his drink, then holds out the one he poured for me. "Are you sure you don't want any?"

"Why would I agree to any of that?" I ask him.

"Because it is the kindest outcome, don't you think? You and Connor get to have your life together, with the resources and comfort that he is due. Rose and Paloma and Sebastian are all taken care of. Trevor, too, I suppose, though I'm sure he'll find a way to squander it. Nick is dead. I will be dead. That's not enough?"

"No, it's not enough," I bite out. "That's not justice."

"Justice, my dear, is not an option," Magnus says with a hint of regret. "I am not going to suffer, no matter what you choose to do. Kill me now and you'll be robbing me of a scant few months of what I'm told is likely to be agonizing pain, while leaving yourself in legal peril. You killed a man today, Theo. Expose me, and I'll endure a great deal of annoyance at the end of my life, but little more. Accept the terms, and you will have all of the protection of any Dalton. We take care of our own, Theo, and that includes you. But only if you agree."

The knife warms in my hand. It would be so easy to let it find the soft parts of him. He says I can't make him suffer? I'm certain I could find a way.

He makes a noise in the back of his throat, like he's forgotten something. "Ah. But I'll tell you what. There is one more thing you are owed, and which I will be happy to grant, if you agree."

"And what's that?" I ask.

"I'll tell you where your mother is buried," he says. My hand jerks in an involuntary spasm. "If you refuse, I promise you—you will never find her. So make your choice."

My mother. My throat closes up. Images swarm through my mind, but I know that they aren't truly my memories. I don't remember my mother's face. I know it from photographs, that's all. She will always be a stranger to me, a ghost. But I could find her. I could lift her up from the cold earth and I could give her a proper burial.

I could say goodbye.

I step toward him, the knife in my hand. He holds his ground. He does not flinch.

I set the knife on the silver tray beside him, fingers uncurling slowly from around the grip.

"Theo?" he says. "What is your decision?"

I walk away from him. Out into the foyer, where the Christmas tree still looms, all twinkling lights and silver and gold baubles. Connor is there, waiting for me.

"Are you all right?" he asks.

I reach out, take his hand. Mine is creased with blood and dirt. His is pale and soft, but he grips me tightly.

"I'm all right," I tell him. I swallow. "And I know what I need to do."

48

The dream comes, as it often does. The buzz of the dragonfly's wings and the red star and the antlered man. I had thought knowing the truth would change it, but it was never a lie to be altered. Only a truth I didn't understand.

Soft pressure against my arm wakes me. The blunt nose of a black-furred dog, her ears pricked with worry. She can always tell. She knows, somehow, to wake me.

"Hey, girl," I say, digging my fingers into Duchess's fur. "It's okay." She huffs, unconvinced, and noses my hand again. Beside me, Connor stirs in his sleep. I slide out from under the covers, quiet as to not wake him, and pad into the living room with Duchess on my heels. The sun is just starting to come up, a seam of light at the horizon. One of those moments where the world seems to pause.

We got married in the spring, Connor and I. Fools rushing in, maybe, but neither of us wanted to wait. It was a tiny ceremony—Harper and Rose as our witnesses at the courthouse, and dinner afterward at our apartment. It's a nice apartment, not far from the bookstore. Smaller than Connor is used to, but then, he's not as rich as he used to be. He salvaged what he could after Magnus cut him off. He thought for a while of giving away most of it to charitable causes, but I convinced him not to. Call it blood money if you want—I figure I earned it, after everything that happened on the mountain.

Everything that happened after.

Magnus kept his word. When the police arrived, it was to arrest me. For ten days, despite Connor's protestations of my innocence, it looked like Magnus's story—that I had killed Olena and Nick as well—would be believed. But Magnus's control over his family was not as thorough as he anticipated.

It was Alexis who broke ranks. It had to be. Rose and Paloma wouldn't do it, not when doing so would condemn Alexis even as it exonerated me. And Trevor—well. He might not be a monster, but he's always been a coward. But they all gave statements, in the end. Told the police exactly what happened, and whose fault it really was.

We don't talk about the trial. Charges have been filed, but it's unlikely to ever actually take place; Magnus is on hospice care, and as he predicted, no one is going to drag a dying man into a courtroom for a twenty-year-old crime—at least not an unfathomably rich dying man with an army of lawyers. And as for Louise, she insists that she knew nothing of what was happening. An old, confused woman, her lawyers say. She walks with a cane now, speaks tremulously.

Paloma sent flowers, after the wedding. She and Sebastian are staying with her family for a while. She and Alexis still speak, but it's hard to say what might happen. What can be forgiven. It's a question I'm still asking myself. Connor visits his sister often. It seems likely that she will escape a prison sentence—she was a minor, and she didn't actually kill anyone.

There will be no justice. Magnus was right about that much. Even Mr. Vance is gone, and though the police are looking for him, I doubt they'll find him. The only thing he left behind was a note, asking someone to look after Duchess, which we have.

"Theo?" Connor calls. He stands in the bedroom doorway, eyes bleary with sleep.

I kept the name. Rowan doesn't really feel like mine. It belongs to a little girl who died in the cold. Theo—that's a name I broke free for myself, and it's the one Connor called me when we found each other again. And so I am Theo Rowan Cahill. As for Connor, he took my name. He wasn't too fond of his own by then.

"Just restless," I tell him. It's the one thing we're allowed to lie about: we pretend it doesn't haunt us, what happened on the mountain.

He walks over to stand behind me, his arms encircling me. I reach up to put my hand on his shoulder, my thumb brushing the knot of scar tissue on one side where the bullet pierced his arm. It has a twin on the other side.

He has scars on his skin now, thanks to me. I'm not the only one with nightmares.

"Come back to bed," he murmurs in my ear.

"I think I'd like to stay up. Watch the sunrise," I say.

"Should I stay?"

I shake my head. "Get some more rest."

He takes me at my word, slipping away again. I walk to the couch and curl up against the arm of it. Duchess doesn't ask for permission before leaping up beside me, settling with a huge exhale. Her head flops onto my lap expectantly.

The sun casts pale orange and yellow against the undersides of clouds. It will already be in the sky over Idlewood, shining down on green slopes, all the snow long melted.

As he promised, Magnus has refused to reveal where Mallory Cahill is buried. A search of the woods has turned up nothing. There's simply too much area, and it's been too long. They wanted to be sure she wouldn't be found. They would have buried her deep.

I will never be able to put her to rest. To say goodbye. But it's summer now.

Wherever she is, the wildflowers are blooming.

ACKNOWLEDGMENTS

As always, I owe an enormous debt to a great many people for their help, support, and hard work in taking this book from a scrawled notebook page titled "Murder Cabin" to an actual book. My earliest coconspirators included Susan Morris, Erin M. Evans, Corry L. Lee, Rashida Smith, and Shanna Germain, who listened as I rambled my way from "So there's this girl and her in-laws are very sketchy and then there are SECRETS and probably someone dies" to something resembling a plot. I am deeply grateful to Lauren Spieller, agent extraordinaire, as well as my brilliant editor, Christine Kopprasch, and the whole team at Flatiron. A special thanks to Karissa Vacker, who has lent her talents as narrator to three of my audiobooks now and has knocked it out of the park every time.

It's sometimes staggering to realize just how many people are involved in bringing a book to fruition, from copy edits to design to publicity to warehouse staff—including a great many people I will never directly interact with but whose work and skill is absolutely essential to the process. And of course it doesn't stop there; I am especially grateful for those librarians and booksellers who have championed my book, and to all my readers. I would write if my only audience were a rock I put googly eyes on and named Paolo, but this way is definitely more fun.

Finally, my endless love and gratitude to my husband, Mike, who makes both excellent mochas and a mean Manhattan, and is thus the ideal writer spouse.

ABOUT THE AUTHOR

KATE ALICE MARSHALL is the bestselling author of *What Lies in the Woods, No One Can Know,* and multiple novels for younger readers. She lives in the Pacific Northwest with her family.